INDIANA JONES™ AND THE GENESIS DELUGE

The Indiana Jones series
Ask your bookseller for the books you have missed

INDIANA JONES AND THE PERIL AT DELPHI
INDIANA JONES AND THE DANCE OF THE GIANTS
INDIANA JONES AND THE SEVEN VEILS
INDIANA JONES AND THE GENESIS DELUGE
INDIANA JONES AND THE UNICORN'S LEGACY
INDIANA JONES AND THE INTERIOR WORLD
INDIANA JONES AND THE SKY PIRATES
INDIANA JONES AND THE WHITE WITCH
INDIANA JONES AND THE PHILOSOPHER'S STONE
INDIANA JONES AND THE DINOSAUR EGGS
INDIANA JONES AND THE HOLLOW EARTH
INDIANA JONES AND THE SECRET OF THE SPHINX

INDIANA JONES™ AND THE GENESIS DELUGE

Rob MacGregor

BANTAM BOOKS
NEW YORK • TORONTO • LONDON • SYDNEY • AUCKLAND

INDIANA JONES AND THE GENESIS DELUGE
A Bantam Book

PUBLISHING HISTORY
Bantam mass market edition published February 1992
Bantam reissue / May 2008

Published by
Bantam Dell
A Division of Random House, Inc.
New York, New York

Cover art by Drew Struzan

ISBN 978-0-553-29502-3

Printed in the United States of America
Published simultaneously in Canada

www.bantamdell.com

OPM 19 18 17 16 15 14 13 12 11 10

This one's for the Megger

Thanks to Ed Smart for his recollections of Chicago 1927.

Do you seriously suppose that we were unable to prove our point when even to this day the remains of Noah's Ark are shown in the country of the Kurds?

Epiphanus of Salamis (A.D. 4th century)

Absolutely anything is possible in this world, but if there's anything that's *impossible* in archaeology, this is it.

Archaeologist Frolich Rainey
on the existence of Noah's Ark

PROLOGUE

October 1917
Petrograd, Russia

The first snow of the season had started to fall less than an hour earlier as Vadim Popov galloped down the wooded lane. A rope tied to the stirrup of his saddle pulled another horse, and on it rode Vadim's captive, a White Russian lieutenant. Blindfolded and gagged, with his hands bound behind his back, the captive soldier rocked unsteadily atop his steed.

They'd been riding for several hours and Vadim was exhausted. But the young Bolshevik soldier knew he was close to the command post and he was anxious to get there before dark. Until he reached the post he was in danger of encountering White Russian soldiers on the road and becoming a captive himself. So far he'd only passed a few wagons, and the peasants had said nothing. Everyone knew the revolution was underway, and the sight of a captured soldier was not so remarkable as it would have been a year ago.

Vadim was a courier who carried messages back and forth from the revolutionary troops to the command post. He had stopped at an inn the night before, where he was to meet another courier, who was to give Vadim additional messages for the revolutionary leaders. It was late when he'd arrived and he'd been unable to find the courier, whom he knew only by the code name Uri.

The next morning the man joined Vadim at breakfast. As they ate, Uri mentioned that the night before he'd begun talking with a man whom he'd momentarily mistaken for Vadim. They shared a few shots of vodka together, and soon the stranger was telling Uri that he was an army lieutenant and was on his way to see the czar.

Vadim knew that the only way a lieutenant would get anywhere near the czar was if he was a courier like himself. "Where is he now?"

"Still here, sleeping, I think. He drank too much last night," Uri said with a laugh.

"Let's pay him a visit."

When the White Russian answered his door, he was still groggy with sleep. Vadim jammed his gun into the lieutenant's stomach, and he and Uri bound and gagged him. They found his diplomatic pouch and looked at its contents. At first, when they examined the photographs and the useless piece of wood, neither understood what they were seeing. Vadim questioned the lieutenant, but he would only say that he was a member of the 14th Railroad Battalion stationed in Turkey. Meanwhile, Uri read the accompanying documents and excitedly explained the importance of what the man was carrying.

That was when Vadim decided he would take the captive to the command post to be interrogated. He was sure the commander of the revolution would want to thank him personally, and if he did, it meant that his future would be bright. The lieutenant suddenly started talking when he realized where he would be taken and told a fantastic story, but it only made Vadim more eager than ever to get him to the command post.

Finally, he told Uri that he'd made a serious mistake talking to the White Russian. Couriers were not supposed to make idle conversation with strangers or drink while on duty. However, he'd said he wouldn't report him if he swore to say nothing about what had happened here. Uri considered what he'd said, then grudgingly agreed and went on his way.

That had been hours ago, and Vadim was wet and cold from the snow. He wanted nothing more than to reach his destination. If he'd been alone, he would've been out of the cold and out of danger by now.

Something was wrong.

He felt it like a stab in the back. He glanced over his shoulder.

"Mother of God," he cursed.

The captive was no longer on his horse, and there was no sign of him on the road. He pulled hard on the reins, turned, and raced back. He'd covered fifty yards before he saw the mark in the snow-covered lane where the soldier had tumbled off. He leaped to the ground and dashed into the woods. It was no problem tracking him, but Vadim was surprised at how well the lieutenant was moving through the trees and underbrush. Then he glimpsed him hobbling across a field and saw that the escapee had managed to lower his blindfold.

Vadim raised his pistol. "Halt!"

The soldier ignored him. Vadim aimed and fired. The bullet shredded bark from a birch tree, missing the lieutenant by inches. Vadim cursed as he raced across the field and plunged into the woods, following the man's tracks. If his captive got away, the accolades he expected to receive for seizing the document would no doubt be muted. He might even be chastised for allowing the White Russian to escape.

The man was starting to drag one leg. Vadim was gaining on him; he was going to catch him. Then he heard the report of a rifle and dived to the ground. How could the bastard have a weapon? His hands were still tied a minute ago.

Voices.

He crawled forward until he saw five or six soldiers who surrounded a body lying facedown in the snow. For an instant he thought he'd run into a squad of the Imperial Army. Then he saw their ragged coats and frayed fur-lined hats and knew they were Bolsheviks like himself, and they'd shot the White Russian.

"Comrades," he called out as he stood up. The soldiers turned and raised their weapons. "That man was my prisoner."

A sergeant approached him. "Who are you?"

Vadim identified himself.

"What's a courier doing with a prisoner?" the sergeant asked suspiciously.

"I was bringing him to the command post. He was carrying documents to the czar."

"What documents?" the sergeant growled.

Vadim adjusted the leather pouch he carried on his shoulder. "I have them here," he answered in an authoritative tone. "I need to get to the command post immediately."

"*Shloosayu*. I am listening," the sergeant said in a stern voice.

Vadim knew he was supposed to give him the password, but so much had happened today that the word slipped his mind for a moment.

"*Mir,*" he finally said, relieved that he had recalled the simple word, which meant village, peace, the world or universe, depending on the context.

The sergeant eyed the satchel a moment, then motioned him to follow.

When they reached the road, Vadim mounted his steed, and accompanied by the sergeant, he continued down the lane. Not more than a mile from where the White Russian had escaped, they turned down a winding drive that ended at a gate where more soldiers waited. The sergeant said something to one of the guards, who looked closely at Vadim, then nodded.

They dismounted and headed along a snow-covered walkway that was scored with boot prints. At the end of the path stood a three-story stone mansion. Smoke curled from a pair of chimneys and soldiers were moving about the grounds. It amazed Vadim that even though they were barely a dozen miles from Petrograd and the czar's palace, the command was firmly ensconced in a baronial estate whose owner had fled from the approaching revolutionary troops.

At the door, there was another exchange with two more guards and they were escorted into an expansive foyer where a fire burned in a huge hearth. Vadim brushed traces of snow from his coat as the sergeant conferred with a captain near the double doors of the mansion's great hall. For an instant, Vadim glimpsed several officers seated around a table. They were probably planning the attack on Petrograd, he thought. The captain, a tall man with a long face, looked over at Vadim, then took the leather pouch and told him and the sergeant to wait.

"What's in the bag? You can tell me now," the sergeant said.

Vadim knew it would be dangerous to reveal anything to the sergeant. "It's not your business."

The White Russian Army had made a great discovery in Turkey, almost great enough to reaffirm his faith. But he was a Bolshevik and he knew that religion was an oppressive force. Maybe there was a God, but it didn't matter. The revolution was going to abolish the wealthy bishops and shut down the churches. Religion, after all, had become nothing more than a conspiracy to keep the proletariat in order.

After Vadim had waited about forty-five minutes, the captain returned and asked the sergeant if he'd looked at the documents that Vadim had carried, or if Vadim had told him anything about them. He shook his head and the captain dismissed him. The sergeant gave Vadim a sour look and walked away.

He was probably hoping he would get credit for my work, Vadim thought.

"Come with me," the captain said.

Vadim followed him down a hall and into a library with walls rising fifteen feet and covered with books. A fire crackled in an immense fireplace. In front of it was an ornate mahogany desk with gold inlaid trim. The high-backed chair behind it was turned toward the fire. As they approached the desk the captain cleared his throat. The chair swiveled about. Seated in front of him was a man with a thick handlebar mustache and penetrating dark eyes. The commander of the revolution. Trotsky.

In his hands were the photographs and the accompanying documents. "Sergeant Popov."

"Yes, sir." Vadim stiffly saluted him.

"Tell me how you came upon this material."

Vadim remained standing as he told his story. He embellished it, making the endeavor sound more daring, and he didn't say a word about Uri's help. He said that after he'd discovered he was sharing the inn with an officer from the Imperial Army, he'd snuck into his room and found the document. Then, while he had been examining it, the White Russian had walked into the room and they'd struggled until he'd overcome the man.

"Excellent work, Sergeant Popov. Has anyone else seen these documents?"

"Just myself." Uri better keep his mouth shut if he knows what's good for him, Vadim thought.

"Did you tell anyone about them?"

"No."

"And do you know what these photos are supposed to be?"

"Yes, sir. Noah's Ark on Mount Ararat."

"Do you believe it?"

Vadim stared straight ahead. He wasn't sure what to say. The question of authenticity had never occurred to him; he wanted the photos to be real. He wanted the discovery to be important. "I think they are what they're said to be. Yes, sir."

Trotsky nodded. "You've intercepted an extremely important document, and I congratulate you. However, it's unfortunate that you've seen the documents and believe so strongly in them."

He realized he'd said something wrong. The warmth had vanished from Trotsky's face. His eyes turned dark and cold. "Well, sir . . . I believe in the revolution. That's what I believe in."

Trotsky wasn't paying any attention. His eyes shifted toward the captain, and he gave a slight nod.

Out of the corner of his eye, Vadim saw the gun. He turned, held up his hand. The captain fired and the bullet ripped through Vadim's palm, pierced his eye, and buried itself deep inside his brain. He took a staggering step backward, shuddered, and collapsed.

1

Celtic Trappings

Spring 1927
London

On the blackboard of the classroom were two vertical lines with bars and curls and rectangles drawn at various intervals, some on the left side of the line, some on the right. The young archaeology instructor, Professor Jones, pointed at the board with his wooden marker. He was in the midst of a lecture on Celtic ogham to the fifteen students in his class. Some of the students looked bored; others were enthralled, busily taking notes. A couple of the women in the front row were passing a piece of paper back and forth and grinning slyly.

The professor's full name was Henry Jones, but he preferred to be called Indy. He had just finished discussing the five letters with bars extending from the right side of the vertical line and now tapped the marker against the letter designated by one bar protruding from the left side of the line. "*Huathe* is the name for the letter *H*. It was represented by the hawthorn tree. To the Celts, it meant cleansing and protection, and it was associated with a period of waiting in which one kept himself or herself away from the hustle and bustle."

Indy could relate to the letter. He felt the same way about himself. He'd felt that way since returning to London last summer after losing the most important person in his life.

He moved down to the letter with three bars extending from the left of the vertical line. "The letter *T* is called *tinne*. It's symbolized by the evergreen holly. It signifies the will and ability to overcome enemies no matter how powerful. The ancient name for holly is Holm and is considered the likely source of the name for Holmsdale in Surrey. It might even be the inspiration for Arthur Conan Doyle's fictional character Sherlock Holmes. As we know, Holmes did quite well in combating his enemies."

He turned to the board. "The letter *C* is *coll*, which—"

"Professor Jones?" A man with a crew cut and a pencil behind his ear raised his hand. "You forgot the letter *D*, the one with two bars. You skipped right over it."

Indy tugged at the lapel of his coat and peered through his black, wire-rim glasses at the *D*, *duir*, the oak, which meant solidity and fortification. There was something about it that he wasn't remembering, or didn't want to remember.

He turned away from the blackboard. "You

know, the interesting thing about the ogham alphabet is not only that the letters contain complex meanings, but that each one can be represented by a hand gesture. In fact, the language was used as a secret way of communicating in the presence of others—for example, the Romans—who would have no idea what was being said."

Indy glanced toward the two women in the front row. "It saved paper, too."

The class laughed, and it seemed that even the skulls in the cabinets with the pottery shards were grinning at the professor's joke. The two women turned red and tried to look attentive.

"Didn't that annoy the Romans when the Celts made these hand gestures?" a man sitting in the second row asked.

"It sure did. No one likes being talked about behind his back, especially when he's standing right there."

Indy frowned at the two women again, who wriggled uneasily in their seats. When he'd begun his teaching career, he had been amused by some of the female students' reaction to him. They apparently expected archaeology professors to be human antiques, not young and virile. But this past year he'd only been annoyed by his flirtatious students. He definitely didn't want to get involved with any of them. He was still hurting from the loss of Deirdre, the love of his life, who had died just weeks after he'd married her.

"The Romans finally had enough of it and outlawed the use of hand gestures," he continued.

An attractive, dark-haired woman raised her

hand. "Does anyone still use the sign language today?"

The question confused him, even though the answer was obvious. "What do you mean?"

"Well, I was thinking about the druids, who go to Stonehenge for the summer solstice. Do they use the hand signals?"

"Not that I know of."

"I have an uncle who is involved with a druid group," said an attractive, but shy, doe-eyed girl.

"Oh? What's he say about hand signals?" She'd never match up to Deirdre, he thought. None of them would.

"Nothing. But he says that the druids set up colonies in the Americas a long time ago, and that some of them are still alive today. Do you think that's true?"

Why did she have to ask that question? "The subject is ogham today. Let's stick with it, and not waste our time on fanciful ideas that some know-nothing druids pass off as the truth."

The woman drew back in her chair. She had hardly spoken during the entire course, and now when she finally had come out of her shell, he'd attacked her. He turned back to the blackboard and stared at it as if he were preparing to make further remarks about the letters.

He felt bad, but the question annoyed him. It made him think of Deirdre again, and their search in the Amazon for Colonel Fawcett, an English adventurer who thought ancient druids had settled in South America. He'd lost Deirdre when their airplane crashed in the jungle, and he knew that as long as he taught Celtic archaeology he would be haunted by her memory.

She had been his best student, a Scot of Celtic descent who spoke fluent Gaelic. Even though she was an undergraduate student, she knew more about Celtic archaeology than most doctoral candidates in the field.

"Okay. Where was I now? Oh, yes. I got up to the letter *C, coll*. This one relates to creativity, imagination, inspiration, and intuition. You may want to reflect on this one awhile before you write your final essay that's due Tuesday."

Everyone laughed, and the bell rang. "Class dismissed."

As the students filed out the room Indy caught the eye of the girl he'd snapped at. "Miss Wilkens?" He motioned to her. The two note passers gaped in surprise. "Listen, I'm sorry if I offended you with my comment. I didn't mean it the way it sounded."

The girl crossed her arms over her books, which were pressed to her chest. She looked embarrassed. "It's all right. I know it . . . it must be hard for you sometimes. We all know about Deirdre, of course. I guess I shouldn't have asked that question. I wasn't thinking."

Indy took off his glasses and stuffed them in his coat pocket. "There was nothing wrong with the question. It's just that I'm not feeling so great today." He glanced up at the clock above the door. "That was all."

"Professor Jones, may I ask you a question?" the girl asked.

Indy gathered up his notes. "What is it?"

"Do you think it's worthwhile for a girl, I mean, you know, a woman to become an archaeologist?"

Indy shrugged. "Why not?"

"My father says it's not a ladylike thing to do. You know, digging in the ground and getting dirty. He thinks I should get married and have kids, and forget about going to graduate school."

He couldn't help thinking of Deirdre again. He glanced up at her, then looked away. "Maybe he's right."

He strode out of the classroom and quickly headed to his office. He didn't understand why Deirdre's death was hitting him so hard today. A year had passed since the tragic incident and he'd been feeling that it was behind him. Maybe the lecture on ogham had opened a door to a buried memory.

Door, *duir*. Something about the ogham word reminded him of the incident leading to Deirdre's death. But he wasn't sure what it was. There was a blank in his memory, a result of the airplane crash. He couldn't recall much of anything that had happened in the jungle, and that especially bothered him because he'd lost the memory of his last days with Deirdre. No matter how hard he tried to recall what had happened, the only thoughts that came to mind were vague images about an Indian village.

He entered the office area and greeted the secretary, a frizzy-haired graduate student who worked for three assistant professors. "I don't want to see anybody."

She shrugged. "No one wants to see you. . . . Not now."

He walked into his office and closed the door. Someday he'd have his own secretary and she wouldn't be so damned insolent. He leaned against the door and rubbed his face with his hands. Then he stared over his fingers at his desk, which took up most of the space in his cramped office. A stack of journals lay on one corner of the desk. His mail was neatly stacked in another. Ungraded term papers were piled in the center of the desk, and a smaller batch of graded ones were to the left. But the papers and journals and mail weren't what caught his attention.

He was peering at two baked clay figurines, one a woman with large breasts and wide hips, the other a man with an erect penis that was half the length of its leg. How'd they get there? They'd been packed away in a box in his closet for months.

The pair had been given to him by Deirdre, who had passed them on from her deceased mother's collection of artifacts. They'd probably been used in Celtic fertility rites, and he remembered how Deirdre had smiled and said: "They represent our love."

But now they were a profanity. They taunted him, and he had an urge to swat them off the desk and smash them against the wall. He moved further into the room and saw that the closet door was open and the box where the figurines had been stored was pulled out of its place on the floor beneath a shelf.

"Francine," he yelled, then walked back into the outer office. "Have you been messing around in my office?"

"Don't bark at me, Jones. I haven't been in your office today."

"Then how did my mail get there?"

"Two of your students were here looking for you during your so-called office hours this morning. They were disturbing me with their chatter, so I told them to wait for you in there. I gave them your mail and told them to put it on your desk."

"What did they look like?"

The phone rang and Francine picked it up. It didn't matter. He was sure they were the two gigglers who were passing notes in class. They'd visited him together last week. They'd asked a couple of innocuous questions about the course, then attempted to pry into his personal life.

He returned to his office, snatched up the figurines, put them back in the box, and closed the closet door. He shook his head in disgust and stopped in front of his bookcase. He stared at the titles and picked up a book called *Buried Treasures of Chinese Turkestan.* He leafed through it, then put it back on the shelf. He needed a change, a new challenge. Something that wouldn't remind him of Deirdre.

But where would he find it? He couldn't just walk away from his responsibilities. Classes were about to end and he was supposed to teach summer school in another week. Then in the fall back to more of the same. Celtic archaeology.

He had to talk to Pencroft. That was all there was to it. He'd ask for a sabbatical. Maybe he'd go to Egypt or Greece or India. Hell, maybe he'd go dig for the buried treasures of Chinese Turkestan. He didn't know, but he was going to do something, something different, and Pencroft would just have to bend a little.

He felt better already. He scooped up the mail,

quickly riffled through it, stopped a moment as he noticed a letter from Jack Shannon, his old friend and former college roommate. He put the letter in his pocket, stuffed the rest of the mail in his backpack, and headed for the door.

He recalled that Pencroft had suggested that he save his backpack for the field and that a briefcase would be more appropriate for the classroom. He was about to leave it behind, then changed his mind. His pack was his way of keeping in touch with a part of himself that was important, and if Pencroft didn't like it, too bad.

"Are you leaving?" Francine called after him.

"I hope so."

At the end of the hall, he approached the department chairman's secretary, a round-faced, middle-aged woman who watched after Pencroft like a mother. "Afternoon, Miss Jenkins. Is he in?"

"Yes. But you can't see him now. He's resting. He has a meeting in half an hour."

"It's important I see him."

"I'm sorry, Professor Jones. You're going to have to make an appointment. How about—"

"Indy, what can I do for you?" Pencroft stood in the doorway of his office. He was a frail, bald man in his mid-sixties. He leaned on a cane and peered through thick black-framed glasses that magnified his eyes.

"Dr. Pencroft, would it be an imposition if I spoke with you for a few minutes?"

"I told him you were resting."

Pencroft patted the air. "It's okay, Rita. Please, come in, Indy. Come in."

Indy didn't hesitate. As he quickly followed

him inside and closed the door he smiled at the secretary, who crossed her arms and shook her head in disgust.

Pencroft hobbled over to his desk and eased himself into his chair. He had spent more than forty years studying Paleolithic man and had become chairman of the department after Victor Bernard had supposedly vanished without a trace on a trip to Guatemala.

Indy knew Bernard had not died in Guatemala, but in Brazil. It was one of Indy's last memories of the Amazon before everything turned fuzzy. But he also knew that no one would believe him. Even his old friend Marcus Brody had thought it was a delusion caused by the plane crash. He'd advised Indy to keep the incredible story to himself. So he hadn't said another word about it, even though he was sure that Bernard had not only been killed by Indians, but had been behind an attempt to murder Indy himself.

"Please, sit down," Pencroft said, and frowned at the backpack as Indy set it on the floor. "Now, what can I do for you?"

Suddenly Indy was tongue-tied. "Well, Dr. Pencroft, it's not that I don't like what I'm doing or that I'm not grateful to be teaching here, but something has come up and I'm not sure, I mean, I don't think I can continue on, and I'm wondering if . . . well, I feel like a sabbatical might be in order."

"Sabbaticals are for tenured professors. Maybe in a few years you might qualify, but right now . . . " He shook his head.

"I didn't really mean a sabbatical in the technical sense. I meant that I need to take a leave of absence."

Pencroft's hand rustled unsteadily through some papers on his desk. "It's interesting that you should bring up this matter about your future with this institution. I've been meaning to talk to you about that very topic."

"Oh?"

"Yes. You see, the academic review board has raised questions about how qualified you are to teach Celtic archaeology."

"What? I've been teaching it almost three years."

Pencroft found the sheaf of papers he was looking for and absently paged through it. "It's your background," he said, uttering each word as if his visitor might not understand. "They don't feel you are sufficiently educated for the task, and between you and me it doesn't help that you are an American."

Indy knew that he had been fortunate to get hired at the University of London. He also was aware that the offer had been related to his discovery of the Omphalos at Delphi, an artifact that he'd belatedly learned was linked with Stonehenge. But all that was in the past. His practical experience outweighed his lack of formal training in Celtic archaeology, and he told Pencroft so.

"The problem is not my qualifications or abilities. I'm just getting stale. I need a break to try something different."

"Let me finish," Pencroft said. "The board also criticized your fieldwork last year. Before Dr. Bernard disappeared last summer, he had submitted an extremely critical report on your work at Tikal."

"But that's got nothing to do with my Celtic teaching." He was tempted to tell Pencroft all about Bernard, but he held back.

"That's part of the problem. Your acceptance of Dr. Bernard's offer to work at Tikal shows that you are not concentrating on Celtic archaeology, and now you tell me that you're feeling stale."

"So what are you saying?"

Pencroft cleared his throat. "If I can make an observation, I'd say that your present feelings are related to what happened to you in the Amazon with Deirdre Campbell last summer."

"That's part of it."

The old professor nodded thoughtfully. "You know, her mother and I were great friends. Her loss affected me deeply. So I certainly understand your feelings, and in fact, I have been considering these mitigating circumstances."

Indy didn't feel much like talking about his feelings with Pencroft, and he didn't appreciate the professor's vague attempt at consoling him. He wished he would get to the point.

"I'm sure you recall at the beginning of the fall term I offered you an opportunity to spend the academic year translating Goidelic manuscripts from the second century B.C."

"I remember." Goidelic was a Celtic dialect, and although Indy had a working knowledge of the language, he was far from an expert. It was not the sort of challenge he was looking for then, or now.

"I made that offer because I thought you might

want to avoid the pressure of teaching after the unfortunate events of the summer."

"I know you did."

Pencroft crossed his arms. "Well, I'm going to give you another chance to work with the manuscripts. I'm sure I can come up with funding for you through the summer. After that we'll examine the progress you're making and decide about the fall."

"I appreciate your offer, Dr. Pencroft. But like I said before, I think there are better people for the job. You see, I was thinking of fieldwork. I need to get away for a while."

"Translating is not always a scholarly task," Pencroft said in an admonishing tone. "Look at Sir Henry Rawlinson. He had to hang over the side of a cliff by one hand and copy the Babylonian cuneiform letters with the other. If his grip had failed, he would've fallen to his death."

"But the Goidelic text you're talking about is in the library down the hall."

"Are you turning down my offer?"

Indy thought a moment. He realized what the consequences might be if he said yes. "I think I am. I need to get away."

Pencroft nodded. "Then I think you understand that your association with the university will terminate with the end of classes."

2

LOOKOUT

During the days of Chaucer, London had been a one-square-mile village surrounded by a Roman wall. Soon, villages took root around the old city with names such as Chelsea, Mayfair, Marylebone, Soho, and Bloomsbury, and gradually the city became a patchwork of these villages. Hampstead was the village with the most open spaces and the highest point of land in London, known as Parliament Hill.

Indy had headed directly for Hampstead Heath, as the village's vast park was called, after he left Pencroft's office. He passed through open fields and clusters of pines, drinking in his surrounding, relieved that he was away from classrooms, students, and colleagues, and when Parliament Hill rose in front of him, he started climbing. The hike was a way of dealing with his frustrations and clearing his mind. He would attain a view of the city, and maybe an overview of his life.

When he reached the crest, he gazed down at

the network of winding streets lined by mansions and terraced cottages. Some were redbrick, others white stucco, and most were garnished with ivy and holly. He spotted Wentworth Place, where John Keats had written "Ode on a Grecian Urn," "Ode to Psyche," "To Autumn," and other poems. He lifted his gaze to the distant spires and buildings and realized that London looked different to him now. He was not only looking at the city from above, but thinking of it in the past tense. His time in England was drawing to an end like the closing chapter of a book. He would miss the characters and the setting, but he was ready to move on. He would leave here this summer, and he wouldn't return in the fall.

As he sat down to rest he slipped Shannon's letter from his back pocket. Jack had moved back to Chicago a year and a half ago, after his father had died. Indy didn't know the details, but he guessed from the little that Shannon had said that his father's death was neither natural nor an accident. Shannon's family was involved in gangster affairs, and death by a bullet was an occupational hazard.

Indy had written Shannon several times, but he'd only received a couple of letters from him. This one was the first he'd gotten since Shannon had written him expressing his sorrow at Deirdre's death. Shannon had said little about his life in Chicago, except that he was playing regularly in a jazz band in a South Side nightclub.

He opened the envelope and unfolded the letter, which was dated May 2, and quickly read it.

Dear Indy,

Sorry I'm so bad at writing. I got no excuses. I'm just too wrapped up in my music and other things. I'm playing now five nights a week at the Nest on Thirty-fifth and State. You ought to see Chicago now. The ole town has really taken to jazz and the blues. You could almost say it's respectable. Well, that's going a bit too far.

Like I said, you should see it. The trouble is that the families are getting ruthless. Since Dad was killed, there's been a shaky truce. I've done my best to stay clear of it, but it's tougher now that Dad is gone. I'm one of the Shannon brothers and the Shannons are in the Business.

I don't know why I'm telling you all of this. Maybe it's a confession. It's a tough line I'm walking and I've had to seek Higher help, if you know what I mean. If things don't work out, I may have to get out of here fast. Maybe I'll show up at your door one of these days. This is your warning. Ha-ha.

Jack

Not unless I show up at your door first, Indy thought. And that wasn't such a bad idea. Going back to Chicago was definitely a possibility.

Last winter he'd attended a conference on Celtic archaeology in Dublin and had presented a paper on Celtic influences in New England. He had focused on stone inscriptions found mainly in Massachusetts and Vermont and compared them to Celtic ones in Great Britain. He'd stopped short of drawing a definite conclusion. His intent had been simply to get Celtic scholars to look at evidence they'd previously ignored. One of the other presenters at the conference had been Angus O'Malley, chairman of the archaeology department at the University of Chicago. He'd been impressed by Indy's paper and had told him that if he was ever interested in returning to Chicago to teach Celtic archaeology, he would find a position for him.

Indy hadn't given the offer much thought. Not until now. He'd always figured he'd move back to the States again; he'd just never known when. Maybe he could join one of the university's digs this summer and start work in the fall. It wasn't a bad plan, and besides, it would be good to see Shannon again, and to find out what sort of "higher" help he was getting. He didn't think that Shannon had turned to religion. He wasn't the type. But then what was he talking about?

The more he thought about it, the more he realized that he was ready to go back. It would be swell living in Chicago again. Maybe he'd even find a girlfriend.

He carefully folded up the letter, returned it to its envelope, and stuck it in his pocket. Heavy clouds were moving in and the view of the city was turning gray and hazy. It was time to go home, he decided, and for the first time in years that meant Chicago.

Jack Shannon leaned against a sooty brick wall at the end of the alley behind the Nest. As the truck motored past him, he glanced at his watch and saw it was two minutes past three A.M. The Nest was closed, but the important business of the day was about to begin.

Both the alley and side street were clear of any suspicious activity, and Shannon hoped the men waiting at the backdoor of the club were ready to unload. He wanted the truck out of here in five minutes or less. Crouched a few feet behind him was another member of the organization, and hidden in the shadows across the alley were two others. At the opposite end of the alley, Shannon's brother Harry and three of his men guarded that entrance. They all had tommy guns tucked close to their sides and were ready to use them. Restocking the nightclub's supply of booze was no routine matter. It wasn't the cops who presented the danger. They were well paid. It was the competition for territory that caused the problems, and right now things were as hot as they could be.

Shannon tried to stay calm by thinking about the woman he'd met earlier this evening before he'd come to the club. Her name was Katrina and the name seemed to fit her personality. He was intrigued by her, and he was looking forward to seeing her again. It had been a long time since he'd met a woman who had made such an impression on him.

Maybe it was because she was so different from the women he was used to seeing at the club. They all had short hair and wore baggy, fringed dresses and layers of beads. They flaunted their cigarettes, snapped their gum, made wisecracks, and drank white lightning when they weren't on the dance floor doing the wicky-wicky-wacky-woo. That was fine, but he'd been around the flappers so much that he fantasized encountering a repressed-Victorian type who would swoon in his arms rather than blow smoke rings across a bar.

Then he'd met Katrina. Her silky blond hair

probably fell to the middle of her back when it wasn't tied on her head. Her clothes were conservative, a high-necked blouse and a long skirt. Yet she didn't seem prudish. She had openly greeted him, her blue eyes studying him curiously as he shook her soft hand. He was sure he'd sensed a longing that was ready to erupt.

But he'd met her at the church just before his Bible class, and it was hardly the place to make a pass. She'd talked about her father, who was meeting with the reverend and who was going to speak at the church in a couple of days. They were planning an expedition to Turkey, where they would search for Noah's Ark.

He'd watched her with such intensity that he'd barely heard what she was saying, and when he'd asked a few questions to keep the conversation alive, she'd finally shook her head and laughed. "I already told you that. Aren't you listening to me?"

"With all my heart," Shannon had replied.

Then the reverend and her father had emerged from the office. She'd smiled coyly and walked off to join them.

She was probably snuggled in bed right now, deeply asleep, while he stood here in the alley with a tommy gun, waiting for trouble. He almost laughed at the contradiction that his life had become. Except it wasn't very funny.

"Hey, look." Richie, the heavyset man behind Shannon, nudged him.

"I see it."

A black Packard was moving slowly down the side street approaching the alley. Just then the truck revved its engine and pulled away from the backdoor of the club; it was coming their way.

"Oh, no," Shannon muttered under his breath.

The Packard had almost slowed to a stop and the truck was picking up speed. He snapped off the safety button. His finger tensed on the trigger. Then the driver of the Packard saw the truck. Shannon raised his weapon, waiting for a window to roll down. But the Packard moved past them and pulled to the curb just as the truck roared out of the alley. It jumped the curb and turned away from the automobile.

The front doors of the Packard swung open and two men in long, dark coats and hats stepped out. Shannon swiveled his gun, still expecting to see machine guns poke out of the coats.

"Don't shoot!" Richie said aloud. "That's Benny Boy."

"What's he doing here?"

"What do you think? Hey, Benny!"

The man turned, wobbled a moment. Then he smiled and doffed his hat, revealing slicked-back hair that was parted in the middle and a thin mustache. "How ya doin', Richie? You goin' upstairs to stick your wicky, too? C'mon."

Of course, Shannon thought, finally relaxing his grip. The bordello next door was open all night.

3
The Nest

Three Weeks Later
Chicago

As the train pulled into the Union Station at Jackson and Canal streets in downtown Chicago Indy watched the throng of people moving this way and that on the platform. The platform was like a huge stage and everyone was performing a part in some incomprehensible play with neither beginning nor end. The dialogue usually ran together with everyone talking at once. Occasionally, an individual's performance would stand out for a few seconds, then the actor would disappear into the masses.

In a sense, the city was an extension of the platform, Indy thought. It was much more complex, of course, with literally thousands of scenes being acted out simultaneously. There were stars and a massive supporting cast everywhere you went. Chicago was a noisy play with the dialogue punctuated from time to time by the staccato fire of tommy guns from the mob, the braying of cattle heading to slaughterhouses, or the grinding and shrieking timbre of industry.

Chicago was discordant and harmonious, drama and comedy, and it played continually around the clock.

Indy had never thought of the city this way when he lived here, but he hadn't spent a night in Chicago for eight years, and he felt like an outsider. He didn't belong anymore. He was an actor without a role. At least for now, he thought as he disembarked from the train.

He'd spent nine days at sea, then had traveled by rail the last three days. It was midafternoon and he felt tired and disoriented. He decided to look for a hotel near the train station and rest awhile. He walked a few blocks over to Sixth and Michigan and found himself outside of the Blackstone. It was famous, luxurious, and expensive. He'd never stayed here, or even thought about it. Rich people from out of town stayed here.

"May I take your bag, sir?" asked the doorman. He was a young Negro, who was dressed like a general, but stood barely over five feet.

"My bags? Oh, no thanks. I don't think I'm going to stay here."

"Why not? Aren't we good enough?"

Indy laughed. "Your hotel's just fine. It's my pocketbook."

"So what? Why not treat yourself for one night? You won't regret it."

"Sounds like you're getting a commission."

"No, but I don't want to work here all my life, either," the doorman said. "I want to get into sales."

"You'd be good at it."

"You mean you're going to stay here at the Blackstone?"

"I wish I could."

"Tell you what. I can get you a suite for the price of a single. What do you say to that?"

"I don't need a suite, and why would you do that for me?"

"Why? Because I know I can do it, and I can see that you're the type of guy who would benefit from my inside information, if you know what I mean."

What the hell, he thought. It wasn't such a bad idea. He'd been given severance pay equaling two months of his regular salary. He'd splurge for a day or two, then he'd find cheaper lodging. "All right. You convinced me."

"Great. My name's Frankie. If you need anything, just let me know."

Frankie opened the door for him, and Indy stopped in his tracks. The elegance was literally breathtaking. His feet sank into the thick carpeting. Massive, intricate chandeliers glistened from the ceiling. The walls were covered with rich woodwork, and there were delicate marble statues everywhere.

He moved to the registration desk and asked for a room. The clerk smiled and told him he was getting the last one available, a single room on the second floor. "A single?" Indy asked.

The clerk gave him a baffled look. "You *are* alone, aren't you?"

"Yeah."

A couple of minutes later, the clerk moved off to get Indy the key. But when he returned, he looked upset. "I'm sorry, Mr. Jones, there's a problem. The room I gave you is already taken. Just a few minutes ago, our guest decided to stay another night. We're completely booked . . . except for one room, but that one is a corner suite."

He laughed, amazed at how Frankie had known exactly what was going on. Then he realized the clerk wasn't offering him any discount. "I can't afford it. I'll have to go somewhere else."

The desk clerk looked disappointed. "Just a minute, please."

He disappeared into an office. Indy watched a middle-aged woman draped in furs and jewelry walk by with two poodles. Two steps behind her was a man in a top hat and tails, carrying an ebony cane with a gold handle shaped like a lion's head. Indy idly wondered how the pair dressed for the evening.

"Mr. Jones, I've talked to the manager and you can take the suite for the price of a single room. Our apologies for the mix-up."

"No problem." Just the kind of mix-up I could get used to, he thought.

"I'll help you with your bags, sir." It was Frankie again.

"Thanks. How did you know what was going to happen?"

Frankie laughed. "When you work at the door, you pick up things. Lots of things."

"So why aren't you at the door?" Indy asked as they waited for the elevator.

"I'm just helping you out."

I bet, Indy thought, and wondered how much change he had. It was payoff time. Same old Chicago. Everyone from the mayor to the hotel doorman had a racket.

A couple of minutes later, Indy was ensconced in an immaculate corner suite with two queen-size beds. He'd tipped Frankie more than he'd expected to pay for a room, but he didn't mind. He was glad the kid had convinced him to stay here; he never would've done it on his own. He flopped down on the bed and within seconds was sound asleep.

In another room of the Blackstone, Katrina Zobolotsky stood in front of the window and brushed her long blond hair. She watched the people moving along the street three stories below. She didn't care for Chicago. She preferred San Francisco, her home for the past six years. But then, her impressions of Chicago had been soured by the presence of the watcher.

She absentmindedly ran her fingers over the velvet drapes and wriggled her toes in the thick carpeting. In her twenty-four years, she had never stayed in such luxurious accommodations. She felt like a princess, but also like a prisoner. She knew he was out there somewhere. Waiting. She and her father couldn't go out without drawing his attention, and he seemed to be everywhere. They would spot him across the street standing in a doorway, only to turn the corner and see him again ahead of them. Waiting. Watching. How he did it she didn't know. Her father was ready to believe that the devil was on their trail, and she didn't blame him.

Maybe it had been a mistake coming to Chicago. But if that were true, then maybe everything was wrong. She couldn't let those kind of thoughts get in her way. She had to believe that what she was doing was right, and that it would all work out.

She turned away from the window and rapped at her father's door. It was dinnertime, and she was sure everything would look better after she ate something. She wanted to believe that. She needed to believe it.

As Indy came awake a phrase was running through his mind over and over again. *D is for duir. . . . D is for duir. . . . D is for duir. D . . . D . . . D.*

"All right. All right," he muttered in his sleep. He'd been away from London and the university for two weeks, but this Celtic stuff was still running through his mind. He blinked his eyes open and looked around. It was dark outside, but the curtains were open and light from the street was shining into the room. He still felt tired, and he had an urge to turn over and go back to sleep. But instead he found the light switch to the lamp next to his bed and tugged on the chain.

He walked over to the radio, twisted the knob, then lay back down. He'd wait until he heard the time before he decided what to do. He didn't feel much like going out, and he could always see Shannon tomorrow. The radio announcer was reading the news and Indy caught the end of a story about federal agents discovering a still in a warehouse a block from city hall in Cicero, a town just outside of Chicago. Then the announcer turned to the national news.

"It's been two and a half weeks now since Charles Lindbergh made his historic flight from New York to Paris and we're hearing more bits and pieces about what it was like on that long and lonely air voyage," he said. "Many of us have wondered how Linbergh managed to stay awake for the thirty-three and a half hours that it took, and now we have an interesting answer. According to a friend of the Lindbergh family, the pilot has remarked on more than one occasion that he felt at times as if he were not alone in his airplane. There was someone else in the compartment with him, an invisible presence, who was guiding him and helping him stay awake."

Indy threw his legs over the side of the bed as the announcer chatted on. He called room service, ordered a steak dinner, and headed to the shower. If Lindbergh could stay awake for the entire trip across the Atlantic, he could damn well stay awake this evening to see his old friend.

By nine-thirty, he'd eaten, dressed, and was ready to go out. As soon as he stepped through the revolving door, a taxi rolled up to the front of the hotel and Indy slid into the backseat. "Take me down to Thirty-fifth and State."

The taxi driver, a Negro in his fifties, peeked over his shoulder at Indy. "Are you sure that's where you wanna go, sir?"

"They're still playing jazz down there, aren't they?"

"Yes, sir. That they are," he said, and drove off.

The area along State Street was known as a vice district as well as the home of much of the jazz that was played in Chicago. It was a Negro neighborhood and was just a few blocks from the Irish, Lithuanian, and Polish neighborhoods, which surrounded the nearby stockyards and packing houses.

Indy gazed out the window as the cab motored along the busy street. He hadn't been here since his college days, when he and Shannon had spent many nights in the neighborhood slipping into the "black and tan" clubs, as the ones catering to mixed racial audiences were called. Usually, they'd ended up at rent parties, where Shannon got his first opportunities to play his cornet with real jazz musicians.

Now jazz, or at least a watered-down version of the gutsy stuff, was being accepted in Chicago and all over. The first movie where the actors were actually talking had just come out; and it was called the *Jazz Singer*, and starred Al Jolson. It was the Jazz Age now as much as it was the Roaring Twenties.

The sidewalks were crowded and he could hear music filtering into the streets from the clubs. As they neared Thirty-fifth, he recognized several cabarets with familiar names: the Dreamland Café, Paradise Gardens, the Elite No. 2, and LaFerencia. Then he saw the New Monogram Theatre and next to it was a building with the words THE NEST lit up in red lights above the door.

"Right here. This is where I'm going."

"You enjoy yourself at the Nest," the driver said as Indy paid his fare. "But watch out in that place. Anything can happen there."

"Thanks for the advice," he said, leaving the driver a tip.

Indy crossed the street, and as he approached the nightclub two policeman looked him over. "Upstairs," one of them said.

"The nightclub's upstairs?" he asked.

"For you it is," the cop answered.

At first Indy didn't understand, then he realized they were telling him that the second floor was for whites. He entered an alcove and was about to climb the stairs when the door suddenly swung open and a Negro couple moved past him. He heard a sultry piano and caught a glimpse of a dimly lit and crowded nightclub: small tables with candles, a stage with green and red lights, a dance floor, and a haze of smoke. He decided to see if he could spot Shannon and catch his attention.

He stepped through the door, but a burly Negro in a coat and tie immediately moved in front of him and pointed to the stairs. "There's plenty of seats upstairs, sir."

"Thanks. I'm looking for Jack Shannon, the cornet player."

The man gave Indy a second look. "You can look at him from right on upstairs. Mr. Shannon is onstage."

Indy handed the doorman two bits, enough to buy a square meal. "Tell him Indy's here from London. Upstairs."

The man nodded. "I'll see that he hears."

The second floor was a horseshoe-shaped balcony with the tables bordering the railing. Indy passed several occupied tables before he found an empty one. The view of the stage was good, so he sat down. Even though the character of the place was similar to the bohemian *boîtes* in Paris, the second-floor patrons wore dark suits with hat brims pulled low, rather than natty sweaters and jauntily cocked berets. But maybe dressing in mobster garb was the craze these days in the Windy City. There was no doubt about the women. They were attired in flapper outfits: short skirts, long strings of beads, hose rolled down to their knees, and unbuckled galoshes on their feet.

He ordered a Coca-Cola from a mulatto waitress, then turned his attention to the stage as he heard the familiar signature of Shannon's cornet and a sassy beat of a jazz drummer. Shannon didn't look any different than the last time Indy had seen him. He still wore a goatee and his red hair was as unkempt as ever. In college, Shannon had stood six-foot-two and weighed a hundred and forty pounds. He didn't look as if he'd added a pound to his wiry frame.

At the end of the third tune, Shannon leaned over the microphone as the applause died down. "Thank you. That was the 'High Society Rag,' appropriated directly from King Joe Oliver himself."

He turned his head to the side and used his cornet like a pointer. "On piano tonight we have our old friend, Mr. Willie 'the Lion' Smith. Let's hear it for him." When the applause died, he continued: "On drums, all the way from New York's famous Rhythm Club, let's welcome Sonny Greer. We're going to play one more now, then take a break. When we come back, some of the Lion's friends are going to sit in with us."

Shannon shaded his eyes with a hand. "You up there, Jones? One of my special friends is here this evening. He won't be performing onstage for us, though. He's a professional ditch digger by trade, fresh off the streets of London."

Indy laughed as Shannon lifted his cornet to

his lips and the band struck up a rollicking tune and the dance floor filled. Indy leaned back in his chair and let the music flow over him. True jazz was the sound of raw emotion, of hard luck and good times. He looked at the people at the other tables on the second floor, watching the dancers below as if they were attending a performance. Some snapped their fingers to the syncopated beat. Others just observed; and for most whites who dared to venture into the neighborhood, that was enough.

A few minutes after the band took its break, Shannon strolled up the stairs wiping his brow with a towel. As he worked his way toward Indy's table he nodded and smiled and paused a couple of time to say a few words to the club's patrons. Indy stood up as Shannon reached his table. They shook hands and clasped shoulders.

"So you're really here," Shannon said. "I got your telegram and could hardly believe it."

"I can hardly believe it myself," Indy said as they sat down. "I feel like it's a dream."

"Well, this ain't Dreamland. That's down the street. No dreaming allowed here."

Indy laughed, and momentarily flashed on his dream. *D is for duir. . . . D is for duir.* It was something about his lost time in the jungle. Whatever had happened to him was like a dream. A dream that was still buried inside of him.

"So what do you think of this place?" Shannon asked.

"I guess it's about what I expected."

"You don't know the half of it, Indy. Believe me."

"What do you mean?"

"We own the place, you know."

"We?"

"Me and my brothers. Who do you think? It's sort of a silent ownership. A Negro manager, you know."

"Really? Then I'm surprised that you won't allow whites downstairs," Indy said. "Back when we used to come down here to listen to jazz, you used to complain about that kind of thing."

"I know. I know. That's one of the concessions I've had to make to my brothers. You see, if we mixed things up, we'd draw attention to the place, and we don't need that. We've got enough trouble as it is."

The waitress set a glass of soda water in front of Shannon and gave Indy another Coke. Shannon reached into his coat pocket and pulled out a flask. "Gin?"

"I see you haven't changed much." Shannon spiked Indy's soft drink, considering the comment as he added gin to his glass of soda water. "Oh, I don't know about that, Indy. You'd be surprised."

"I guess you've gotten closer to your brothers," Indy said, attempting to gauge Shannon's involvement in the mob.

"That's not really what I was thinking of, but yeah, I have gotten closer to the family. It was a necessity, you could say."

Indy knew that Shannon had moved into the family house, which he shared with his mother and one of his brothers, who had a wife and a couple of kids. "You still like living back home again?"

"It has certain advantages." Shannon ran a hand through his thick, unkempt hair. "I wish I could invite you to stay at the house, but it's just not the best idea right now."

"No problem. I've got a room already. I'm staying in the Blackstone Hotel." The last thing he wanted to do was take up space in a house that was probably already overcrowded.

"You're kidding. Hoover stayed there when he was in town."

"I believe it. It's quite a place, even if I can only afford it for a couple of nights."

"So how long you staying?"

"I don't know. It all depends. I'm going to see about a teaching job at our old alma mater, if you can believe that."

Shannon looked astonished. "What about your job in London?"

"What job?"

"You quit?"

"More or less. I couldn't take it anymore. I felt haunted. I'd even see Deirdre walking across the campus. Of course, it was never really her. Just someone who looked like her."

"It's a damn shame what happened," Shannon said. "I know things weren't always great with you two, but I thought right from the start that she was the one."

"She was. That's the problem. But it's over now, and I've got to put it behind me."

"Well, I'm glad you're back, but I'm a little surprised that you would want to teach at the university, especially after that run-in with Mulhouse over Founding Fathers' Day."

Indy waved a hand. "God, I'd almost forgotten

about that little episode. That's ancient history."

"I suppose. But if you had to do it over again, would you still hang those dummies?"

Indy dredged his memory. The two of them had hung effigies of George Washington, Thomas Paine, and Benjamin Franklin from lampposts to protest the university's mandatory participation in Founding Fathers' Day activities and assignments. When Indy had been caught, he'd nearly lost his degree.

"You know, when time passes, you look back at things that seemed important and you realize that they weren't such a big deal after all."

Shannon sipped his drink. "I see, so you're getting older and wiser."

"No, listen. At the time, I thought I was trying to make a point about heroes. You know, if the British had won, our revolutionary heroes would've been criminals. But I realize now that the real point I was making was that celebrating freedom should never be required of anyone. That's not what freedom is about, and Mulhouse was just plain wrong to force us to participate."

"I guess you're right. I always looked at it as your way of making a stand against mediocrity, because that's what that whole celebration . . ."

Shannon stopped as he stared down to the first floor at three men in stylish suits and hats who just walked into the club. The husky doorman was attempting to direct them upstairs.

"Looks like they don't know the downstairs is off limits for whites," Indy said.

"They know. They're looking for me." Shannon stood up and backed away from the table.

"What do they want?" Indy asked as he rose from his chair and trailed after Shannon.

"Oh, probably my life."

4

NIGHT AFFAIRS

Katrina and her father were leaving the restaurant when she saw the watcher again. He stood across the street, huddled under a streetlight. "Look, Papa. There he is. Do you see him?"

"Don't look at him. Just get in the taxi."

She slid across the backseat, but couldn't help stealing another glance at the mysterious man. He stood well over six feet, but he didn't look tall because of his bulk, which probably surpassed two hundred and fifty pounds. He had a square jaw and wore a hat and a trench coat. He was too far away now, but she'd already seen his icy blue eyes. He stared at the taxi and didn't move. She felt an involuntary shiver and was relieved when the taxi pulled away from the curb.

A few minutes later, they stopped in front of the Blackstone. But as soon as she stepped out a chill raced up her spine. She saw him. He was standing less than fifty feet away under the outside light of a shop. She stared, and saw the clothes, the same features, the square jaw, those terrible eyes that seemed to bore right through her. How had he gotten here ahead of them? It was impossible. But there he was. Waiting. Watching.

She was about to say something to her father as they entered the lobby, but she could see by his tense expression that he, too, had seen the watcher. It was better not to exacerbate the situation. Stay calm, she told herself.

"Papa, I'm tired. I think I'm going to go to bed early," she said when they reached their suite.

"That's a good idea. We have a big day tomorrow. And don't worry about him. We're safe here."

"I know. See you in the morning." Katrina kissed him on the cheek and retired to her room. She sat on the edge of her bed and paged through a magazine, waiting. She heard the water running in her father's bathroom, then the toilet flush. Finally, a faint creaking of springs told her that he'd settled into bed. She waited another few minutes, then turned off the light and quietly slipped out the door. She walked quickly down the hall to the elevator and descended to the lobby.

She identified herself to a desk clerk and told him what she wanted. He asked her to step around the counter, then escorted her into a room where dozens of built-in safes lined the walls. She took the key from her purse and searched the walls. She was confused because all of the safes looked too small. They were fine for jewelry and cash, but not for the sort of valuable her father had placed here.

"The number, madam?"

"Three twenty-three. I don't remember—"

"The lower level."

"Oh, there it is." Larger safes lined the wall along the floor. She tried the key and was relieved when it worked. Carefully, she withdrew a canvas bag, closed the door to the safe, and thanked the desk clerk.

She started to leave the room, but then turned back to the man. "Could someone accompany me to my room, please?"

The clerk gave her a puzzled look. "Our hotel is perfectly safe, madam."

You don't know about the watcher, she thought. "I'm sure it is, but I'd still like someone to walk with me."

"Of course." The desk clerk raised his head and snapped his fingers. "Frankie."

A young Negro man in a fancy doorman's uniform hurried over to the desk. "Please accompany Miss Zobolotsky to her room."

"Yes, sir."

He wasn't even as tall as she was, she thought.

"Evening, madam. Can I carry the bag for you?"

She drew back. "No, I'll carry it."

Frankie shrugged, then led the way to the elevator.

Katrina wasn't expecting trouble; there were too many people around. But she wasn't going to take any chances. As they rode up in the elevator it occurred to her that the doorman might have noticed the watcher.

"Frankie, can I ask you a question?"

"Yes, ma'am."

"I'm wondering if you noticed a certain man outside the hotel this evening." She described the watcher to him.

"Oh, that guy. I asked him if he wanted a room, but he just ignored me. Not a very friendly fellow."

"Have you seen him around before?"

"Just the past couple of days. There are two of them, you know."

"What?"

"Yeah. They look alike, even dress alike."

So that was it. She felt relieved that at least part of the mystery had been solved. It wasn't the devil, just twins. But her relief was only momentary. She still didn't know who they were, or what they wanted. "Did you notice anything else about them?"

He gave her a sly look. "Well, you see, I sort of snuck up on them earlier this evening and listened to them. I wanted to know what they were talking about."

This kid was great, she thought. "And what did they say?"

"I don't know. They spoke in some foreign language. Maybe Lithuanian. We got some of them folks here, you know."

Russian, not Lithuanian. That was her guess.

"Do you know them?" Frankie asked.

"I just happened to notice them," she said, and gave him a well-deserved tip as she stopped at her door. She quickly unlocked the door and slipped into the room. She stood in the darkness, listening. When she didn't hear any sounds from the adjoining room, she moved silently over to her bed and shoved the bag underneath it. She opened a dresser drawer and patted the inside of it until she found her nightgown.

As she changed in the bathroom she felt like a kid trying to get away with something. She didn't like doing anything behind her father's back, but it was better she did this alone. She was concerned about what would happen tomorrow. She needed some reassurance that it was going to work out. She opened the canvas bag and reached inside it. She removed an oblong object and slowly unwound the cloth that was wrapped around it. Finally, she closed her eyes and pressed it to her breast, and waited.

Indy followed Shannon as he quickly walked over to a red door in the corner. Shannon tapped on it three times, and after a moment it swung open. Another hulking doorman looked them over. He was a light-skinned Negro with wavy hair, and his arms and chest looked as if they were about to burst out of his tuxedo.

"He's okay. He's a friend," Shannon said, nodding toward Indy. The doorman was the only Negro in the smoky, crowded room. In the center under hanging lights were three gambling tables in full operation. A young woman walked up to Shannon. She wore a gingham baby romper with a big bow in the back, high heels, and pink and blue silk ribbons in her bobbed hair that were as large as her head. Her face was heavily made up and she carried a tray with several drinks on it.

"Hi, Jack. Whiskey for you and your friend?"

"No thanks." Shannon moved toward the tables. As Indy trailed him he noticed several more women, all dressed in identical costumes. Some were moving about the room with drinks or cigarettes, others were seated on couches talking with men who were smoking and drinking.

"What's going on, Jack?" Indy asked as Shannon stopped by one of the tables and looked around.

"Just wait a minute, will ya?"

"Would you like to get into the game, sir?"

Indy turned to see a handsome man with slicked-back hair and a thin mustache. He wore a tuxedo like the doorman, but was closer to Indy's size. "Ah, I don't think so. Not right now."

"Benny." Shannon motioned to the man. "If three mugs carrying lead in their jackets come in asking for me, tell them you haven't seen me. Okay?"

The man nodded. "Of course, Mr. Shannon."

Shannon motioned to Indy and they moved past the tables and over to another door. This time there was no doorman to question them. They hurried down a dingy back staircase and into an alley behind the club.

"Okay, Jack, what's going on?"

"It's a long story," Shannon said, walking rapidly down the alley.

"Give me a hint."

"Wait till we're inside."

Shannon knocked on a door at the next building. After a few seconds, Indy heard someone ask who it was, and Shannon gave his name.

The door opened a couple of inches and a face peered out. A tall woman in a cocktail dress smiled at them. "Hi, Marlee."

"Why, hello, Jack. Is this business or pleasure or both?"

"Neither. We just want to come in for a while. We'll stay out of the way."

"Anything you want."

As they stepped inside and closed the door Marlee looked at Indy, a question mark on her face.

"This is Indy, an old friend."

The woman extended a long hand with painted nails, then she turned away and motioned for them to follow. They moved down a dimly lit hallway and into a room that looked like a harem. Yards of silk with swirls of pink and blue floated in waves across the ceiling. More silk was draped over a couple of Tiffany lamps. The opposite wall was a mirror covered by a sheer material that gave their reflection a dreamy look. It took a moment before Indy noticed the pink couch with three women seated on it. They all wore silky robes; their faces were masks of makeup. One of them stood up and her robe slipped from her shoulders. She wore a lacy teddy and high heels.

"Not tonight, Cheri," Shannon said.

"Is this what I think it is?" Indy asked.

"Of course it is. The family protects it," Shannon explained.

"Seems like it's the other way around to me," Indy commented.

"I mean we protect the place from police raids," Shannon said, sounding annoyed. "That's the only way a bordello can stay open. Ain't that right, Marlee?"

"You got it. Now is there any service we can provide you gentlemen?"

"Just give us an empty room where we can get out of sight."

She smiled knowingly. "Oh, I get it."

"I don't think you do, Marlee, but show us the room anyhow," Shannon said.

They followed her around the corner and down a short hall. "This one has a king-size bed."

"Thanks." Shannon closed the door and locked it.

There was a sink in the corner and a bed, which nearly filled the room. Indy walked over to the window and saw that it looked out onto a brick wall. He peered down and saw a fire escape about ten feet below.

"Well, here we are locked in a bordello with no women and no view."

"Welcome back to Chicago," Shannon said as he stretched out on the bed and propped up his head with his hands.

Indy sat on the windowsill and crossed his arms. "Okay. I'm waiting to hear all about it."

"All right," Shannon began. "Those guys we saw are from the syndicate."

"What syndicate?"

Shannon laughed. "You certainly have been away a long time. The syndicate is an alliance of families in Chicago who got together and mapped out their territory for the liquor business. Dad refused to join, because he didn't get along with the Sicilians and didn't hide the fact. He paid for it. He was ambushed and shot along with two of his men in a restaurant in Cicero."

"I didn't know the details. I'm sorry," Indy said.

"Yeah, well. It hit me pretty hard, because

Dad and I weren't on the greatest terms after I moved to Paris. I was the black sheep, you know."

"But you always said he understood."

Shannon shrugged. "I guess he did."

That wasn't the case with Indy's father. He didn't understand why Indy had become an archaeologist, and it seemed that he didn't much care about him anymore.

"Anyhow, Harry, my oldest brother, took over and worked out a deal to join the syndicate. We got a piece of the South Side."

"Wait a minute. How could he join the syndicate after what happened to your father?"

"Don't think he liked it, Indy. He didn't one bit. But it was the only thing he could do. It was that or get out of the business, and if we did that, the cops would've been all over us."

"For going straight?"

"For losing our power base."

"So why is the syndicate after you now?"

"After Harry took over, we bought the Nest, but the club, you see, was a few blocks outside of our territory. So we worked out a special deal with Johnny Torrio, the head of the syndicate. The problem is that Johnny's out of the picture now. Replaced by his former chief lieutenant, and he says the Nest is his territory."

"You mean for liquor?"

"Yeah, but it don't make no sense for us to run the club and gambling room and not control the booze."

"You keep saying 'we.' Does that mean you're involved?"

"Sure it does. If I'm here in Chicago, there's

no escaping it, Indy. It's a fact of life."

"What do your brothers say about this problem with the Nest?"

"They say to hell with Alphonse Capone. If we give an inch to him, he'll go after more of our territory, and push us right off the map."

"Sounds like trouble."

"That's what I was getting at in the letter I wrote you."

"What are you going to do?"

Shannon shrugged. "I don't know. But I've been praying a lot on it."

"Praying?"

"Every day, Indy. On my knees."

Indy was quiet a moment. "I would say you were joking, but I don't think you are."

"I'm not. I've taken up the Bible. I'm serious about it."

"When did this all come about?"

"After Dad's death."

Shannon didn't seem very anxious to talk about it, but Indy was curious. "Tell me about it."

"I just started thinking about things. I'd already decided to stay, and I knew that if things didn't work out right, I'd be joining Dad real fast. I just felt I was being called. It was time for me to listen to what God was saying to me."

"But, Jack, how can you justify being religious and reading the Bible and being involved in the mob and everything that goes with it? Hell, we're sitting in a bordello."

"I'm a sinner, Indy. I'll be the first to admit it. I sin every day. But the Lord died for our sins, and that means there's hope."

That sort of summed it all up. What could he say?

"Well, no offense, but it sounds to me like this religious stuff isn't having much effect on your personal life."

"What do you mean?"

"I mean instead of going around talking about how much you sin, do something about it."

"We're all sinners, Indy. Plain and simple. You can't get around it."

And if you think otherwise, that's probably a sin, too, Indy thought. He was having a hard time adjusting to Shannon's new approach to life, as well as to the surrounding circumstances. In the past few minutes, he'd learned that his old friend was actively involved in his family's illegal businesses, that he was being pursued by some vicious mobsters, and that he'd found a refuge in religion.

"What are you going to do about those guys with the guns?"

"I'll leave that up to God. It's totally in His hands."

"Then why did you run?"

"Because I'm weak. I let my fear control me."

"Cut the crap, Jack. It was your instinct. And you were right."

Indy heard voices in the hallway and a door open and close. "How does this protection racket work, anyhow?"

"It's two dollars a trick. The girl gets eighty cents, twenty cents goes to protection, and the house gets the other dollar."

"Swell deal." Indy's head jerked at the sound of shouts and a scuffle outside the room. "What's that?"

"They found us."

Indy moved over to the window, pulled it open. He stretched a leg out the window toward the fire escape. "Jack, c'mon. Move it."

Shannon's face was contorted with the anguish of some private battle. It was as if part of him wanted to flee and another pinned him to the bed. "There's nothing easy about following the path of the Lord," he said.

"Let's talk about it later. Now get over here."

Suddenly there was an ominous thud and the door shuddered. Indy was now in a fix similar to Shannon's. He was torn between dropping to the fire escape and staying with his friend. The door crashed open, and from his perch Indy saw a blur of movement and a gun aimed at Shannon. He pulled his leg back into the room and dived headfirst, tackling the gunman. They rolled over amid shouts and grunts.

Someone kicked him in the side. A hand grabbed him by the hair and jerked him to his feet. He was thrown against the wall and kneed in the crotch. He took a wild swing, and connected. But hands immediately grabbed his arms and twisted them behind his back.

He expected to see the three thugs, but instead he was surrounded by cops waving billy clubs and aiming guns.

"Oh, isn't this sweet," one of them said. "Which one of you is supposed to be the girl?"

Shannon was shoved over next to him and they were both handcuffed.

"They don't look like sissies to me," one of the cops said. "I can always spot 'em. They were probably just waiting for the girls, and we spoiled their fun."

"I don't know," another one said. "You can't tell these days. Some of 'em even have wives and kids."

They were pushed out in the hall and hustled out of the bordello. Indy found himself in the back of a police wagon with Shannon and Marlee, several women in robes, and two other men.

"Jack, I thought you said you protected the place. What happened?"

"Isn't it obvious? Capone's taking over. He bought out our protection."

5

VISITORS

"I wonder how things are going at the Blackstone?" Indy said from his bunk in their barren jail cell.

They were charged with lewd and lascivious behavior, resisting arrest, and disorderly conduct. They wouldn't get out until morning at the earliest, and all Indy could think about was his empty suite at the Blackstone.

"Count your blessings."

"My blessings? What blessings are they?"

"I'm just saying we were lucky it was the cops and not the capos who got us, and we were lucky they were real cops."

"Yeah. I feel real lucky."

Shannon stared across the cell at Indy. "Okay, I'm sorry about this. When we get out of here, I think it might be a good idea if you just stayed away from me."

"Jack, cut it out."

"I'm not kidding. Things are getting out of

hand. Just look where we are now, and like I said, we were lucky."

Indy grinned. "And you always said I was the one who pulled you into dangerous waters."

"I guess I'm getting back at you."

Indy understood how Shannon had latched onto religion. But it was so uncharacteristic of the Shannon he knew that he asked how it had happened.

"How did what happen?"

"The Bible stuff."

"One of the guys who plays at the Nest one day invited me to the church. He said they needed a horn player. I thought it was going to be like playing at a bar mitzvah. You know, go play, collect your money, and go home. But when we got there, everyone welcomed me in a way that was real genuine. I don't know; it just made me feel real good. It turned out the minister had been a barrelhouse piano player from the old days before he'd turned to God."

"Oh, yeah?"

"I guess that sold me on the church. I just felt comfortable and there were other musicians there, too. Pretty soon the Bible started making sense to me. It was like a part of me needed it and I was ready."

"How is it different from going to Mass?"

"No comparison. This church doesn't have all the ritual. I mean you can stand up and shout if that's what you feel like doing. It's just a lot freer."

"Is the minister a Negro?"

"Sure. It's a Negro church."

"Are you the only white guy in the congregation?"

"There're a few other whites in mixed marriages who belong. But I'm the only Irishman. Ambrose, the minister, says the race of the congregation members is about as important as the color of socks you wore yesterday."

"Well, if you like it, why not?"

"Indy, it's given me a new way of looking at things. It really has."

He could tell Shannon was sincere, and that was fine with him. He just hoped his old friend didn't get so caught up in his new religious ways that he became intolerant toward anyone whose beliefs were different.

"Just do me one favor, Jack. Don't ever try to tell me that the world was created six thousand, eight hundred, and twenty-three years ago on a Tuesday morning."

"Wasn't it on a Thursday morning?" Shannon laughed. "All right. That's a promise. I may think it, if that's what the good book says, but I won't try to make you believe it."

A minute passed in silence, then Shannon spoke up. "You know maybe this isn't such a bad thing being in jail together."

"What do you mean?"

"We're getting a chance to talk and we haven't done that for a long time."

"That's true."

"I hope you get the job at the university. It would be great to have you around again. At least, after things settle down."

"The only thing about the job is that I'd be teaching Celtic archaeology again, and like I said, I'm not sure I want to do that now."

Shannon nodded. "You know, maybe you should get back into translating inscriptions. You're good at languages," he said.

"Why do you say that?" Indy asked suspiciously.

"Oh, I don't know. I was just thinking that something like that might bring you closer to your father again. I think it's important to have a good relationship with your parents, especially your father."

"Jack, don't worry about me and my father. I know that situation better than you do, and translating inscriptions is no way to win his affection. Not at this point, anyhow."

"No, I suppose not."

"Besides, I already turned down a chance to do that very thing. That's what got me fired."

"I thought you quit."

"It was sort of a mutual agreement. I just don't care much about translating dead languages for a living. It can drive you nuts."

Shannon pondered his comment a moment. "Why do you say that?"

"It's the truth. Ogham doesn't use vowels. Ancient Greek doesn't use punctuation, and sometimes it reads one direction on one line, then the other direction on the next one."

Shannon shrugged. "Yeah, but you like a good mystery."

"Listen, when I say that it can drive you crazy, I mean it. Have you ever heard of George Smith?"

"What instrument does he play?"

"None that I know of. Around the turn of the

century, Smith became one of the most renowned decoders of ancient languages when he translated cuneiform found at the ruins of Ninevah."

"Wait a minute. I'm a jazz musician, remember? What language is cuneiform? I never heard of it."

"It's not a language; it's an alphabet that was used for several languages: Babylonian, Assyrian, Sumerian, and Persian. That's part of what made decoding them so tough. It's got wedge-shaped characters that are so different from any other alphabet that for a long time it was thought to be a decorative motif. But finally cuneiform dictionaries were discovered with translations in several languages."

"So where does this Smith guy fit in?" Shannon asked. "Did he find the dictionaries?"

"No, that was Rawlinson. What Smith did was translate cuneiform that was found in the palace library of the Assyrian king Ashurbanipal."

"A library with books?"

"Books made out of clay. The inscriptions were baked rather than printed."

Shannon shook his head and laughed. "Indy, it amazes me that you know all this stuff."

"It's not as amazing as the way you can pick up a cornet and actually make music."

"Nothing to that. But this stuff is sort of interesting. Those people you're talking about are from biblical times, aren't they?"

"Biblical times and long before it. But let me finish what I started to tell you. Smith was translating a broken-off section of a book when he realized that he was reading the story of the Flood."

"You're kidding. You mean the one Moses wrote about—Noah's Ark in Genesis?"

"Right. But the version that Smith was translating was written long before the Hebrew one. The amazing thing is that it was the same story, except for the names of the deity and of Noah."

Shannon suddenly let out a whoop and stood up. He raised his hands above his head and shook them. "Oh, yeah. Praise the Lord."

Indy looked up in alarm. "What's wrong?"

"I just had a revelation."

"What are you talking about?"

"I can't believe it. Oh, yes. I do believe it."

"Jack, calm down. . . . "

"Listen. Noah's Ark, Indy. That's it. Hallelujah! I'm receiving the Lord's word. I think you're supposed to go to my church with me tomorrow night."

The pressure of everything that was happening with Shannon's family was getting the better of him, Indy thought. "Jack, just sit down. Take a deep breath."

Shannon laughed. "You think I'm crazy, don't you? But you're wrong. Tomorrow night, Indy. It's important."

"Jack, I told you that it's fine with me if you want to get religious. Praise the Lord and read the Bible all you want, but don't try to drag me to your church. All right?"

"But you don't understand. Tomorrow evening there's a man, a special guest, who's going to talk, and I think you should hear him."

"Why?"

"The name of his talk is 'The Genesis Deluge.' He's going to talk about Noah's Ark. In fact, he climbed Mount . . . Mount . . . "

"Ararat."

"Right. He climbed Mount Ararat and found Noah's Ark."

"Or so he says," Indy said without enthusiasm. "Think about it, Jack. Let's be rational. If he really found Noah's Ark, don't you think the whole world would know about it by now? Hell, it probably would've been carted down off the mountain and put on exhibit in the world's fair."

"Indy, give the man a chance, will ya? You're judging him before you've heard what he's got to say."

"I've heard enough already. Noah's Ark is a legend, a myth. It's not a wood boat that you can climb up and look at, for chrissakes."

Shannon looked acutely disappointed. "You don't even want to hear about it, do you? You're so concerned about us so-called Bible thumpers forcing you to believe something that you won't listen to anything we have to say. Maybe he did find Noah's Ark. Can't you even consider it?"

Indy held up a hand. "Okay, I'm sorry."

He knew Shannon was right. He was reacting to Jack just like many of his former colleagues would react to some of his own experiences. Experiences he himself couldn't explain or quite grasp. He'd never told any of his colleagues about what had happened to him at Stonehenge beyond the barest details. He'd said nothing about the enigmatic influences of a stone called the Omphalos, and not a word about his strange chat with a kindly old man who claimed to be Merlin the magician. It wasn't that he didn't have the courage to talk about those encounters; he just considered them personal experiences. Besides, since he didn't fully understand them himself, how could he convince anyone that they were real?

"I'll tell you what. If you can get us out of here, I'll gladly go with you tomorrow night."

"That's great. Don't worry. We'll get out by morning. That's a promise."

"One other thing," Indy added.

"What's that?" Shannon asked warily.

"Do me a favor, and don't shout any more hallelujahs in my ear."

They both laughed, and Indy realized their friendship had just been reaffirmed.

Morning was still hours away, so Indy decided to get some sleep and forget about what had happened. He was just about to stretch out on the bench when Shannon spoke up.

"Say, you never finished your story about this guy named Smith."

"Oh, yeah." Shannon's enthusiastic outburst had made him forget all about Smith.

"You said he translated a book that gave the same flood story, but was a lot older."

"Right. The man who built the boat and saved the animals was called Ut-naphishtim."

Shannon looked perplexed. "Then there were two Noahs?"

"I don't know. But that's not the point. What I was getting to was that the work was so consuming for Smith that it did something to his mind. After he finished making one crucial translation, he told his colleagues: 'I am the first man to read this text after two thousand years of oblivion.' Then he started making some strange grunting sounds and ripped off his clothes. He died a little while later. He was only thirty-six."

"You're making this up."

"No, I'm not."

"You think he was possessed by the devil?"

"No. It's like I said, translating old languages can drive you nuts, and I don't want to follow in Smith's footsteps."

"I see your point, but—"

Just then the gate of the cell block creaked open, and Shannon leaped to his feet. "Maybe we're going to get out of here sooner than I thought."

Indy heard footsteps and suddenly a guard appeared at the door with the key. "What did I tell you?" Shannon said, turning to him. "You see, God is with us."

But Indy was looking beyond the guard. He saw three men in dark suits with hats pulled low over their brow. He was almost certain they were the same trio who'd come to the Nest in search of Shannon.

"You got visitors, fellows," the guard said. "Mr. Capone would like to talk to you."

The three men moved into the cell and the guard turned his back. Two of the men pulled short clubs from inside their coats. The third one, a round-faced man with dark, mean eyes, crossed his arms and smiled. Indy had been away, but he knew he was standing face to face with Al Capone. His picture, as well as his notoriety, had made the papers in London.

"So Jack Shannon, your big brother has been ignoring me, and here I thought we had an agreement about territory," Capone said.

"I'm a musician. I don't know what you're talking about."

One of Capone's henchmen thrust the blackjack into Shannon's gut. Indy stepped forward and the other thug clubbed him in the kidneys. Both men crumpled to the floor of the cell.

One of the thugs jerked Shannon to his feet and pressed his blackjack under his jaw. "Let's not play games, Shannon," Capone said. "Just answer my questions."

"What do you want from me?"

"This is your lucky day, Jack. I'm going to go real easy on you tonight. You're going to be my messenger boy for your big brother Harry. You got that?"

Shannon nodded.

"Good. You see, the Shannons broke our agreement. That was real stupid. But I'm going to try one more time to talk some sense into you. You tell brother Harry that there'll be no more Shannon booze in my territory, and you tell 'em that from tonight on I get half of the gambling take at the Nest. I heard you guys are doing real well, so we're going to share it, like buddies. You got that?"

Shannon tried to say something, but the blackjack cut off his windpipe.

"You either like it or join your dear old dad. You got that, Jackie Boy?"

Indy wobbled to his feet. "Let him go."

Capone stared at Indy. "Who is this guy, Shannon, another punk horn blower?"

Indy took a swing at Capone, who jerked his head back just in time. The thugs instantly slammed into Indy, knocking him to the floor. They pounded him with fists and clubs again and again until he couldn't feel a thing.

"Stop it," Shannon yelled. "You're killing him."

"Enough," Capone said. "Pick him up."

The thugs grabbed Indy by his shirt and pulled him to his feet. Indy could barely see, but he knew what was about to happen. Capone drew back his arm and slammed his fist into Indy's jaw, and that was the last thing he remembered.

6

The Gospel Truth

When Indy awoke the next morning, he found himself on a bed with white curtains draped around it. He vaguely recalled being carried on a stretcher and transported by ambulance to a hospital. He sat up, wincing as pain shot from his shoulders and arms, up his neck, and into his jaw.

He heard voices from beyond the curtain and recognized Shannon's. He tried to make sense of what was being said, but he only picked out disjointed words and phrases. "Possible concussion . . . bruises . . . lucky . . . no fractures . . . examine . . . later."

He heard footsteps as someone walked away. "Jack? You out there?"

Shannon pushed aside the curtain. "You're awake. How you feeling?"

"How do you think?"

"I was just talking to the doctor. He said it could've been a lot worse."

"Yeah, maybe if I'd been run over by a truck. I see we're out of jail."

"We were officially released about an hour ago. The charges were dropped."

"Why was that? Because they let goons in the cell to beat us up?"

"No. Because one of the circuit judges is a special friend of the family."

"Convenient."

"I thought you would think so. The doctor's going to be back around lunchtime to check on you. I guess you should stay here a couple of days."

"No thanks. I'm not in that bad of shape." He threw his legs over the side of the bed and tried to ignore the pain. "Hand me my clothes."

Shannon chuckled as he reached down on the lower shelf of a steel tray for the clothing. "I had the feeling you wouldn't want to stick around here."

"I've got to get my things out of the Blackstone before I go broke."

"Don't worry about it," Shannon said offhandedly.

Indy pulled on his pants. "What do you mean don't worry about it?"

"I extended your stay a couple nights. It's all taken care of."

"You did?"

"The family's got a little credit at the Blackstone, you could say."

"Huh. Well, in that case, thanks. How are you feeling?"

Shannon rubbed his side. "I'm okay. You're the one they laid into."

"So what are you and your brothers going to do about Capone?"

"Good question. I've got to talk to them today. It's not going to be an easy decision, I know that."

"Good luck."

"Say, do you still want to see Dr. Zobolotsky tonight?"

"Who?"

"The guy who found Noah's Ark. He's a Russian doctor. He lives in San Francisco now. Escaped after the Bolsheviks took over."

"Oh, yeah," Indy said unenthusiastically. It was about the last thing on his mind right now. "You think it's going to be worth it?"

"I can't promise you anything. But I'd really like you to go. As a favor for me. Besides, you ought to see his daughter, Katrina. I'm in love with her and I only met her for a few minutes."

"In love, uh?" Indy grimaced as he pulled on his shirt. Shannon was an independent sort who was not quick to fall in love. In fact, he'd only heard Shannon say he was in love once before.

"Yeah, I think I am. I really do."

Indy didn't give a damn about seeing the girl or her father. But he knew there was no way he could back out, especially after Shannon had covered his room at the Blackstone. "Now tell me again why he's speaking at your church?"

"I don't think I told you in the first place. He was originally going to talk at a Lithuanian church over on Wood Street. But the pastor backed out after he realized there was going to be publicity about it. Most of his parishioners have families back in the old country and they're afraid this sort of thing could cause trouble for them."

"The Russians don't run Lithuania."

"Give them time," Shannon said. "I hear they've got big plans for Europe."

Indy looked around for his shoes. "So your minister volunteered his church."

Shannon found Indy's shoes under the bed and handed them to him. "Not a Russian or Lithuanian immigrant in the congregation," he said with a grin. "But we've opened the doors to the Lithuanians and anybody else interested for this event. It should be interesting."

"All right. I'll take it easy today and see you there tonight."

"Great. I've got a real good feeling about this, Indy."

"What do you mean by that?"

"Something is going to come out of this for you. I'm almost sure of it."

Probably a good laugh, Indy thought.

The man read the article in the *Chicago Tribune* for the second time. He read it slowly and carefully, making sure that he understood every line. He had lived in America for ten years, but his English was not as good as it could have been. The article was about plans to search for Noah's Ark on Mount Ararat. The mountain was located in Turkey, his homeland, and he had to do something to stop this Zobolotsky before it was too late.

"What are you reading there? You look like you're going to start the paper on fire with that stare."

Ismael looked up at his young wife, Jela, whose dark hair fell over her shoulders. She had just put their year-and-a-half-old son into his crib for his afternoon nap. "Take a look."

She read over the article much more quickly than he had, then looked up at him. "What are you thinking?"

"This can't be allowed. It's not time for the Ark to be found. You know the scriptures. The savior has not returned."

"Don't talk like that. You're not carrying the future of the world on your back. If that man wants to go to Turkey, you can't stop him."

"But he must be stopped."

"Ismael, please. You have your family to think about. Maybe he'll change his mind or maybe he won't find it. Don't ruin your life over something like this. Think about our children."

She was right. Maybe nothing would come of it. But he would contact his brother right away and warn him. Hasan was difficult to reach, but he knew someone in Istanbul who would get a message to his brother.

He pushed away from the table.

"Where are you going?"

He took her hand. "Don't worry. I'm just going to send a cable to Istanbul. Hasan must be told. He will take care of what must be done."

Humidity clung to the air like a cloak, but a fresh breeze was blowing off the lake as Indy left the Blackstone and headed up Michigan Street. It had rained late in the afternoon and the streets were slick and glistening. Shannon's church was located about a mile south of the hotel just off Michigan, and he'd decided to walk.

He was glad now that he'd committed himself

to going out. The walk would give him a chance to clear his head and work out the aches and pains. It was probably not what a doctor would recommend, but he knew his body and his ability to recover from injury better than anyone.

After all, he'd spent the day in the hotel soaking in his bath, resting in bed, and ordering room service. He was still sore, but he felt surprisingly improved from this morning. He took his time, though, and he wasn't going to make it a late night. He wanted to be ready to see Angus O'Malley tomorrow.

He'd called the archaeology department at the university that afternoon and was told O'Malley was out of the office. When he identified himself, the secretary told him that O'Malley had received his telegram and was interested in seeing him as soon as possible.

"That's fine with me," Indy had said, and made an appointment for two-thirty.

"Oh, wait a minute. Dr. O'Malley just walked in the door. Let me tell him you're on the phone."

"Indiana, how are you?" O'Malley's voice boomed so loudly that Indy had to pull the receiver away from his ear.

"I'm fine. I just got into town yesterday." *Fine* wasn't exactly the right adjective to describe the way he felt. But he certainly wasn't going to tell O'Malley that Al Capone and a couple of his henchmen had beat him up in jail last night after he'd been arrested in a bordello. "And please, just call me Indy."

"Well, I'm glad you called . . . Indy. I was very pleased to get your telegram. The timing couldn't be better. It just so happens that one of my staff is leaving quite unexpectedly and I have a part-time position open this summer, if you're interested."

"I think I might be. What about the fall?"

"By then I should have the funding for a full-time assistant professorship for you, if you're willing to stay on with us."

"That sounds great." O'Malley, it seemed, was actually true to his word.

"There is one thing, Indy. I can't assure you that all of your classes will be in Celtic archaeology. We like our staff to be as versatile as possible. In fact, this summer you would be teaching an introductory course with an emphasis on North American archaeology."

"Oh, well, I suppose I could manage." He tried his best not to sound gleeful at the unexpected and welcome development.

"Don't worry about it. I'm sure you can handle the course with ease."

"I would think so."

"I see you're scheduled to come in at two-thirty tomorrow. I have another appointment just before that, but I don't expect it to take long at all."

"I'll see you then," Indy said, and rang off.

No, he wouldn't mind getting away from the Celts for a while. Not at all, he thought, as he neared his destination.

The Gospel Chapel of New Life didn't look like a typical church. There was no high steeple or sharply sloping roof, no stained glass or arched windows, and no impressive doors. It was an unimpressive two-story brick building, where a dozen or so people were filing through the door ahead of him. He followed them inside and up the aisle past rows of wooden seats that were already filled.

He'd no sooner entered the church than he heard Shannon's cornet accompanied by a clarinet and a piano. The three-piece band was set up in a corner near the front of the church. The music was intended as a soothing background sound and it was one of the more tranquil horn pieces he'd heard Shannon play in a long time. The usual flurry of sixteenth- and thirty-second-note runs had been replaced by long, drawn-out notes that made Indy think Shannon was moving in slow motion. Gone was the dissonance that seemed almost part of his instrument. In its place was a smooth, flowing sound that rippled gently over the assembly.

Although Indy would've preferred sitting near the rear, all the seats in the back half of the church were filled, mostly with whites, who, like himself, were probably attending the church for the first time. He found a seat a few rows from the front and sat down. Shannon nodded to him and continued playing. Indy wondered how Shannon's meeting with his brothers had gone. He'd ask about it when the evening's address was over.

Just as Indy was starting to wonder how long the music would go on, a robed choir rose in unison to its feet and began to sing "Swing Low, Sweet Chariot." The congregation sang along. When "Michael, Row the Boat Ashore" followed, Indy realized the evening was going to extend longer than he had hoped. Halfway through the song, someone began to shout "Noah" in place of "Michael" and others quickly joined in. Then the pace quickened as the choir swung into a lively gospel song in which the crowd answered each line with the same two words.

"Won't you ring old hammer?
HAMMER RING
Broke the handle in my hammer.
HAMMER RING
Got to hammering in the Bible.
HAMMER RING
Gotta talk about Noah.
HAMMER RING
Well, God told Noah
HAMMER RING
You is a-going in the timber
HAMMER RING."

Suddenly people were rising to their feet, first the Negroes, then slowly the whites. They clapped their hands and shouted their response. A large, Negro woman tugged at Indy's arm, pulling him to his feet, and he joined the clapping. Shannon set his horn down on the piano and joined the call and response, and he grinned as he caught Indy's eye.

Finally, the musical warm-up came to a close and a Negro man who looked to be in his mid-fifties strode to the pulpit. He greeted the audience and many of them greeted him right back. He introduced himself as Ambrose Hinton, the pastor of the church, and welcomed all the new faces.

"Tonight we have a very special guest with us. During the war, Dr. Vladimir Zo-bo-lot-sky was a lieutenant in the White Russian Army and was stationed near Mount Ararat in Turkey. Mr. Z, as I like to call him, brings a message of great importance, not only for this assembled audience, but the entire world."

As he spoke his voice grew louder and stronger. "It is a message that not only documents the truth of the word of God as spoken through the Bible, but is a direct message from the Almighty, who is telling us here and now to reaffirm our faith and belief in Him, because it will ultimately be rewarded. O Lord, you know we're listening to you."

"Amen," several people shouted.

"I usually have more to say," he continued in a quieter voice, "but this is such a momentous occasion that I will now yield the pulpit to our honorable speaker so we can all hear his wonderful story."

"Hallelujah," someone cried out.

"I hope that's for our speaker and not for my quick departure," Hinton said. Laughter rippled through the crowd.

A slender man with sandy hair walked out with his spine held straight and his shoulders back. He moved as if he were in a hurry to reach the pulpit. He shook hands with Hinton, then moved behind the pulpit.

"Praise the Lord," someone shouted before the Russian had a chance to say anything.

"Yes, praise the Lord," Zobolotsky responded in accented English. "I am very glad to be here with you this evening."

"We're glad you came," someone responded.

Indy wondered what the Russian thought of the church. The Gospel Chapel of New Life, with its freewheeling style of music and the shouts from the assembly, was no doubt a far cry from the Russian Orthodox Church or any other church in his homeland. But Zobolotsky was not a timid man. He rose up on his toes and leaned forward over the pulpit as he spoke. His voice was strong and easily carried to the back of the room.

"Thank you, my friends, for inviting me. I am happy to have the opportunity to talk to you this evening about a great wonder," he began.

"During the war, I was an officer with the Nineteenth Petropovlovsky Regiment, which was stationed in a very isolated province of Turkey. Our mission was to guard the Aratsky Pass from the Turks, who were aligned with the Germans. It was very cold when I arrived there and I remember thinking about how I missed my home and wished I was there. Or actually any place but where I was. Then one day, it was late in 1916, something very startling happened. A pilot named Roskovitsky was flying over the mountain they call Ararat, and when he returned he said that he saw a great wooden ship up near to the top. Well, I knew my Bible stories and I knew that the mountain was the one where Noah landed."

Zobolotsky paused and looked over the audience. The place was quiet now. A chair squeaked; someone cleared his throat and the sounds seemed to fill the room.

"I thought to myself that this pilot probably knows the Bible, too, and he's playing a joke on us. I am not a pilot, so I did not know him very well. But about a week after I heard the story, I saw Lieutenant Roskovitsky in the village and asked him what he had seen on the mountain. He became very serious and told me that, yes, it was a ship. His copilot was there with him and he said he saw it, too. I said, 'Well, maybe it was a big rock,' but both men said they saw wood beams. They were convinced it was a boat.

"Then Roskovitsky said I should see it for myself and invited me to fly over the mountain with him. So three or four days later, I joined Roskovitsky and two other officers, and I was very impressed with what I saw. It did look like a ship, maybe a very large submarine. But I asked myself, why would someone be building a submarine way up here on the mountain?"

He paused again and his eyes scanned the attentive audience. "I was very curious about what I saw, but to be truthful, all I wanted at that time was to go home to Harbin and my family. Every day I prayed that today I would hear that the war was over and we were leaving. Several months passed and finally we were told that the Nineteenth Petropovlovsky Regiment would be returning to Russia. I was so happy that I nearly wept when I heard the news.

"Then two days before the regiment was to depart, the colonel gathered all the officers and told us that the Fourteenth Railroad Battalion had arrived with orders from the czar to climb the mountain and find Noah's Ark."

"Hal-le-lujah," several people shouted in unison.

"Well, that's not what I said," Zobolotsky responded. "My first thought was that no one could climb to the top of that mountain. Good luck, boys, I said to myself. Then the colonel looked us over and I saw his eyes stare right at me. He said that the battalion would need a medical doctor to join them, and the next thing I knew—how do I say it? The colonel volunteered me to stay behind with the battalion. I was very disappointed. Only later I realized it was God's will that I stay. God's will, and of course, the colonel's, too."

The audience laughed, and Indy chuckled along. At least Zobolotsky wasn't boring.

"The next week one hundred soldiers were picked to climb the mountain. We were divided into two groups and we soon found ourselves marching up different sides of the mountain. It was a very difficult climb that took us two days. During the second day, it seemed that we were almost to the top. Then we would reach another crest and see that there was more mountain ahead of us. Finally, late in the afternoon we crawled to the top of a ridge, and there we saw it. The Ark was resting in a saddle of the mountain between the two peaks. The soldiers from the other group had already reached the ship and we could see them walking around it and on top of it."

"Oh, Lord," the woman next to Indy whispered.

"So we hurried down, moving faster than we had gone all day. When we arrived, everyone was amazed that there was actually a ship here on the mountain. We were fourteen thousand feet above sea level. It was huge, and the entire ship was covered with a thick layer of pitch that had preserved it, so that most of the ship looked in very good condition.

"I saw that the door had fallen off and it lay next to the ship. It was partially burned and I thought that lightning must have hit it. I went inside and looked around, and that was when I knew it must be the Ark. There were three decks and on each of them were cages. Lots of cages of different sizes."

Oh, brother, Indy thought. This is entertaining, but it was getting to be a bit much. Moses had written the story of Noah around 1475 B.C., supposedly about fourteen hundred years after the great deluge. Even if a wooden ship could somehow still exist after almost five thousand years, finding Noah's and finding it virtually intact was just too good to be true.

Zobolotsky explained how the soldiers meticulously measured the Ark, drew diagrams of the exterior of the ship and each of the three interior decks, and took numerous photographs. "We were all very excited about what we had found, and a message was sent to the czar. Later, a full report was prepared with the drawings and photographs, and it was carried by messenger to the czar's palace. Unfortunately, we know nothing of what happened to the messenger or the report. You see, about the time he would have arrived in Petrograd the czar was overthrown in the Bolshevik Revolution."

Swell, Indy thought. A testimonial, but no evidence. Zobolotsky turned and motioned toward the side of the church. An attractive, young blond woman walked toward the pulpit carrying a canvas bag. She passed the bag to Zobolotsky, who laid it on the pulpit and removed something that was wrapped in cloth.

"I had the feeling that I should take something of the Ark with me just in case anything happened to the rest of the evidence. So when no one was looking, I took a piece of wood from the broken door and quickly hid it in my pack."

He stepped aside; the woman took his place and began to slowly unwind the cloth. She must be his daughter, Indy thought. He glanced over at Shannon and saw a look on his face that he hadn't seen since they were in college and Shannon thought he'd found the love of his life, a music major who was fascinated with jazz and infatuated with Shannon. She was just right for him, but when she'd found out about his family, she'd suddenly broken off their engagement.

Everyone leaned forward for a better look. "Now you will see it," Zobolotsky said. "Here, my good friends, is a piece of Noah's Ark." The woman lifted a blackened, oblong object above her head. It was about the length and thickness of her forearm. Everyone was quiet; some people bowed their heads in silent prayer, others held their hands out toward the piece of wood as if to be closer to it or to soak in its sacred energy.

Zobolotsky could've found the stick behind the church for all Indy knew. He shifted his gaze from the piece of wood to the woman. He could see why Shannon was so taken with her. She hadn't said a word, yet Indy almost felt as if he knew her. She was innocent, honest, dedicated, and compassionate. He didn't know how he knew this, but he would be surprised to find out otherwise. For a moment, he thought her eyes met his, then she lowered the object. As she rewrapped it and returned it to the canvas bag, Zobolotsky finished his narrative.

"Soon I will be leaving the United States and going back to Turkey, where I will climb Mount Ararat again. I know I must go back. I have no choice. The sacred Ark is pulling me. There are dangers, of course, but I know I am under the guidance of the good Lord. Someday I hope you will invite me back and I'll tell you all about my return to the Ark. Thank you."

As Zobolotsky and the woman walked away from the pulpit the audience rose to its feet and applauded loudly. Indy stood and watched the pair until they disappeared from sight. He didn't know quite what to think. It was an interesting performance, but what was the point? What did Zobolotsky expect to gain from it?

He was sore and tired and ready to go back to the hotel, and the sooner the better. He'd say hello to Shannon, then he'd be on his way. But the evening's entertainment wasn't quite over yet. The choir was on its feet again, and as the applause started to die, the vacuum was filled with the lyrics of another lively gospel song.

"Ol' Noah's lookin' for his mountaintop,
Goin' let that dove go fly flippety flop.
When that bird come back round with a sprig
You bet Noah's goin' dance all over that rig."

The crowd clapped to the beat, and hardly anyone left until the song was over. Finally, as the rows of chairs emptied, Indy walked over to Shannon, who was wiping his cornet with a towel.

"So what did you think, Indy?"

"I enjoyed it. Glad I came."

"What did you think of Katrina?"

"The girl?" Indy shrugged. "A real heartbreaker, I'd guess."

"Thanks for being so encouraging."

"Well, you know how it goes sometimes."

Shannon laid his cornet in its case. "Let's see if we can talk to them. You could have a chat with Dr. Zobolotsky about the Ark, and I could get to know Katrina better."

Indy held up a hand. "I don't think so. I've heard all I care to hear for tonight."

"Really? You mean to say that if Dr. Zobolotsky offered you a chance to go with him to Mount Ararat on his mission, you wouldn't jump at it?"

"First of all, archaeologists don't go on missions. They go on expeditions. They're scientists, not part of a church."

"All right, all right. But answer my question. Would you go with him if you had the chance?"

"I'm not interested in missionary work. Besides, there's a real good chance I'm going to be teaching right here in Chicago this summer. I'll find out for sure tomorrow."

They headed down the aisle toward the door. "I don't know, Indy. I just had the feeling that you'd be more excited about this."

Indy didn't say anything more until they stepped outside. "Do you really think Zobolotsky found Noah's Ark, Jack?"

"You heard what he said. You think he'd lie in a church about something like that?"

"It's not a lie exactly. I think he saw what he wanted to see. Or believes. That's all."

"Yeah, I suppose," Shannon said, sounding disappointed. "C'mon, Mr. Scientist, I'll give you a ride to your palace."

They climbed into Shannon's Model-T runabout and pulled away from the curb. "I thought you sounded good tonight, Jack. It was a different style for you."

"Thanks." Shannon seemed fatigued. His shoulders slumped, his jaw was slack.

"So how'd things go with your brothers?"

Shannon shrugged. "Not so good. We had a talk, but I don't know what's going to happen. Things could get violent very easy."

"Can't you do something to stop it?"

"Any suggestions? I'm out of them."

Indy didn't know what to say. As they slowed to a stop in front of the hotel Shannon leaned back in his seat. "The way things are going I may get to heaven before you. But I'll blow my horn when I see you coming."

7

The Reflecting Pond

It was his first time back on campus since he'd graduated, and Indy couldn't help feeling uneasy about it. Even though eight years had passed, he still remembered how he'd been treated during his last days here. But why even think about it? Mulhouse had retired; Founding Fathers' Day had been dropped. Yet he still felt an undeniable undercurrent of tension as he approached the campus.

He passed the university bookstore, peered in through the window, then crossed Ellis Avenue. He walked past the administration building where he'd been interrogated by Mulhouse and some of the regents. He could still picture himself sitting at a long table on the top floor and facing his gray-haired accusers. His gut tightened as if he were up there now doing it over again. He walked along the south side of the building through a narrow passageway and into the quadrangle.

The university, with its neo-Gothic buildings,

looked the same as he remembered it. But there were differences. The students, for instance. They looked very much like the ones he'd been teaching in London, but seeing them here made him realize how much he'd changed over the past eight years. Not only were the students no longer his peers, they looked like kids.

As he strolled across the campus he tried to recall what he'd been like in his student days. One thing struck him. Even though he'd gone on to get a Ph.D. and had already experienced life as few people ever do, he felt he knew less now than he had in his undergraduate days. But back then he had everything figured out. He knew the answers, whether it was about politics or linguistics, love or war. But in his present ignorance about all of those topics, Indy knew he was far wiser than he had been at age twenty-one.

He passed a building where he had taken many of his language classes, then climbed the steps of the one housing the archaeology department. The clock in the waiting room outside of Angus O'Malley's office read two-twenty-three when he arrived. He introduced himself to the secretary, a young woman with short, straight hair and bangs that framed a thin face with closely set eyes. He guessed she was a student working a part-time job.

"Dr. O'Malley has a couple of people with him, but he's expecting you."

Indy sat down and picked up an alumni magazine from a stack on the table and paged through it. After a few moments, he glanced up and saw the secretary watching him. He smiled and looked back down at the magazine.

"I understand you might be joining the staff," she said.

"I hope so."

"You took your degree here, too, didn't you?"

"Yeah."

"Dr. O'Malley sent for your grades."

"Really? They weren't very good."

"I know. You took a lot of tough courses, though. All those linguistic courses are tough. Especially Anderson's 301 course. He still fails nearly half the class every semester."

Swell. The secretary knew more about his academic record than he could remember. He turned the page of the magazine, hoping she'd get the hint. He wondered how much emphasis O'Malley would put on his undergraduate grades. He'd never been too concerned about his grade-point average. It wasn't until he was in graduate school that he'd started getting *A*'s in most of his classes.

"As long as you don't take advantage of your position, everything is fine here," the secretary said when he didn't respond.

Indy looked up from the magazine. "Excuse me?" She leaned forward and gave him a conspiratorial look.

"The professor you'll be replacing got fired because he was making advances at the girls in his classes and fixing their grades if they went along with what he wanted."

"Well, I guess I don't have to worry then," he whispered back to her. "I don't fix grades, and I'm not the least bit interested in extracurricular activities with my students."

"Oh. That's good."

From the tone of her voice, she sounded disappointed. She'd probably hoped he would wink at her or something and say that he would have to watch himself. Ever since Fitzgerald had written about petting on college campuses in *This Side of Paradise*, there'd been a controversy raging about the morality of college coeds. The professor in question probably had been caught researching that very question himself, and no doubt in great depth.

He heard voices as the door of O'Malley's office opened a few inches. "I'm sorry I can't be of any assistance, but I'm sure you understand we have our priorities," O'Malley said.

"Well, you're missing a great opportunity," someone else said.

Indy knew that voice. Then the door swung open and he saw O'Malley and Vladimir Zobolotsky. They paused, letting Zobolotsky's daughter step through the doorway.

"You'll regret your decision," the woman said in a firm voice.

The pair swept past Indy, followed by O'Malley. "Well, I'm sure I will, if you are successful," O'Malley said as they paused in the outer doorway. "Good luck and thank you for stopping by."

Indy studied the shapely legs of the blonde as he tried to recall her name. When his gaze climbed her body, he saw she was staring back at him, a scowl on her face. Then she turned on her heel and was gone.

Katrina, that was it. Lovely Katrina. What the hell were she and her father doing here? Probably after money. O'Malley was the chairman of the department, after all, and he'd have a list of contributors who might back the expedition.

O'Malley let out a long breath and shook his head. "What a story. You wouldn't believe it. So how are you, Indy?"

Indy stood up and they shook hands. "Great. Let me guess, he's going to look for Noah's Ark."

"You must have read about him in the papers."

"No. I heard him talk last night."

O'Malley looked surprised. "You actually went to that church to hear him?"

"A friend invited me."

"Oh. So what did you think about Dr. Zobolotsky's claims?" O'Malley asked as they walked into his office.

"Probably about the same thing as you did. They don't make myths out of wood."

O'Malley laughed. "Well put, Indy. Well put." He pointed at a chair. "Please, sit."

"I suppose he wanted you to fund his expedition?"

"Actually, he wasn't looking for money. In fact, quite the opposite. He was willing to pay. He wants to authenticate his expedition with the name of a major university behind it." O'Malley shook his head in disgust. "I don't care how much money he offers, I would never send any of my staff on such an expedition. The university would be the laughingstock of the academic world."

"If he's got money, I'm sure someone will take him up on it."

"No doubt. The world's full of fools." O'Malley cleared his throat and opened a file folder on his desk. "Now, about our business." He stared at a piece of paper for a long moment and seemed to hesitate. A frown creased his forehead. He tapped his desk with a pencil.

Indy wondered what the hell he was doing. Maybe it was something about the salary. He hadn't even thought about that. It better be competitive; he wasn't about to work for peanuts.

O'Malley ran his hands over his face, then looked up. "You know something, Indy? As much as I would like to hire you, I just can't do it."

The last three words hit like a blow to the gut, and it was harder than anything dished out by Capone or his thugs.

"Why not?"

"After I talked to you yesterday, I sent for your records. They arrived this morning." He rapped his pencil against the file folder. "Everything is in order, except . . . It seems you were involved in an unfortunate incident here at the end of your senior year. I think you know what I'm talking about."

Founding Fathers' Day, Indy thought as his hopes plummeted. "That was a long time ago, and President Mulhouse is—"

"I know, I know. But the university has a long memory about such things, and whether Mulhouse is here or not, it doesn't really matter. You embarrassed the institution and your name is on a list."

"What list?"

O'Malley hesitated. "It's a list of . . . "

"A list of people you can't hire because they think for themselves. Right?" He stood up.

"That's swell, Dr. O'Malley. I think I've heard enough. No sense wasting time, mine or yours."

"I'm sorry, Indy," O'Malley said, rising from his chair. "There's nothing I can do about it."

"Nothing that won't shake the walls of this hallowed institution, but I guess you're not about to do that. Nice to see you again."

He walked out without looking back. So much for his new job. So much for living in Chicago. He was ready to get out of the city. He didn't know where he was going, but he didn't want to stay around now. The university didn't want him, and even Shannon didn't think it was a good idea for them to see each other.

He crossed the quadrangle and headed for a tree-lined roadway on the east side of the campus. He felt like a ship without an anchor. Up until now his life had been relatively structured, with either his studies or a teaching job forming the backbone of his existence. But now there was nothing, not even a family to speak of.

He reached a path veering to his left from the roadway and followed it. The trail wound past a quiet pool of water officially known as Botany Pond. He walked over to it and stared into the glassy water. His reflection wavered like a mirror in a funhouse. He sat down on the grass and wondered if the students still called it the Reflecting Pool. In his undergraduate days, he'd stared into the water, thinking about his problems, problems with girls mostly. Now he couldn't even remember which girls had been of such concern to him.

At the moment, they were the least of his worries. What the hell was he going to do? Where was he going to go? He couldn't go back to London, and Paris was out of the question. He was jobless and his savings wouldn't last forever. Damn, I shouldn't have stayed at the Blackstone, he thought. Maybe he should go to New York and see his father. But they hadn't spoken for a long time, and his present circumstances would just prove his father right. He could just imagine the old man telling him he knew all along that archaeology was not the proper field for him. "And now look at you, Junior: no job, no career. You're a disgrace."

No. He wouldn't see his father. But maybe he would go to New York. He could stay with Marcus Brody for a while, and Marcus would probably give him a job working in his museum until he found something else. Marcus, after all, had helped him out of other jams. But that was the problem. He'd taken advantage of Marcus's kindness too many times already. He had to strike out on his own.

He picked up a pebble and tossed it in the pool, shattering his reflection. He pushed off from the ground and continued down the path. He passed under the wrought-iron gate at the entrance to the campus and turned right on Fifty-seventh Street. One block down at the corner of Fifty-seventh and University, he paused to look at Mandel Hall, a massive building with an ornate theater filled with rich, dark wood and gold-leaf trim. It was also the home of the student union and was another spot where he'd spent a lot of time, especially during his freshman and sophomore years when he lived in a dormitory a few blocks from here.

He recalled meeting a farm girl here, whose name he had forgotten. They'd talked awhile and then walked back to their dormitories together. He continued on, following the same route that he and the girl had taken. He remembered his heart thumping as they'd turned onto Woodlawn and headed along the dark street hand in hand.

Grace. That was her name. He still remembered that she spoke with a south Illinois accent and that her parents had frowned on her moving to Chicago on her own. They'd been disappointed that she hadn't married her high-school sweetheart. The things you remembered.

Stately brick mansions lined Woodlawn. They'd been built in the 1890s and were inhabited mostly by professors. Not much chance now that he would ever occupy one of these majestic residences, he thought. But then, it had never occurred to him that he would live here.

If there was any house along Woodlawn that he would like to live in, it was the one built by Frank Lloyd Wright. It was a Prairie-style house that was built on a pedestal, instead of above a basement, and it had a cantilevered roof projecting out over the lawn.

He remembered Grace saying that she would live in that house one day, and if he ever came by he should stop in and see her. Back then everything seemed possible. Now he saw things differently. Grace didn't live in that house, and even if she did, they wouldn't have anything to say to each other.

He'd gone out with Grace a few times after

that first night. Then the school year had ended and he'd never seen her again. She'd probably married that old boyfriend, or someone from her hometown. By now she had a couple of kids in school and maybe lived on a farm. The good life, he thought. But almost any life sounded good when you didn't have one. He didn't have much of anything.

He was only a block from the dormitory where he'd lived for two years, but there was no reason to look at it. Besides, the sullen, leaden sky had finally started to drizzle. He turned on Fifty-eighth and walked over to University Avenue. On the corner was the Oriental Institute, another place where he'd spent numerous afternoons. Its exhibits focused on the history, art, and archaeology of the ancient Near East—Assyria, Mesopotamia, Persia, Egypt, and Palestine.

He headed up the walk to the entrance, passing two men wearing trench coats and hats. He overheard one of the men. Indy didn't understand what he'd said, but knew he was speaking Russian. He glanced back at them as he opened the door, but both had turned away.

He meandered past displays of statuary, pottery, and bronze busts, some dating back to the second millennium B.C. He was about to enter a room featuring artifacts from Mesopotania when he stopped short. Directly across the room from him stood Zobolotsky and Katrina.

The pair was huddled to one side of a tablet and conversing in soft voices. Indy moved quietly into the room and acted as if he were examining a statue. He edged closer until he could hear them better. Zobolotsky was speaking Russian just like the man outside. Indy spent a few months in Russia when he was a kid, and he had spent his mornings studying the language. As a result, nearly twenty years later, he could still pick up words and phrases.

Zobolotsky: "I just don't understand it."

Katrina: "Don't worry. It'll work out."

"But where do we look?"

"Father, I think . . . " The woman stopped in midsentence and turned toward Indy as she realized he was standing behind her eavesdropping. "What is it?" she snapped.

Indy looked blankly at her as if he didn't understand. "Pardon me?"

"What do you want?" she asked in English.

He glanced at the tablet in front of them and saw it was inscribed with cuneiform. "I want to look at the tablet. It's cuneiform, you know."

"I'm sorry." She stepped back. Her features softened as she smiled. "It's just that you surprised me."

Now that he was so near her, he was suddenly curious about her. She had a heart-shaped face with high cheekbones and a narrow chin. Her skin looked baby soft, and her eyes were blue, watery, deep. Eyes that could cast a spell, and what man would fight it? Her lips were luscious and full and matched the color of the ruby silk scarf that was draped over her shoulders.

"Can you read cuneiform?" she asked.

"Nobody really reads it," he replied, noticing how her long black dress accented the flair of her hips from her wasplike waist. "A few people translate it. It's slow, painstaking work."

"You sound like you know something about it," Zobolotsky said. The Russian looked older today. His sandy hair was tinged with gray, and his eyes were deeply creased at the corners. He was hunched over like a very old man.

"A bit."

"Do you know how important this tablet is?" Zobolotsky asked.

Indy stepped forward and peered at it. He saw that it had been broken into two pieces and fitted back together. He had no idea what the cunieform said and started reading the printed translation next at it.

> "I caused to embark within the vessel all my family and my relations,
> The beasts of the field, the cattle of the field, the craftsmen, I made them all embark.
> I entered the vessel and closed the door . . .
> From the foundations of heaven a black cloud arose . . .
> All that which is bright is turned into darkness . . .
> The gods feared the flood,
> They fled, they climbed into the heaven of Anu,
> The gods crouched like a dog on the wall, they lay down. . . . "

He stopped reading and stared at the tablet, the actual cuneiform tablet with the story of Utnaphishtim. "Well, this is quite a coincidence," he said, his tone hushed.

"What do you mean?" Katrina asked.

He took a step back, but kept his gaze on the tablet. "Just the other day I was telling a friend of mine about this very tablet. I had no idea it was here in Chicago. After I told him the story of how it was found and translated, he asked me to go to his church and hear a talk about the search for Noah's Ark."

"You mean . . . " Zobolotsky began.

"Yes. I was there."

"I thought you looked familiar to me," Katrina interjected. "I must have seen you there. Who are you?"

"Excuse my daughter," Zobolotsky said. "Are you an archaeologist?"

"Yes." His voice seemed a bit too loud, as if he needed to convince them as well as himself. "I've been at the University of London for a few years. But I'm taking some time off now."

"Interesting," Zobolotsky said, and stroked his chin as he studied Indy.

"Wait a minute," Katrina said. "I know where I saw you. You were just now in Dr. O'Malley's office."

"That's right. I had a meeting with him right after you left."

"We did not find him very cooperative," Zobolotsky said.

"As a matter of fact, I didn't either," Indy said, and couldn't help but laugh.

Katrina looked mystified. "What did he say about us?"

"What makes you think he said anything to me about you?"

"Because you were at the church. You must have said something to him."

Indy nodded. "He's very skeptical about your expedition."

"He doesn't understand how important it is," Zobolotsky said.

"What do you think?" Katrina asked.

"I have some questions about it."

Indy tried not to sound too harsh. Katrina touched something in him that had been buried for months. He felt a magnetic attraction to her that was startling in its intensity. He'd forgotten all about Shannon's fascination with her. For every second that he remained in her presence, the strength of her magnetism doubled, then tripled, as though she were a mathematical law unto herself and he was nothing but a number she shuffled around in an equation.

"What are they?" her father asked.

For a moment, Indy didn't know what Zobolotsky was talking about. "Why do you want to go back there if you've already climbed the mountain and seen the ship?"

"It's important that we document its existence."

"You've already got the piece of wood," Indy said.

"The wood means nothing to the nonbelievers. People like O'Malley look at it and tell me I'm lying, that I could have found it anywhere. It proves nothing to people like him. Do you understand?"

"Perfectly."

"But they cannot ignore photographs. Katrina is a very good photographer and will prove to the world that the Ark exists."

So she was going along. That changed everything. He was no longer merely curious about their expedition; he *needed* to know about it.

He tried to concentrate on Zobolotsky. "Why is it so important to you?"

The former soldier straightened his back. "Because the world must know, and when it is known, all the false governments that have outlawed God and religion will collapse."

"I see." So it was political as well as religious. Science took a distant third place.

"I'm not saying the government under the czar was the best possible, but the Bolsheviks are taking away the freedom of the people to even think for themselves," Zobolotsky explained.

"Yeah," Indy said without enthusiasm. "It's none of my business, but how can you afford this expedition?"

"I am a successful doctor. I've saved my money for a long time."

"So when are you leaving?"

"Soon," Katrina said. "Do you think you might want to join us?"

"Me?" Indy smiled. His better judgment told him to say no. But then again he didn't have anything else planned, and the allure of Katrina was unmistakable. "It sounds interesting, but you'd have to understand that my participation would be purely a scientific one." That comment wasn't entirely true, but Zobolotsky didn't have to know how Indy felt about his daughter. At least, not right now.

"Of course," Zobolotsky said. "Are you ready to leave tomorrow morning?"

"That's kind of short notice."

"How long do you want?" Zobolotsky asked.

He thought a moment. What else did he have to do except say good-bye to Shannon? He shrugged. "Tomorrow morning is fine."

"Wonderful." Katrina was literally beaming.

"We're staying at the Blackstone," Zobolotsky said. "Do you want to meet us there tomorrow at eight?"

"The Blackstone? I guess I can manage."

As Indy walked away he felt elated at the turn of events and amazed by the series of odd coincidences he'd encountered. He'd made two stops this afternoon, at O'Malley's office and the institute, and he'd found Zobolotsky and his daughter at both places. Now it turned out that they were staying in the same hotel. It must mean that he was on the right track, that he was supposed to join the expedition. At least, he hoped that's what it meant.

He pushed the door open and headed down the sidewalk. A drop of rain struck his forehead, then another. He recalled the two men in trench coats and wished he was wearing one. But he didn't have far to go. He was going to walk over to Shannon's house and tell him the news. He was sure that Shannon would be pleased to hear that his so-called revelation about Indy and Noah's Ark was turning out to be true.

8

BULLETS

Boris Kaboshev stood near the entrance of a basement bookstore across the street from the Oriental Institute, and watched the man in the sport jacket head down Fifty-sixth Street. He'd seen him at the university when the man had walked into the same office that Zobolotsky and his daughter had disappeared into. He wanted to know who he was and why he had followed them here.

"He was at the church, too," Boris said to his twin brother, Alexander. "That's where I've seen him before."

"Come to think of it, I've seen him, too," Alexander asked. "He's staying at the Blackstone."

"Get down," Boris hissed as he spotted Zobolotsky and Katrina leaving the Oriental Institute. They backed down the stairs and into the bookstore as the pair moved in their direction. When they were sure that the father and daughter weren't coming into the bookstore, they climbed the stairs back to the street and saw them flag down a taxi.

"They're going to Turkey soon," Alexander said. "Then it will be over for us and we can go back to the shop."

"Not necessarily, Alex. They may want us to stay on this one a little longer."

In fact, Boris had been told that if Zobolotsky left the country, he and Alexander were to follow them and complete their mission in the appropriate way.

"Let's see if we can catch up to the other one," Boris said. "I want to see where he's going."

Alexander grunted and they stepped out into the drizzle and hurried after the man in the sport jacket. Boris knew that Alexander didn't want to follow the man any more than he'd wanted to watch the Zobolotskys. Alexander hadn't said anything lately against their work, but Boris knew that his brother would be happy living like a normal person. But Alexander kept forgetting that they weren't normal people.

The two Russian immigrants operated a small printing plant on the South Side and actively kept in touch with other Russians who had come to the United States after the Bolshevik Revolution. But unlike most of the others, Boris and Alexander had not fled Russia because of their fear of the Bolsheviks. On the contrary, they were Bolsheviks and followers of Leon Trotsky. They were here in the United States on behalf of the revolution.

Their job was to keep track of Russian immigrants who might be working to overthrow the Bolshevik government. Their current mission was to watch Zobolotsky and his daughter, and to follow them wherever they went in Chicago.

Zobolotsky was a known associate of the New Russia Movement, a group of czarists who hadn't given up the idea of returning their homeland to the ways of the past.

The father and daughter had arrived in Chicago five days ago, but had acted like tourists until the day before yesterday when the newspapers ran an article about Zobolotsky and Noah's Ark. At first, the news had puzzled Boris, but he'd soon realized that the whole thing must be a propaganda ploy by the NRM. The discovery of Noah's Ark would lend credibility to the Bible, and that was counter to the revolution. Religion was the opiate of the masses, and the discovery of a boat on Mount Ararat would only confuse people, which is just what these czarist dogs wanted.

It would be easy to get rid of Zobolotsky and his daughter, but the orders were not to kill Russians in the United States. A murder would attract attention and might expose the network of spies who worked in the country. If the Zobolotskys left the United States, then it was another matter.

"Where's he going now?" Alexander asked as the man disappeared into a park.

"How should I know?"

They crossed the street and followed him. Boris was almost certain that the man was not a Russian, even though he hadn't heard him say a single word. When he knew for sure, he would act. After all, he was free to eliminate any non-Russian who might be aiding the enemy's propaganda efforts.

* * *

If archaeologists in the distant future ever excavate Chicago, they might puzzle over the odd remains of buildings constructed in the style of ancient Greek architecture. No doubt someone would mistakenly hypothesize that the Greeks discovered America and built great structures in the middle of the country at least two thousand years before the birth of Christ. Indy mulled over the thought as he cut through Jackson Park and passed the Palace of Fine Arts. The museum, which from the air looked like a giant geometric bird, was one of several buildings constructed in the Greek Revival style for the World's Columbian Exposition of 1893.

He walked down the drive to the entrance of the museum, crossed Fifty-sixth Street, and headed down Cornell Avenue. The Shannon family home was just a block away, a short walk from the University of Chicago and a few blocks from Lake Michigan. Indy knew the neighborhood well from his days at the university, but he'd never seen the Shannon home. It was built the year after he and Shannon had graduated, and Shannon's father had bought it a few years later.

He figured it would be better to talk to Shannon at the house rather than wait until this evening when he'd be at the nightclub. Besides the fact that Shannon would be busy, the last thing Indy wanted was another encounter with the likes of Capone, and from what Shannon had said, that was a distinct possibility.

Indy slowed his pace and looked around. He was sure he was on the right block, but he couldn't find the house. Where it should have been was a huge estate surrounded by an ominous-looking iron fence that resembled rows of upright spears. Barely visible through a wall of trees was an immense mansion, and at the entrance to a driveway was a gatehouse.

He saw someone watching him from the gatehouse and decided to ask for directions. As he approached the gatehouse he saw a pair of German shepherds tied on leashes to the iron fence on either side of the driveway.

A brawny man with thinning hair and no neck to speak of had stepped from the gatehouse. The tenseness in his body suggested that he might reach into his suit coat for his weapon at any moment.

"What can I do for you, fellow?"

"I'm looking for the Shannon residence. It's supposed to be—"

"You found it. What do you want?"

Indy stared up the drive, which curved in front of a three-story, red-brick manor set back fifty yards from the road. It looked like a fortress not a home.

"Well?" the gatekeeper asked when Indy didn't immediately respond.

"I'm here to see Jack Shannon."

"He expecting you?"

"Not really. But I'm an old friend."

"What's your name?"

Indy told him.

"I heard about you," the man answered in a tone that was neither hostile nor friendly. "Hold up your arms."

"What?"

The gatekeeper stepped forward and patted

him down, searching for weapons. "You're okay. Wait here."

The man moved back inside the guardhouse and wrote something down on a piece of paper. He lifted a small wooden box from a peg and stuck the paper inside it. He called one of the dogs, bent over, and secured the wooden box to a hook on its collar. Then he said something in the dog's ear and unleashed it. The shepherd instantly sprang away and scampered toward the house.

"Your messenger?"

The gatekeeper nodded.

"What if nobody sees him coming?"

"Listen."

The dog barked at the front door and a few seconds later a man stepped outside and bent down.

"Smart dog," Indy said.

"Vicious dog. With the right command, he'd tear out your lungs."

Indy cleared his throat. " I'll take your word for it."

The conversation lapsed, but the gatekeeper didn't retreat to his house. He kept an eye on Indy and the remaining shepherd did the same. Indy paced about as he waited. The drizzle was still coming down, and an occasional raindrop ran over his jaw and down his neck. At this rate he wouldn't have to worry about taking a bath for a while.

"We need to find out who lives there," Boris said as he watched Indy pace back and forth in front of the gatehouse. He and Alexander were crouched behind a hedge halfway down the block and across the street.

"Maybe it's one of the czar's nobles," Alexander answered.

Boris shook his head. "We would know." That was the advantage of the print shop. He printed a newsletter for Russian immigrants, and he heard all of the gossip.

Alexander took a pair of opera glasses out of his pocket and focused on the man. "Maybe we're wasting our time. Maybe this guy doesn't have anything to do with Zobolotsky and his expedition."

"He must," Boris snapped. The guy had stuck his nose into the wrong Russian's business. Now he'd become Boris's business.

Finally, Indy heard a bark and saw the dog race toward the gatehouse. For an instant, he thought the shepherd was charging right at him. He held his ground and tried not to show any sign of fear. The dog leaped the last ten feet and skidded to a stop in front of the gatekeeper. The man calmly reached down and unhooked the box as if deliveries by dog were an everyday occurrence. He opened it and unfolded a piece of paper.

"Jack's waiting for you." He jerked his head toward the house. "Go around to the porch door on the left side."

"Thanks."

Indy moved carefully past the dogs and strode toward the house. He knew that the Shannons were successful in their enterprises, which were a combination of legal and illegal businesses ranging from bootlegging and gambling to trucking and laundry-and-linen delivery. However, he'd never thought of Shannon as wealthy or living the sort of opulent life that this estate symbolized. After all, Shannon had lived in one-room apartments for years in Paris and London. Now, though, he had an idea why Shannon hadn't said much about the place. It embarrassed him.

Shannon was standing in the doorway of the porch, and he didn't look very pleased to see him.

"Indy, I told you not to come here."

"No, you didn't. You said I couldn't stay here."

"Yeah, well, what do you want? It's not the best time to stand around and bullshit. I'm sort of busy."

Indy was surprised by Shannon's wariness. "I just came to say good-bye. I'm leaving in the morning."

Shannon stepped out on the porch. "Where're you going?"

"To Turkey with Zobolotsky."

Shannon looked puzzled. "You changed your mind, I see."

Indy shrugged. "It didn't work out with the university. They dragged up that old episode with the dummies. I should've known."

"Jack!" Someone called him from inside the house.

"Who the hell you talking to out there?"

"It's Indy. He's here from London," Shannon called out.

A man with slicked-back red hair stepped outside. Indy recognized Shannon's oldest brother. Harry was a couple of inches shorter than Jack and at least twenty pounds heavier. Indy hadn't seen him since he and Shannon were in college together, but he didn't look much different. He'd always been mature and savvy, and now he was the head of the Shannon family.

"How's it going, Harry?"

He glared at Indy and it was obvious even before he spoke that he didn't want him around. "You know, you're calling at a bad time. We were just on our way out. We've got some business to attend to."

"I was just leaving. Good to see you again, Harry. Jack. Nice house." He nodded, stuffed his hands in his pockets, and walked off.

"I'll walk you down to the gate," Shannon said, then glanced at his brother. "Meet you out front."

"Make it fast," Harry said tersely. "And Jones. I hope you don't think you're going to drag Jackie Boy off to Europe again, because little brother here is settled down and part of the family. You understand?"

"Yeah. I sure do."

Shannon joined Indy and they walked in silence for a few steps. "I'm sorry about Harry. He's under a lot of pressure."

"I understand."

"Hey, look, I didn't mean to make it sound like you're not welcome here. It's just that things are a little tense right now, and we do have some business to take care of."

"You don't have to apologize, Jack."

"So you're going to Turkey after all. What about Katrina? What's she going to do while her father's gone?"

"She's going, too. She's the team photographer."

Shannon stopped near the gate. "Oh, ain't that

just sweet. I should've known. That's why you're going."

"That's not true, Jack."

"You telling me that woman had no effect on your decision, that you just happen to want to climb some mountain in Turkey to look for a boat. I don't buy it."

"C'mon, Jack, I'm an archaeologist. This could be an important discovery." Indy knew he didn't sound very convincing. He couldn't hide anything from Shannon for long. "Besides, you wanted me to go look for the Ark. Remember?"

Shannon's eyes narrowed. "I wanted you to go with her old man, not her. You knew how I feel about Katrina."

"But she's not your girl, Jack. You hardly know her."

"You'd steal my girl right from under me. Nice friend you are, Jones."

"Jack, come on," Indy said.

"Get out of here, will you? Go have your fun."

That was when Indy noticed the bulge under Shannon's jacket. "What's that you're carrying?"

"That's my business."

"Don't let Harry push you around, Jack."

"What do you care?"

A shiny Cadillac moved slowly down the drive toward them. Suddenly, he understood. "I can't believe it. You're going out on a hit, aren't you?"

"I said stay out of it."

"You're going after Capone, aren't you? Don't do it, Jack."

"We're doing what we have to do. We've got to do it before he does it to us. It's just business."

Indy shook his head. "Is this what all your Bible study has taught you? To go out and kill anyone who gets in your way?"

Shannon grabbed Indy by the lapel and shoved him.

"Just get out of here. You got that? Get out!"

"You're some friend, Jack," Indy spat as he backed through the gate.

He heard a growl and out of the corner of his eye saw one of the shepherds dashing toward him. Then it leaped. The dog struck him on the shoulder and chest and knocked him off his feet. He saw snapping fangs and raised his forearm just in time to block the beast from ripping out his throat. The animal grabbed his arm and shook it.

A shot rang in Indy's ear, the dog squealed, then shuddered and collapsed on top him, its jaws still clamped on his forearm. He pushed off the dead weight. Shannon stood over him, his revolver in his hand.

"Get back, Gretel." Shannon snapped at the other dog, which was straining at its leash, fangs bared. "You shouldn't have cursed me like that, Indy. That was his command to kill."

"Sorry." Indy held on to his injured arm and backed away from the other dog. "And thanks."

"He was my favorite dog," Shannon said, staring down at the lifeless shepherd. "Richie, get him out of here."

"Right away." The gatekeeper pulled the dog out of the driveway.

Indy didn't know what else to say.

"Are you hurt?" Shannon asked.

"No, but another few seconds and it would've been another story."

"What is this, Jackie?" Harry was standing next to the Cadillac, which had stopped at the gate.

"Hansel attacked Indy. I had to kill him."

Harry shook his head and looked disgusted. "Get in the car. Now!"

"Harry, I'm not going."

"What do you mean you're not going?"

"That's what I said."

"Are you part of this family or not?"

"I didn't like killing Hansel, and I don't think I'll like killing people, either."

Harry reached into the car and pulled out a tommy gun. He aimed it at Shannon. "Get in the car, Jack."

"Or what? You gonna shoot your brother, Harry?"

Harry lowered the tommy gun. "No, I've got a better idea. If you don't get in here, I'm going to give you an ugly little hairlip so you never play that horn of yours again. You got that?"

"Jack, get in here," another brother shouted as he stepped out from the passenger side.

"Stay out of this, Jerry," Harry snarled.

Just then a Packard slowed in front of the driveway. Indy took one glance and saw tommy guns sticking out the windows.

"Harry!" the gatekeeper yelled as he pulled a gun from his coat.

Harry's eyes widened until they were as large as the Packard's tires. He swung up the tommy gun. "Sonuva...," he growled, and was hit by a burst of gunfire.

Indy tackled Shannon and they rolled over near the gatehouse as the chatter of machine-gun fire filled the air. The gatehouse windows shattered; bullets tore through the wood walls and ricocheted off the iron fence inches above their heads. Shannon lifted his head; Indy grabbed him by the neck, smashed him to the ground.

Tires screeched and the Packard roared away. It all had happened in less than ten seconds. Slowly, Indy and Shannon picked themselves from the ground. Bodies and blood were everywhere. The gatekeeper and the two shepherds lay in pools of blood on the driveway. The burly man was coughing and spitting up blood.

"Oh, God," Shannon yelled. "Oh, God." He rushed toward the car. "I knew it. I knew this was going to happen."

Jerry was draped over the hood of the Cadillac, his blood streaming down the fender. Harry was sitting on the ground next to the car; his face was blood-splattered, his hands were crimson.

Shannon dropped down next to him. "You're going to make it, Harry. You're going to make it. We'll get you to the hospital."

Blood trickled from Harry's mouth. He lifted a hand. "Your fault, Jackie Boy. Your fault."

He slumped over dead.

9

Flaring Passions

"I'm sure he is the right one, Papa," Katrina said as they headed toward downtown and the hotel.

Zobolotsky gazed out the rain-splattered window of the taxi. "I hope so."

"What's wrong?"

"He seemed almost too eager, and I wonder about his background. If we had more time . . . but the Lord sometimes works in strange ways, and he did tell us we would find our archaeologist here in Chicago."

She never contradicted her father when it came to his beliefs, but she wasn't so sure that the Lord had anything to do with it, at least not in the way her father thought.

As a child, she had received impressions about things that were going to happen to her and other people around her, and when she'd told her father these things, he'd said that only the Lord could prophesize. At school, her teachers told her that no one could see the future, and so at age six her visions had stopped.

Years passed. Then, after her father came home from the war, he showed her the piece of wood from the ship on Mount Ararat, and it was as if she were a child again. When she'd held the Ark wood for the first time, she'd described the ship in detail. Things her father had seen, and other things he knew nothing about. For example, she'd told him that people in the village had climbed the mountain from time to time over the centuries to collect pitch from the ship, which they used as sacred amulets. Her father was impressed, then astonished, and from that day on he was convinced that the Lord spoke through her.

She didn't know quite what to think of this. But she figured that the Lord had some helpers. She liked to think that it was old Noah himself who spoke through the wood. She never told this to her father, though, because she knew that to his way of thinking, it was either the Lord Himself, or the devil.

Images came to her every time she held the wood. She had seen her father talking to crowds of people about the Ark, and she saw people rejoicing and returning to their faith in God, and she had witnessed it coming true right here in Chicago. She had also seen her father climbing the mountain again, and she'd sensed that many people waited to hear about the expedition and to see the proof they would obtain.

Other times the visions confused her and

made little sense. One recurring image continued to puzzle her. She was moving through a strange valley where everything was white and distorted, and it was both dark and light at the same time. In the vision, she was being taken to a place against her will.

But the future was by no means a well-paved road with no surprises. Things continued to happen to her and her father that she hadn't foreseen. Three months ago, they'd been ready to set off on their expedition when two nights before they were to leave, their sponsors held an emergency meeting and decided they would require Zobolotsky to bring along an archaeologist. The decision had disappointed them, but Katrina knew that it also made sense. It would help document their discovery, or, rather, her father's rediscovery of the Ark.

But they'd run into one barrier after another in their search for a reputable archaeologist. It seemed that no university was willing to endow her father's quest with credibility. Finally, she'd held the Ark wood one evening and asked where they should go to find the person they needed, and she'd heard the name clearly in her mind: the University of Chicago. They'd left the next day.

Since their arrival, she'd become increasingly anxious that the chairman of the archaeology department would be like the rest of the archaeologists they'd talked to, and it would mean that she'd been wrong. But when she'd taken out the Ark wood from the safe two nights ago, she'd felt the presence of the one who would join them, and she'd reconfirmed it the next night in the church. She'd sensed him there in the audience, and as she'd held the Ark wood above her head she'd tried to pinpoint him. But she'd been distracted when she'd spotted the twin watchers seated near the back of the church, and she'd lost her concentration.

"You like him, don't you?"

She smiled and turned her head away. During the past couple of years, Papa had started asking her about her feelings about men and it always embarrassed her. If her mother were still alive, she would have readily volunteered her thoughts and feelings. But Mama had died shortly after her father had returned from the war and she'd never confided in him in the same way.

"I think . . . he's interesting." She hardly knew him. The other man she'd met since they'd arrived in Chicago, the one who'd played the cornet at the church, was interesting, too. Jack—that was his name. There was a certain helplessness about him that appealed to her. She sensed that Indy was hiding something. It was almost as if a protective crust were hardening around the man's feelings, and she wondered what was behind it.

"It's okay if you like men. It's time you started thinking about finding a husband, you know. It's what God wants for His children when they grow up."

"Papa, I don't want to get married to anyone. I've told you that." She knew her father liked to hear her say that. He was proud that she was still content to live with him.

He laughed as the taxi pulled up to the curb in front of the hotel. "You will, Katrina. You will. All little girls grow up. But I want you to watch out for this Jones. I don't want him to hurt you."

As they entered the lobby Zobolotsky headed directly to the security room and unlocked the safe containing the Ark wood. "What are you doing, Papa?"

"I'm going to bring it up to the room."

"Do you think it'll be safe?"

"The Lord will protect us."

A few minutes later, Katrina sat on the couch and waited for her father. She knew that getting the Ark wood from the safe meant that he had a question and would want her to hold it again.

When he had taken a seat on the chair across from her, she picked up the cloth-covered Ark wood and carefully unwrapped it. She turned it over in her hands. It wasn't much more than a splinter of wood sixteen inches long and a couple of inches thick. On one side it was coated with a dull black resin. On the other side the wood was rougher, and it was apparent that it had been broken off from something larger.

She held the wood in her hands and closed her eyes as her father recited a prayer. "We thank Thee Lord for Your help. We are Your humble servants and we wish to serve You in all things. Please guide us now in the direction we should follow. We rely on Your wisdom and we trust it. Thank you, Lord, for listening to our humble petition. Amen."

Katrina held the Ark wood to her breast and rocked gently forward and back. She breathed deeply, exhaled, and let go of all thoughts. She drifted just above sleep, and it wasn't long before she saw an image of Jack, the horn player.

At first, she just saw his face. Then she realized that he was looking down at her, and slowly she was drawn into the scene. The impressions were more than just visual. She could feel, hear, and sense his presence. It was as if she was really with him. And how she was with him!

His face was just above hers, his lips were parted. He leaned down and kissed her. She returned his kiss and hugged him tightly. They were lying down very close to each other, and a hand grazed her breast, then ran down her belly and along hip and thigh.

"Katrina."

She looked up and saw that it wasn't Jack. . . . It was Indy.

"Katrina . . . "

This time she knew it was her father's voice. She blinked her eyes open. Gasped for breath. He was staring intently at her. She laid the Ark wood down on the coffee table in front of her.

"Well?"

"I'm . . . not sure." It had seemed so real. But why had the faces changed? What did it mean? She was confused and flustered. And now she was embarrassed, too; Papa had been sitting here calmly watching her. She wondered what sounds she had made, and what her body had done.

"You must have seen something. You were so . . . intense. You were whispering to someone."

Not only whispering, she thought.

"What did I say?"

"I couldn't understand, but I know who you were talking to."

"You do?"

"It was the Lord, wasn't it?" Zobolotsky said. "You were talking with the Lord."

"I think he said Indy is the right one."

"Are you sure?"

She didn't like the way he was looking at her as if he doubted her. She was tempted to ask him if he doubted the word of the Lord. But she couldn't say it. "I think so."

She slowly rewrapped the Ark wood in the cloth and tried to make sense of what had happened to her. Maybe the devil had fanned her passion. No. She refused to believe that. The act of love was not the devil's work. She knew that much. Then it dawned on her. The Ark was about survival and so was lovemaking. The only thing was, it hadn't really happened. She'd imagined it. But maybe she had also foreseen what was to be. But with which man?

Then her father dropped the bombshell. "I don't think Jones is the one, Katrina. There's something about him that I don't like. Let's pack and leave right now."

"But, Papa!"

"If it wasn't clear to you, he's not the one we want."

"But I think it was clear. It's just that . . . "

"Just what?"

"Nothing."

He laid a hand on her shoulder. "You'll see, Katrina. It'll work out. There are lots of universities in New York. We'll find an archaeologist there. And this way we'll also be rid of those two Trotskyites. I'm sure you'll be glad of that."

Katrina didn't answer. She moved over to the closet and started to pack.

They were both covered in blood and surrounded by the carnage. Shannon was hugging Harry's body, crying and babbling to the dead man as Indy tried to comfort his friend. Indy knew he had to do something. They were vulnerable. The mobsters could swing by again before the cops got here. Given what had happened in the jail, he didn't trust the cops, either.

"Jack, we've got to get out of here. C'mon. Right now."

"What are you talking about. I can't go anywhere. I can't just leave my brothers like this here."

"Let them go, Jack. It won't do any good."

"We've got to help them."

"There's nothing we can do for them. Think about yourself. Your life is in danger. You've got to get out of Chicago."

"Where am I going to go?"

"Come on to the hotel with me. You'll be safe there until morning. We'll figure out what to do."

Indy grabbed Shannon by the arm and pulled him away from the bullet-riddled car where his brothers lay dead. A siren wailed in the distance. They hurried down Cornell until they reached Fifty-third, then cut over to Lake Park Avenue.

A trolley was approaching. Perfect timing, he thought. They'd be downtown in ten minutes. They leaped on and the trolley rolled ahead. There were a dozen people on board and everyone was staring at them. Indy looked down at his shirt and hands and over at Shannon. Christ. Their clothes and skin were streaked and stained with blood. They couldn't walk into the Blackstone this way. They'd be stopped before they'd gotten ten feet, and the police would be called.

"Let's get off," Indy said as the trolley slowed.

"What in the world happened to you boys?" an elderly woman asked.

"The slaughterhouse, ma'am," Indy said. "The slaughterhouse."

"What are we doing, Indy?" Shannon asked after they hopped down from the trolley.

"I don't know, but we've got to get cleaned up."

They backtracked until they reached Jackson Park, where they headed to a pool near the Palace of Fine Arts. The day was overcast and cool, and the park was nearly deserted. Indy took out a handkerchief, wet it in the pool, and washed his face and hands as best he could. He wrung out the handkerchief, then gave it to Shannon, who made an attempt to wash away the blood.

Shannon handed him the handkerchief and stared blankly ahead. He was in shock. They needed to get to the hotel. Their faces were fairly clean, but their clothes were another matter. They needed to do something about them before they walked into the Blackstone.

Then he spotted the two men in trench coats. The same two men he'd seen outside the museum. Who the hell were they, and what were they doing here? As he and Shannon ambled away from the pool Indy watched the men out of the corner of his eye, and an idea came to mind.

"You still got your gun, Jack?"

Shannon nodded.

"Good. See those guys over there? When I say 'now,' pull the gun on them. You hear me, Jack?"

"I hear you," Jack said in a monotone, then followed Indy toward the pair.

As they neared them the men veered away. "Hey, fellows. How much you want for those coats?" Indy yelled.

The men stopped and turned. "What?" one of them asked.

Indy saw they were twins. "We need your raincoats."

"I don't know what you are talking about," one said in accented English.

"We don't sell our clothes on the street," Twin Two said as they started to move away.

"Give us those coats. Now!"

The men stopped and turned. Although Indy was sturdy and muscular, he was no match for these guys. They were at least fifty pounds heavier, two or three inches taller, and their necks looked as large as his thighs.

Indy glanced at Shannon. "Now," he repeated.

Twin One grabbed Indy by the collar of his shirt. "Maybe it's time you see some of your own blood."

The gun was suddenly in Shannon's hand and it was aimed at Twin One's head. He knocked the man's hat off with the muzzle, revealing a completely bald head. "Let go, and move away if you want to keep your cue ball on your shoulders."

The man did as Shannon said.

"Now both of you, get those coats off or I'll shoot them full of holes with you inside."

Indy was surprised by Shannon's recovery. It seemed the moment the twin had grabbed him, he snapped out of the shock and lethargy from the gunfight and deaths.

The twins shrugged out of the trench coats. "Drop them at your feet," Indy said. "Now start walking. Move it."

As soon as the twins had walked a few yards Indy grabbed the coats. "Let's get the hell out of here."

Without another word, they dashed out of the park until they were back on Lake Park Avenue. They pulled on the coats as they spotted another trolley coming. Both of them were lost in the extra-large raincoats, but it didn't matter.

They climbed aboard the trolley, and no one paid them any heed. Ten minutes later, they entered the lobby of the Blackstone. The belts on their raincoats were tightened, and their hands were inside the deep pockets discreetly holding the hems above the carpeting.

The elevator was waiting. "Howya doing, sir?"

Indy saw that it was the doorman, who was now manning the elevator. "Hiya, Frankie. I thought you worked at the door."

"I'm a man of many talents," Frankie answered. "Today I run the elevator. But to tell you the truth, sitting in this little room all day is boring. But don't tell my boss I said so."

As the elevator rose Indy was struck by an idea. It seemed so obvious. It was just a matter of getting Shannon to agree to it, and he didn't think that was going to be too difficult. "Say, Frankie, I was talking to a young lady earlier today, a Miss Zobolotsky. Do you know which room she's in?"

Frankie grinned. "Of course. She and her father are in the suite right above you."

The elevator stopped and they headed down the hall to Indy's room. "Jack, why don't we both go to Turkey?"

"You want me to go to Turkey with you?"

"Why not? What better place to hide out. And don't forget, Katrina will be with us."

"That's right. It's definitely worth considering, that is, if Zobolotsky will take me."

Indy unlocked the door to the suite. "If they want me, then they're going to have to take you, too. Simple as that."

Shannon slapped him on the back. "That's great. You are a friend."

"Of course I am. C'mon. Let's get out of these clothes and go upstairs for a chat."

10

The Getaway

Katrina tapped her foot impatiently as they waited for the elevator. The arrow above the door had gone from the first to the third floor and stopped. But now she heard the whining of the motor and the arrow edged toward four.

She hadn't even bothered arguing with her father. It was no use. He was stubborn, and he would do as he saw fit. But she didn't understand why he'd changed his mind about Indy so suddenly. Maybe it was a look on her face or a word she'd uttered while she'd held the Ark wood. Something had made him decide to cross Indy out.

Finally, the door creaked open, and the elevator operator nodded to them. He was the same young man who had accompanied her to the room on the night she'd gotten the Ark wood from the safe.

"May I help you with your bags, Miss Zobolotsky?"

"No, they're very light. Thank you."

She was carrying her handbag and a small luggage case while her father held the bag with the Ark wood and a suitcase. They would send a bellboy for their other bags while they checked out.

As the door closed and the elevator descended she felt the gaze of the operator on her. She gave him a rueful glance to let him know she didn't like being stared at.

"Miss Zobolotsky?"

"Yes," she answered stiffly. *Don't say a word about the other night*, she silently commanded.

"There was someone just asking about you."

"Who?" Zobolotsky asked.

"Mr. Jones."

"When was he here?"

"He's here now."

"Where?"

"Katrina, that's enough. There's no need to say anything further to him. It'll just complicate things."

"But, Papa. What's wrong with him?"

"I don't think he would be a good influence on you."

She was tempted to say something about how all little girls grow up, as he'd put it, but she wouldn't do it in front of the elevator operator.

The door opened and Zobolotsky grabbed his suitcase and ushered Katrina toward the desk.

"Mr. Jones is gonna be disappointed," Frankie said to himself as they walked away. "I do know that."

Indy tried not to laugh as he looked at Shannon, who was wearing a pair of his pants that were several inches too short and a shirt that was too loose. "Well, that'll have to do until we can get you some new clothes. Let's go upstairs."

They headed down the hall and waited for the elevator. "One floor up," Indy said.

Frankie made a face. "You're not going to see Miss Zobolotsky, are you?"

"Something wrong with that?"

"Yeah. They checked out about fifteen minutes ago. They're gone."

Indy held out his hand to keep the elevator door from closing. "Did they say why they were leaving so fast?"

"No, sir, but I think Mr. Zobolotsky was afraid of something."

"Any idea where they were going?"

"They didn't say, but my guess is the train station."

"Thanks." Indy and Shannon quickly backtracked to their room.

"I wonder what he was afraid of," Shannon said.

"Let's go find out. I'll pack and we'll be out of here in five minutes."

"But I don't have any luggage," Shannon protested.

"Good. You can help me carry mine."

Katrina sat glumly by the window as the conductor made his last call for passengers. Indy should be here with them. But now it was too late. They were leaving without him, and that was as good as telling him they didn't want him along.

The turn of events was giving her second thoughts about the expedition. If she was wrong about Indy, then maybe she was wrong about everything. Maybe she had thought Indy was the right one for the expedition because he was young and handsome, the very reason her father didn't want him along. Likewise, maybe she had foreseen her father going to Turkey and climbing Ararat just because she knew that was what he wanted to do. Maybe it was impossible to foretell anything.

What if the Ark wood was nothing but a piece of old firewood, and her visions just a recurrence of childhood fantasies? What if there was no Ark? But Papa wouldn't lie. He must have seen it. Unless . . .

Something about her father's story bothered her. It was something she knew, but couldn't quite place into context.

It didn't take long for Indy to realize that the chances of finding Zobolotsky and Katrina were slim. One of the first weekends of the summer was approaching and the train station was so crowded it looked like everyone in Chicago was trying to get out of the city. "I say if we don't see them in another few minutes, we just hop a train and get out of here," he said.

"Let me buy some clothes at least," Shannon said. "And I should go to the nightclub and get some money. I just can't leave empty-handed."

"Jack, don't be stupid." They moved along the platform past clusters of travelers who were boarding trains on either side of them. "If you go back to the nightclub, you're as good as dead. And we can get you some clothes in another town. They do sell clothes outside of Chicago, you know."

Shannon ignored Indy's sarcastic comment. "Capone and his henchmen are probably lying low. They're not going to bother me."

"Uh, Jack, from what I remember, Capone said if you didn't play by his rules, it was curtains. I believe the guy. I think he keeps his word when it comes to killing his enemies."

Shannon shrugged. "I don't know, Indy. Where would we go, New York?"

"Hell no. If there's a hit on you, New York would be as bad as Chicago. Maybe worse."

"Listen to you. You sound like one of the Shannon brothers yourself. God, I'm finally corrupting you."

"Cut it out, Jack. I've had my fill of gangsters. You know that."

Indy had told Shannon all about Julian Ray, the New York bookmaker and mobster who had placed odds against Colonel Fawcett's return to civilization with evidence of a lost city in the Amazon. Indy had belatedly learned that his own boss, Victor Bernard, was a compulsive gambler and had joined forces with Ray to keep Indy from ever reaching the Amazon. Ray's thugs and Bernard himself had narrowly missed accomplishing their goal.

"If New York is out, then where do we go?" Shannon asked, as if New York were the only alternative to Chicago.

"I've got an idea. Why don't we got to the Upper Peninsula of Michigan? You know, on the other side of the lake. We'll get a cabin in the woods for a while."

"Yeah, and what are we going to do for money? Chop wood? Forget it, you know me, I like cities."

Indy was about to suggest that Shannon get used to rural living for a while when he spotted a familiar face. It was one of Capone's henchmen who had beat them up in the jail. "Look over there. On your left, by the next car."

"I see him, and I just spotted his buddy across the way by the other train. I say we do a one-eighty and move on."

"Good idea."

They turned and started walking at a steady, but unhurried pace so as not to draw attention to themselves. They reached the end of the train and walked over to the next set of tracks, where a train hissed and belched a burst of smoke as it prepared to leave.

The conductor yelled, "All aboard," and rattled off a list of cities to the east, ending with New York.

As they moved along the platform the train started rolling out of the station. If Zobolotsky was getting ready to leave for Turkey with or without an archaeologist, it would make sense for him and Katrina to go to New York. But Zobolotsky and his plans were a secondary concern. Indy just wanted to stay alive.

Shannon grabbed Indy by the arm. "Hold it. More trouble ahead."

The platform was crowded, and it took Indy a moment to spot them. It wasn't Capone's henchmen, but the twin thugs. And the pair was heading right for them.

Indy and Shannon turned and tried to lose themselves in the crowd. "Too bad we left the raincoats in the hotel room," Shannon said. "We could bargain with them."

"Somehow I don't think they're the bargaining types. I don't know who they are, but I don't like them much."

When Indy glanced over his shoulder, he saw that the twins were closing the gap. Then he glimpsed Capone's men moving toward them from the other direction. One of them pointed, and they charged toward them.

"I think we're in big trouble, Jack." The train was picking up speed. The last car was approaching, and it was their only hope. "Hop aboard," Indy yelled.

They both rushed after the car as it passed them, each of them swinging a bag. Indy leaped and grabbed the railing. He dropped his bag on the rear platform of the car and reached for Shannon. He was racing after the train, and the two thugs were right behind him. Indy leaned over and stretched as far as he could. His fingers brushed Shannon's, then he grabbed his hand and pulled him up onto the bottom step.

One of Capone's men lurched for the railing just as one of the Russians did the same from a different angle. The two men collided, tumbled to the platform, and their companions tripped over them.

"See you, guys."

Indy didn't mean it literally, but he was right

in the case of the Russians. They would see them again.

Katrina was peering forlornly out the window when she saw the Russians about to board the next car.

"Look, Papa. It's those twins again."

"Just what we don't need," he growled.

The men hadn't harmed them. Hadn't done anything, but Papa was right about them. They must be Bolshevik spies. Then, to her surprise, one of them pointed to something along the platform and instead of boarding the car they hurried away. She craned her neck.

"What are they doing?" Zobolotsky asked.

"I can't tell."

The train started to roll forward. Whatever the distraction was, it was working to their advantage. A few more seconds and they'd be free of them.

"I see Indy!" She nearly shouted the words. "He's out there."

Indy and another man were racing for the train, and the twins were chasing them. But so were two other men. She couldn't believe what she was seeing. How did they know about Indy, and who were the other men? For that matter, who was with Indy? She'd only caught a quick glimpse of him, but he looked familiar.

She tugged at the window, but it wouldn't go up high enough for her to stick her head out. She squashed her cheek to the glass. She couldn't see Indy or the other man any longer.

"What happened?" Zobolotsky asked.

"I don't know. No, there they are."

"Who?"

"The Russians. They didn't make it. We're free of them."

"And Jones?"

"I don't see him, Papa. But I think he's on the train. He was with another man, too. He looked familiar. I know who it was. It was the man from the church—Jack. The one who played the cornet."

"I don't like this. I don't like it at all."

"Papa, don't you see? This is the way it was supposed to happen. They got rid of the Bolsheviks for us."

Her father was a cautious man, but she could tell by his pensive expression that he was mulling over what she'd said. He reached for the door handle. "You wait here. I'll be right back."

"You know, Indy, it's too bad this train isn't going to take us to the Upper Peninsula of Michigan," Shannon said as they moved along the aisle looking for an empty seat.

"Okay, okay. So maybe it wasn't the greatest idea. But at least it was a destination."

Indy stopped abruptly and Shannon bumped into him. Zobolotsky had just entered the car and was standing five feet in front of him. He was staring directly at him and he didn't look a bit surprised. "We seem to have a way of bumping into each other," Indy said.

"You got that right," Shannon said, not realizing that Indy was talking to someone else.

"What are you doing here?" Zobolotsky asked.

"Right now Jack and I are just trying to find a seat."

Zobolotsky nodded solemnly, then looked past Indy at Shannon. "I met you in the church the other day. You were talking to my daughter."

"Right," Shannon said. "Is she here with you?"

Indy heard the eagerness in his voice and gave him a sharp look.

"Why don't you two join me and Katrina in our compartment?"

"Sounds good to me," Shannon said.

As Zobolotsky moved ahead a few steps Indy turned to Shannon. "Take it easy," he whispered.

When they reached the compartment, Zobolotsky stepped inside first, then held the door open for Indy and Shannon. "I think you both remember Katrina."

How could I forget? Indy thought. She looked between them and he swore she was blushing.

"I saw you catching the train." She was looking directly at Shannon. "Jack. How are you? I didn't know you two knew each other."

"We've met." Shannon's gaze was locked on Katrina.

"It was quite a race to catch the train," Indy said as he settled into the seat across from her. Shannon started to sit down next to Katrina, but Zobolotsky directed him to sit next to Indy. Damn you, Shannon, Indy thought as Zobolotsky sat down next to his daughter, but he directed his words at the expedition's leader. "I guess you decided to leave early."

When Zobolotsky didn't answer, Indy continued. "My guess is that it had something to do with those bald-headed twins. Am I right?"

"They're Bolshevik spies. Trotskyites. I've had it up to here with them."

"We would've contacted you from New York," Katrina said.

Indy nodded, and wondered how they would've done that since he hadn't told them how to reach him.

"We're glad you're here now, aren't we, Papa?"

Zobolotsky stared at them, but didn't say anything.

Indy cleared his throat. "I'm not too excited about getting involved in any political battles with Bolsheviks, but my friend here can help. Right, Jack?"

Shannon still couldn't take his eyes off Katrina. "What's that, Indy?"

"I said you can help with security."

"Oh, yeah. Sure."

Zobolotsky stiffened. "What makes you think I want to take you two with me to Ararat? This isn't a vacation, you know."

"Because you need an archaeologist, and your time is running out. You've got some opposition, too, and you need protection. That's where Jack comes in."

Indy didn't know whether or not Zobolotsky's time was running out, but he spoke as if he did and he hoped his dramatic flair would capture the ex-soldier's attention.

Zobolotsky peered at Shannon, who was doing his best to pay attention now. "He doesn't look like someone who could protect himself, much less anyone else."

"Are you kidding?" Indy responded. "I know you're living in San Francisco, but I'm sure you must have heard of the notorious Shannon gang of Chicago's South Side."

Zobolotsky looked perplexed.

"I think I've heard of them, Papa," Katrina said, and smiled at Shannon.

"Jack is one of the brothers. He knows a lot about protection."

"We do need protection, Papa." Katrina's voice was soft. "You've said it will be dangerous."

Zobolotsky reflected a moment, then reached forward and patted his daughter's leg. "All right, you can both come with us. We can use the extra help."

Indy and Shannon watched Zobolotsky's hand as it rested on Katrina's thigh, and both had the same thought: they wished it was their own hand.

11
LIFE IN THE BAZAAR

Two Weeks Later
Istanbul

"Nefis . . . simit, simit."

The words echoed in Indy's head as he rolled over in bed. They were shouted from somewhere outside of their hotel room.

"You awake?" Shannon asked.

"Sort of."

"Take a look at this." Shannon was leaning out the window.

The view of downtown Istanbul was dramatic, a skyline of domes and minarets silhouetted in the orange glow of the early-morning sunlight. But that wasn't what had caught Shannon's attention.

"Nefis . . . simit, simit."

Across the street baskets were being lowered down on ropes from several windows to a waiting vendor. The man pulled donut-shaped objects from a stick and placed them in the basket.

"You woke me to see that?"

"What's he selling?" Shannon asked.

"I don't know. *Simits*. I guess. Some kind of bread."

Indy spotted a kid lowering a pail from the adjacent building. "What is it? *Bu nedir?*"

The kid turned his head and gave Indy a puzzled look. "Ah, English. What time is it?"

"Too early. What's he putting in your pail?"

"Good morning. How are you today?" the kid responded in slow, accented English. "Is Turkey beautiful? Yes?"

"He's avoiding your question," Shannon said, and laughed.

Suddenly an arm shot out the window and the kid was yanked out of sight. A moment later, a girl of about eleven or twelve leaned out and pulled up the pail. She glanced over at Indy and smiled. "My little brother does not know English, only phrases. Are you going to get *simits* for breakfast?"

"What are they?"

"Hot bread. It's very good. You will like it."

"I wish I had a basket."

The girl pulled her basket into the window. "That's okay. I will bring *simits* to your door."

"You don't have to do that."

"Oh, yes. You are *misafir*."

"Okay. *Tesekkur ederim*."

Indy pulled his head back in the window. "Breakfast is on the way."

"What did you say to her?" Shannon asked, looking mystified.

"She's going to deliver the *simits* because we're guests in her country. I said thank you."

"I didn't know you spoke Turkish."

"Enough to get by," Indy said as he pulled on his clothes.

"Teach me something."

"All right. *Turkce bilmiyorum.*"

"*Teurk-chech bihl-mih-yohrum,*" Shannon repeated. "So what's it mean?"

"I don't speak Turkish."

"Oh, great. Just in case there's any doubt about it. Right?"

"You got it."

A few minutes later, there was a knock, and when Indy opened the door, the girl was holding a tray with tea and *simits*, donuts of hot bread covered with sesame seeds. She wore a ragged dress and her long, dark hair was braided.

"I hope you like Turkey," she said as she set the tray down.

Indy thanked her and handed her some change, which she slipped into her pocket.

"What's your name?" Shannon asked.

"Sekiz."

"That's a number," Indy said.

"Yes, of course. Number eight, because I am the eighth child in my family."

"Lots of kids," Shannon said.

"There are eleven."

"Do you go to school?" Indy asked.

"No, it is not possible now. I work in my father's leather shop in the bazaar."

"Do you sell boots?" Shannon asked. "I need a pair of boots."

"No, boots are on another street. We sell bags. We make them, too."

"You like the job?"

She shrugged. "Someday I want to be a tourist guide. I can tell you all the best places to see, if you want."

Katrina suddenly appeared behind the girl,

materializing like a ghost. "Am I interupting something?"

"No, come in." Indy was surprised to see her.

Katrina had said little to him or Shannon during their trip. She'd stuck close to her father most of the time and had spent hours alone in her cabin on the cruise from New York to Athens. His attempts at conversation usually ended with Katrina excusing herself for one reason or another. Shannon hadn't had any better luck getting to know her, and he was just as baffled by her behavior.

"We're just getting our breakfast and a little conversation," Shannon said. "This is Sekiz. She lives in the next building."

"*Gunaydin.*" Katrina smiled at the girl.

"Good morning to you, too, kiddo," Sekiz answered.

Katrina laughed, then turned to the men. "I just want to tell you both that Papa and I are going out to arrange for our permits and transportation. He's hoping he can get all the paperwork done today or tomorrow at the latest."

"Swell," Indy said.

He was interested in seeing Istanbul, but he was even more anxious to get moving as soon as possible. They'd been waylaid for five days in Athens as the Zobolotskys had visited family members living in the city. Indy and Shannon had spent their days wandering around the city and most of their nights in tavernas drinking ouzo. With each drink they recalled another incident from the time they'd spent in Greece together a few years ago. They toasted Greece, their friendship, the mysterious Katrina, and the Zobolotsky family reunion. The Never-Ending Family Reunion, they'd dubbed it.

But it had finally ended, and now they were in Istanbul. But that didn't mean they were ready to climb Ararat. Besides the matter of permits, they had to traverse the length of the country to get to the mountain. Turkey was shaped like a foot, with Istanbul located near the toes, and Ararat at the heel.

"Do you need help?" Indy asked after a moment.

"Papa said it will be best if it is only two of us so as not cause confusion." She smiled shyly at him. "I'll tell you all about it at dinner." She looked over at Shannon. "Both of you."

"Aren't we lucky," Indy said when she'd left. "We're going to hear all about the Turkish bureaucracy tonight."

"At least she's coming out of her shell," Shannon said. "It gives me hope."

A man with a thick mustache that reached from ear to ear stood across the street from the hotel and munched on *simits* as he listened to a small clutch of men chatting near a storefront. His name was Hasan and he was enjoying the exchange of ideas. The men were arguing about the need to change the alphabet from Arabic to Latin and the value of becoming a Westernized nation. Most of the men, Hasan observed, had thought that modernization of the nation was a good idea, but now that it was actually taking place they were having second thoughts. He was glad to hear it. Even though he'd been educated in London, he was bound to Ottoman tradition and didn't appreciate the changes that had been sweeping through Turkey in recent years. He was a victim of the changes, but he was fighting back.

Hasan's attention was distracted as an older man and a young woman left the hotel. He nodded to another man who stood in a doorway a few yards away and watched as the man followed the pair. Hasan would wait and see what the other two foreigners would do. He'd been waiting patiently for several days for the arrival of the expedition, and he didn't mind waiting another few minutes or even hours. The plan was ready. It was only a matter of exactly how and when it would be carried out.

After breakfast, Indy and Shannon headed to the Covered Bazaar, a maze of tiny shops, restaurants, mosques, and workshops. As they entered one of the gates they passed under a huge gold armorial emblem. It was from the days of the Ottoman Empire, and a reminder that the old ways were still close at hand. In spite of the confusing array of narrow, winding streets that led into one another, there was an order to the market. On one street they passed dozens of vendors selling copper pots. On another street, the only product being offered was used Korans. Still another street was well stocked with thousands of yards of colorful fabrics. It went on like that, street after street, block after block. There were rows of stalls stocked with sheepskins, alleys of bangles and beads, and the world's only street that exclusively sold portraits of Mehmet the Conqueror.

"I remember Zobolotsky saying that this wasn't a vacation, but I can't help feeling like I'm on a vacation," Shannon said glumly.

"Enjoy it while it lasts."

"But I don't like being a tourist. Not unless I was with Katrina. Then I wouldn't mind."

Sometimes Shannon acted like a kid, and whenever he did, Indy just ignored him. He was as anxious as his friend to move on, but he didn't mind Istanbul. It was a vibrant, friendly city, if somewhat chaotic to a Westerner. In a way, it was more accessible to outsiders than the Northern European cities. The people here were more willing to stop and answer a question, even if they didn't know the answer, and more often than not they asked a few questions of their own. They didn't expect you to know their language and were pleased when you made an effort to speak it. He remembered Turkey from a visit he'd made when he was a kid, and he was pleased that his youthful impressions were still true.

When they reached the cobblers' lane, Shannon just stared at the array of footwear that surrounded them. They were finally lured into one of the shops by a cup of mint tea, and while the aged proprietor helped Shannon try on boots his son tried to convince Indy to buy a pair. When Indy failed to show any interest, the dark-eyed young man moved his stool closer to Indy and told him about a special kind of boot.

"You see, it has an extra layer of leather on the inside where you can hide things you don't want the customs people to see. You understand?"

Indy had no idea what he would want to

hide in a boot from customs. "Tell me about it."

"I thought you would be interested. You see, I can sew the packets of powder right into the lining for you, and you can make big money when you get back to your rich country. You understand?"

"What kind of powder?"

"The heroin. You know, from the poppies."

"No thanks." Indy set down his tea. "Jack, make sure you don't buy any boots with an extra lining inside."

"That's the least of my concerns," Shannon said. "They don't make boots here for size-twelve feet."

The proprietor's son wasn't ready to give up yet. "Look at this." He showed Indy the bottom of a boot, twisted the heel, and a three-inch blade slid out of a hidden groove.

"Now, *that's* interesting." Indy examined the heel. "You think you could do that to my heel?"

The young cobbler smiled. "Before you can say Ali Baba."

A few minutes later, they moved on to another shop and then a third before Shannon finally found a pair of boots. They'd been offered cups of tea at every stop, and by the time Shannon made his purchase, they'd also attracted an entourage of onlookers who watched their every move.

"I think we're the center of attraction today," Shannon commented.

"They don't see tall, skinny guys with red hair every day."

"I guess not. I wish I had my cornet. I've give them an earful of Chicago jazz."

"I bet you would. Let's go look for a restaurant." As they moved on, the onlookers trailed after them.

"You think we're in trouble?" Shannon asked, glancing over his shoulder.

"Naw. They're just curious. That's all. The market's safe."

"Then why are you carrying a gun and a whip, and why did you get a knife put in your boot?"

"Just in case I'm wrong." Indy turned and everyone watched him as if he were about to perform a trick. "Where's a good restaurant in the Covered Bazaar?" he asked the man standing nearest to him.

The Turk thought a moment and everyone was quiet. Someone made a suggestion, then all of them were suddenly talking at once as if the choice of restaurants was a serious matter of dispute. Finally, the man waved everyone back. "My name is Hasan," he said in accented English. "I will guide you to a very good restaurant on Kahvehane Street."

Indy wondered why the man didn't have anything better to do, but then he realized that judging him by his own Western standards was probably meaningless. "Okay. Let's go."

As they moved through the market the man asked why they had come to Turkey. He was muscular, in his late thirties, with a face adorned by a full mustache that curved around his cheeks and melted into his sideburns. He had large, dark eyes, a long chin, and a hawk nose.

"We're going to climb a mountain," Indy said offhandedly.

"Why do you want to climb a mountain?" Hasan asked

"To look for a boat," Indy quipped.

"Indy!" Shannon shook his head.

"What's wrong?" Indy asked under his breath.

"Too many eyes watching and ears listening."

When they arrived at the restaurant, Indy reached into his pocket, but Hasan raised his hand and shook his head. "No charge. You are guests in our country."

"*Tesekkur ederim*," Indy said, and tipped his fedora.

The dining room was crowded, so they took a table outside on the porch. "Nice guy, that Hasan."

Shannon ran a hand through his auburn mop. "I wonder."

"Wonder what?"

"What he was after. I didn't trust him."

"Why not?"

"His eyes."

"Cut it out. You're just not used to seeing Turks."

Shannon gazed out at the nearby cluster of shops and the activity on the street. "Don't get me wrong; I like this place. Life in the bazaar sort of appeals to me. But I know a suspicious character when I see one."

12

Aya Sophia

At the waiter's recommendation, they both ordered *cerkez kebabi circassian*, a dish consisting of peas, lamb, potatoes, eggplant, tomatoes, and peppers in a sauce. When it arrived at the table, it was accompanied by bulgur pilaf, beans, and bread.

Indy noticed a furrow on Shannon's brow and asked him if the food didn't agree with him.

"No, it's tasty. Real tasty. I was just wondering why they changed the name of this place from Constantinople. I mean if they renamed Chicago, people would go nuts."

"*Stin poli*," Indy said as if that explained everything.

"So what's that mean?"

"That's Turkish for 'in the city.' The phrase was used so much here that people just stopped calling it Constantinople, and *stin poli* became Istanbul when the Ottoman Empire died after the war."

"Why did the empire die?"

"Why does any empire fade? The world changed. Constantinople was the center of a great power for centuries, first under the Byzantine, then the Ottoman rule."

"What made this place powerful?" Shannon asked.

Indy dipped his bread in the sauce, took a bite, and swallowed. "Mostly because it's located on both the land and sea routes between the East and the West."

"So it was a rich country."

"Yeah, but the sultans milked the wealth from their provinces to pay for their palaces and fortresses, mosques, and all the excesses."

"What about now? It seems to me like there's a lot of confusion."

"There is. Mustafa Kemal is remaking the country. The last of the sultans were banished with the Ottoman Empire five years ago. They've got a constitution now. Polygamy was abolished. No one is supposed to wear fezes anymore, and now the Latin alphabet is replacing the Arabic."

"Why can't they wear fezes? I kind of like them," Shannon said.

"They're a reminder of the sultans and harems and the backwardness of the Ottoman Empire."

"If you take away someone's hat, you're only gonna make him mad," Shannon said.

Indy laughed. "You're probably right there."

Shannon sat back in his chair and crossed his arms. "Have you ever forgotten anything?"

"What do you mean?"

Shannon made a snatching motion with his hand. "You're always pulling facts out of the air like they're just there for the grabbing."

Indy shrugged. "Makes me sound intelligent. It's a requirement of my profession. Sometimes at least."

"Hell, until yesterday, I didn't even know that Istanbul used to be Constantinople or Byzantine."

"Actually, only part of Turkey was Byzantine, but it was all Roman."

"See, that's what I mean."

By the time they'd finished lunch, the onlookers had lost interest in them, and they left the Covered Bazaar unaccompanied. They crossed Sultanahmet Square, passing pools and fountains and flower gardens. Just ahead of them was the Byzantium church known as Aya Sophia, which in English meant Divine Wisdom.

"You want to go take a look at the church?" Indy asked, looking up at the Aya Sofia.

"What's so special about it?"

"Look at it. It's supposed to be the most impressive dome ever built. In the sixth century, there was nothing like it in the world. The Byzantines said it was suspended from heaven by a golden chain."

"I don't like looking at old churches. It's just a shell. The spirit's in the word, not the building."

Indy shrugged. "I didn't say we were going to look at God."

"I think I'll go the telegraph office and see if there're any cables for me. You want me to check for you?"

"Sure. Why not?"

While they were in Athens, Shannon had cabled his mother to tell her he was okay and to ask what had happened in Chicago after he'd left.

Indy wasn't expecting any cables, not unless he got one from Marcus Brody. He thought about his conversation with Brody in New York as he headed toward the Aya Sophia. Indy had explained the latest developments with his teaching career, and he'd told him about the expedition he was about to embark upon. Brody, who was usually open to the unusual, surprised him. He thought Indy must be desperate to join such a farfetched undertaking and offered him a job in his museum. Indy had thanked him and gently turned down the offer.

"Have you checked this Dr. Zobolotsky's credentials?" Brody asked.

"Not really. I know he's saved his money for years to finance the expedition. He's very religious and anti-Bolshevik. He thinks that proving the Ark exists will help bring down the revolutionary government."

Brody frowned and shook his head. "I hope you know what you're doing. Let me check on this man myself."

"That's not necessary, Marcus."

"No, no. I insist. I'll cable you in Istanbul if I come up with anything. Please be careful. This sounds like it could be dangerous." Then Brody's frown had vanished. "When you're in Istanbul, don't forget to visit Aya Sophia. Think about me when you're inside that incredible church."

Indy smiled to himself as he entered a side door of the church. Instantly, his gaze was literally pulled up to the dome one hundred and eighty-one feet above the floor. Flanking the great dome was a network of smaller semidomes, vaults, arches, and columns leading to the ground. It was impressive, Indy thought, but it was also barren and cold. The church's gold-leaf mosaics and chandeliers were stripped away, as was its golden altar. Oddly, it was the crusaders who had sacked the church of its gold in the thirteenth century, and the Moslems who had repeatedly overseen its repairs when it seemed destined to crumble to the ground. Now it was neither Christian nor Moslem, but a symbol of monotheism.

In spite of its lack of embellishments, the beauty of the structure itself still remained. On the capitals, atop the columns, were monograms of Justinian, who rebuilt the original fifth-century church after it was burned to the ground in the Nike Revolt. As Indy walked under the dome, a lone figure in the massive ancient building, he could almost hear the walls reverberate with Justinian's words upon the completion of the Aya Sophia: "Solomon, I have surpassed thee!"

The massive columns had come from even more ancient structures, the red ones from the Temple of the Sun in Baalbek, the green from the Artemision of Ephesus. He gazed up at a pair of green columns in the center of the gallery at the far end of the church. The two columns marked the spot where the empress used to worship.

He glimpsed the ghostly figure of a woman as she moved between the columns. She was turned away and seemed to examine something on the wall. Her hair was long and loose. For a moment, he imagined it was a spectral figure of an empress returning for a visit. Then she was caught in a beam of light from one of the upper windows and Indy recognized her.

"Katrina!" His voice echoed between the walls.

She gazed down at him and placed a finger to her lips. He turned up his hands as if to ask what she was doing here. She leaned forward between the columns and motioned for him to join her.

Elated, he crossed the floor to the ramp that led up to the gallery. When he reached the top, he saw her camera perched on a tripod. The rest of her photography equipment lay in a canvas bag inside a cart, which she'd wheeled into the church.

"What a surprise," he said. "I thought you were going to be busy with paperwork."

"It was too boring. We were just waiting in offices and Papa knew I wanted to photograph the church, so he said it was all right for me to go." It was the first time he had seen Katrina without her hair tied back or on top of her head. Her hands were folded in front of her and a faint smile brightened her angelic, heart-shaped face. The more he was around her, the more intrigued he became. He imagined that she was keeping some deep secret and yearning to tell him. Maybe this would be the moment when the tension between them would collapse and her secrets would spill.

"Look at this mosaic. It's Empress Zoë and her husband. Her third husband. His face was painted over the second one."

"That's the way it goes," Indy said.

"If I get married, it'll be forever," Katrina said softly. "How about you?"

"I was married once, and thought the same thing."

"You were?"

At first, he didn't feel like talking about it, but he'd brought up the topic and he could see that she was curious to hear about his marriage, so he told her about Deirdre.

When he finished, she looked up, obviously moved by the story. "I'm so sorry, Indy. I didn't know."

"It's okay. It's over now."

"Will you never love another woman?"

He reached out and took her hand. Without a word, he leaned toward her, kissed her gently on the lips. Then he abruptly pulled his head back as he heard footsteps on the ramp and a muttering of voices. A few minutes ago, he'd thought he was alone in the church. Now it sounded as if the gallery was about to get crowded.

"I'd better go," Katrina said, and turned away from him to pick up her camera.

But she wasn't going anywhere, at least not on her own. A half-dozen men appeared at the top of the ramp, and they didn't look like they were here for the mosaics. They stared intently at Indy and Katrina as they fanned out. They were garbed like no one Indy had seen in Turkey: baggy pants made of thick raw cotton and long tunics, which were tied about their waists with brightly colored sashes. But what made their appearances particularly peculiar was their headgear. They each wore a tall, black hat that made them look like they were at least seven feet tall.

"You guys looking for someone?" Indy asked.

No one answered. Indy tried some more happy talk, hoping that if he didn't take them seriously, they wouldn't present any danger. "What's with the hats? You hiding your fezes?" Again, no one responded. Not the right thing to say, he thought.

Then Indy recognized one of the men from the bazaar. "Oh, it's you. Hasan, isn't that your name? Thanks for the recommendation on the restaurant. My friend and I enjoyed our meal."

The man stroked his thick mustache. "It was your last."

Swell. The men closed in on them. "Things are getting little dicey," he said to Katrina as they edged back toward the railing. She said something to him under her breath.

"I didn't catch that," he muttered.

"They're going to kill us."

"No, just him," Hasan said.

"You wouldn't kill anyone in a church, would you? That could cost you in the long run."

"We are guided by Allah," Hasan said. "We act upon his commands."

The men were within six feet of them; Indy's back was pressed to the railing. One of them kicked the tripod that Katrina had abandoned and the camera crashed to the floor. One of the others dumped over the contents of the cart, and for a moment Indy glimpsed what he thought was the ark wood wrapped in a cloth.

"Why is He commanding you to pick on us?" Indy asked. "We haven't done anything."

"You told me yourself that you are here to climb Ararat to find the Ark."

"Did I say that?"

"It's not time yet to find the Ark."

"We're not planning on stealing it." Indy kept an eye on the men as they edged closer. "We just want to take a few pictures. We probably won't even find it."

Indy could see there was no use arguing with him, but he had to try to talk his way out of the situation. The chances of saving himself and escaping with Katrina weren't good. "Okay, we'll talk to the leader of the expedition, and tell him your concern. Maybe you'd like to meet with him yourself."

"You don't understand. We are not going to talk about it. You are not going to Ararat."

If they didn't want to talk, then it was time to act, Indy figured. He reached inside his jacket and pulled out his .455 Webley. "Stop right there. Fun's over for you guys and just starting for me. I've got a bullet for each of you." He hoped he sounded convincing.

The men stopped, then drew their own guns. "Hey, no fair." Indy put his revolver away.

He didn't waste another second. Drastic measures were required and he didn't hesitate. He executed a backward somersault over the rail and caught the base of the railing with one hand. He dangled a moment, then hooked his arm through the railing. With his free hand, he unhitched the whip from his belt. Just as one of the men kicked at his arm, he unfurled the whip and snagged the nearest green column. The rope curled around it; his intent was to grasp the other end and slide down the column.

But it didn't work out that way. The end of the whip didn't reach all the way around. It fell limply down the column. "So much for that," he muttered, and winced as a boot struck his forearm with another blow. Katrina's screams echoed through the church, then fell silent.

He couldn't hang on much longer. Another kick would do it. He could try to climb down the column, but the chances were he would simply fall. His head was just below the base of the gallery floor, and as he twisted he saw iron rungs leading under the floor to the wall.

The structure had been reinforced several times over the centuries and the rungs were probably part of the reinforcements. He jammed the handle of the whip in his mouth, grabbed the nearest rung, and unhooked his arm just in time to avoid another kick. His arm throbbed; he could barely hang on to the rung. But in times of great danger, the body reacted in seemingly superhuman ways. And this was one of those times.

Hand over hand, he climbed until he reached another column. But this one's circumference was smaller. He snapped the whip around it and grabbed hold of both ends in one hand. He positioned his feet against the column and let go of the last rung. As he skidded downward, the whip started to slip from his grasp, but he snagged it with his free hand. He slid rapidly down the column, the whip cutting into his palms. He struck the stone floor and dropped to his hands and knees.

As he started to get up he saw a pair of legs in front of him. Before he could react, a boot connected solidly with his jaw. He fell over backward, struck his head against the floor, and another boot slammed into his groin. Nearly blind with pain, he rolled over, tried to stand up. A rope tightened around his neck; no, not a rope. His whip. He was being strangled with his own whip.

He gagged, clawed at the air with his hands. A tall hat dropped to the floor. The whip tightened, cutting off his air. He struggled, but he was losing his strength. He saw dark, beady eyes, a hawk nose, and a thick mustache that was twisted by a grimacing expression.

Then everything went black.

13

Cocoon of Pleasure

He was floating under the great dome. He felt warm, comfortable, relaxed. The dome was spinning and he smiled. Suspended from heaven by a golden chain, Indy thought. Or did he speak the words? He didn't know, didn't care. Nothing mattered. Not now. Not ever.

He was on his back, gliding effortlessly. So easy. He felt hands on his arms and legs and realized he was being carried away. He wondered who was carrying him. They were taking him out of the dome, but he didn't want to leave. It was too nice here. He told himself to fight, to get away, but his body wouldn't listen to him. It felt too good.

What did it matter where he was going or who was carrying him? He laughed. It was just a free ride. Go with it. No problem. No problem at all.

Then the dome was gone and the bright sun seared his eyes and he was being held up and dragged down a street. He wanted to scream. A blur of color and forms moved past him. People.

He should say something to them. But what and why? Was something the matter?

Katrina.

He remembered being with her and then he recalled the men with the tall hats. He'd tried to get away, but something had happened. His throat. He vaguely remembered being strangled by his whip. He moved his head, felt a burning in his throat; the skin on his neck was raw. But he was breathing now, so what did it matter? Nothing mattered. Not even Katrina. But why didn't anything matter? He should be concerned.

Morphine.

They'd drugged him. That was it. He had to do something . . . something . . . but . . .

The bright light and crowd vanished and he was tossed inside an enclosed wagon. He was lying on something soft, and a wave of good feeling swept over him. Everything was all right again. He closed his eyes as he felt the wagon moving. He smiled to himself and drifted.

Indy blinked his eyes at the gray canvas ceiling. Faint light oozed around him. He felt the motion of the wagon bouncing over a rough road. He could hear men's voices speaking Turkish. He rose up and saw vague shapes huddled together. Men. Someone saw him and spoke sharply. Immediately, the men moved toward him. They pushed him down, pulled at his arm, and held him down so he couldn't move. He felt a sharp stinging pain in his forearm.

Several seconds passed as he tried to grasp what was happening. Where was he? Who were these men? He had to remember; it was important. Of course. He was drugged, and these men...

Time stopped. The tension drained from his muscles. He was drowsy and floating. A cocoon of exquisite pleasure wove its threads around him. He felt something being wrapped around his eyes. Didn't matter. Nothing could hurt him. Everything was perfect in the cocoon. No desires, no pains, no concerns.

The darkness was complete, but through its thickness Indy heard a jumble of words. Not Turkish. Not English. A woman's voice. Speaking softly near his ear. She was speaking Russian, and it took a while for him to make sense of any of it. Then he recognized a few words, enough to know that she was praying.

"Katrina," he whispered.

"Indy, are you all right?" she said in English.

"It's so dark."

"Wait."

Fingers on his face tugged at something and suddenly blinding light beamed in his eyes. He squinted and slowly his eyes adjusted. He saw Katrina staring intently at him. Her hair was loose and wild as straw, and right then, she was the most beautiful human being he'd ever seen. Then the pain hit him.

"God, my head feels like pulp. They must have drugged me."

"Shh. Not so loud."

The wagon had stopped. "What's going on? Where are we?" he whispered.

"They're outside. I think they're changing horses again."

"Again?"

He dimly recalled incidents with men moving about, incomprehensible activities that were just part of a long dream. He still felt groggy, but he was getting back in control of himself. He knew the morphine was wearing off because now he cared about what was happening to him and Katrina, and he wanted to do something about it.

"We've been traveling three days now. They only drugged me the first day.

"Who are they, anyhow?"

Katrina looked away.

"What's wrong? Did they do something to you?"

She shook her head. "No, it's my fault that you're in this mess. We didn't tell you everything."

"What do you mean?"

"When we were in Athens, it wasn't for a family reunion. There was a big meeting of the NRM."

"What's that?"

"The New Russia Movement. They're the ones who are sponsoring the expedition. They're placing a lot of pressure on Papa to make sure that we find the Ark. They really think that its discovery will topple the godless Bolsheviks."

So there were things going on, as Indy had suspected, that she and her father had kept to themselves. He should've known. Zobolotsky had given him enough hints. "But what's that got to do with those guys in the church?"

"Don't you see? They must be agents of the Bolsheviks. They don't want us to get to Mount Ararat."

Indy nodded, but he wasn't so sure about the identity of the men. Something about them was vaguely familiar and he didn't think it had anything to do with Bolsheviks.

"Where are they taking us?"

"I don't know. But look outside." Katrina moved over to the canvas wall and held open a tear in the fabric that was several inches long.

Indy leaned forward, his face close to Katrina's. He blinked, then ran a hand over his eyes. He didn't believe what he saw. The drugs must be still affecting him. It was a dream landscape. It looked as if a giant had molded the land from white clay, creating mountains and hills and strange forms like nothing he'd ever seen. There were buildings made of the white clay, but they were like no buildings he had ever seen. Some were jagged and peaked, others smooth and egg-shaped.

The nearest one had walls that bulged out as if the giant had sat on the flat roof while the clay was still wet. The door was squat and arched, and two small children stood in front of it staring at the wagon. But what was even more peculiar was that to the right of the structure was the strangest monument Indy had ever seen. It looked like a ten-foot-high needle of white stone with a boulder resting on its tip. In the background, a cliff rose from the surreal landscape, and it appeared to have windows carved on its face.

He drew back from the slit. "Do you see what—"

"Yes. I see it, too. It's very unusual."

"Unusual? The place looks like a nightmare."

"Then it's my nightmare, too. I've seen this place when I've held the Ark wood. Several times. Now I know it's a real place."

"Let's not try to figure it out. Let's just get the hell out of this wagon."

"But how?"

Indy pulled off his left boot and twisted its heel. He shook the boot, but nothing happened. Then he hit the heel against the floor of the wagon, and this time a three-inch knife blade fell out. He slipped the boot back on and found the rip in the canvas covering. Carefully, he made a horizontal slit, then a vertical one, while Katrina held the canvas together at the top.

"You ready?"

"I don't know," Katrina said. "It'll be dangerous."

"It's dangerous staying here, too." He didn't want to leave her behind, didn't think he would do it. But he needed to cajole her into action. "You coming with me or not?"

"Well, yes. I guess so, but . . ."

"Then let's go. Run toward that house or whatever it is. We'll get it between the wagon and us and then head for that cliff."

He pulled the flap inside the wagon and stuck his head out. A man with a rifle stood about ten feet away, a complication Indy hadn't noticed when he'd peered through the tear. But the guard's back was turned to him, and Indy had the advantage of surprise. He somersaulted out of the wagon, sprang to his feet, and just as the guard turned he jabbed the blade against his throat. In Turkish, he ordered him to drop the rifle. The man followed his orders. Then Indy stuffed what was left of his blindfold in the man's mouth.

"One more thing," he said, and slammed his fist into the man's face. The guard staggered, but stayed on his feet. "Must be the drugs," Indy muttered, and leaned over to pick up the rifle. The guard dived and tackled him around the ankles just as Indy was about to scoop up the weapon. Indy kicked hard, and his boot caught the man under the jaw. This time he dropped to the ground, out cold.

Indy grabbed the rifle and helped Katrina, who was halfway out of the wagon. "Let's go," he hissed.

The house with the bulging walls was less than fifty yards away, and he was about to sprint for it when a shout from behind stopped him in his tracks. "Hold it right there. Drop the gun, Jones."

It was Hasan and he held Indy's own revolver to Katrina's head. Indy dropped the rifle and two other men moved around the other end of the wagon and grabbed his arms.

"So you didn't get enough morphine, Professor Jones," Hasan said. "We'll have to experiment a little with you."

Indy and Katrina were dragged back into the wagon, and a few minutes later Hasan reappeared. One of the men pulled up Indy's shirt sleeve. Indy struggled and slipped free, but two other men quickly pinned him to the floor of the wagon.

Hasan leered at him as he held up a syringe. "This should take care of you for a while. It's a mixture of morphine and a certain herb we call the beautiful lady."

Belladona, Indy thought, fighting a wave of panic. It was a hallucinogenic drug, and if he was given too much of it, he'd die, and lose his mind in the process.

"You might really like this, Professor, if it doesn't kill you."

Hasan had already promised to kill him, but Indy had never suspected it would be by an overdose of drugs. "You no good sadistic...."

"This is for the sultans of old." Hasan stabbed the needle into his forearm.

Indy tried to fight off the drug by talking, but a pleasant glowing feeling began to envelope him. He felt powerful, on top of the world, and drowsy at the same time. "I'll be whatever I want to be, thank you." His voice was slurred. He giggled; he couldn't help it. "Where are we going?"

"To my harem, of course. You'll be there soon enough."

Hasan's voice was a liquid bubbling of sound. Indy smiled and closed his eyes. He'd never felt so relaxed, so good. He wanted to laugh at the absurdity of the situation, but he couldn't quite remember what the situation was. It didn't matter. He felt like his being was in a million places at once and it all felt wonderful.

Shannon sat on the edge of his bed and opened his Bible to the place that was marked with the unopened cable he'd picked up for Indy. He wondered if he would ever get a chance to deliver it.

He read the short passage from the second

book of Corinthians yet another time. They were the same words that had saved him from despair more than once during the last few weeks in Chicago. He'd memorized the words, but they seemed stronger to him when he read them.

My grace is all you need; for my power is strongest when you are weak.

That was exactly how he felt: weak and helpless. Indy and Katrina were missing, and he had no idea where to look for them. All that he could do was pray and hope that Zobolotsky would turn up some clue. The words blurred on the page. Got to do something, he thought. He knew damn well that if he was the one who had disappeared, Indy wouldn't be reading the Bible or any other book. He'd be out looking for him.

He stood up; the Bible slipped to the floor. He walked over to the window and stared down at the street. Someone out there must know what happened. He just had to find the right person. He turned from the window, intent on going out, but stopped before he reached the door. Who was going to listen to him? He and Zobolotsky had already spent two days scouring the market for them. He didn't speak Turkish, and even if he did, the chance of finding that one person who could help was like hunting for the proverbial needle in the haystack, and Istanbul was not the easiest haystack to dig through.

He looked down at the floor. The Bible had fallen open to a passage from the Acts of the Apostles. He picked it up and started to read a verse from Acts 8 in which an angel of the Lord spoke to Philip. *Get yourself ready and go south to the road that goes from Jerusalem to Gaza. So Philip got ready and went.*

Was that a message for him? Was he supposed to go south? But he was in Turkey, not Palestine. He kept reading.

En route Philip encountered an Ethiopian eunuch who was reading from the book of the prophet Isaiah. When Philip asked if he understood what he was reading, the eunuch asked for help interpreting the scripture, which read:

> He was like a sheep that is taken to be
> slaughtered;
> he was like a lamb that makes no
> sound when its wool is cut off;
> he did not say a word.
> He was humiliated and justice
> was denied him.
> No one will be able to tell
> about his descendants,
> because his life on earth has
> come to an end.

Shannon snapped the Bible closed. If that was a message to him, then Indy was dead. There was no reason for him to go anywhere. But the Bible had always given him hope, not despair. There had to be something here for him to grasp onto. His thumb was still in the book and he opened it again. The rest of the verse explained how Philip told the eunuch of the Lord and how he baptized him when they came upon water.

That was it. Indy could be saved. Shannon wasn't in Jerusalem and Indy wasn't in Gaza, but it didn't matter. He would go out in search of Indy, and the Lord would lead him. If Philip could save the eunuch, then just maybe Jack Shannon could save Indy.

He stuffed the Bible in his bag and started packing. This was going to be a true test of his faith, but he was looking forward to it. If he found Indy, he would know that the Lord worked miracles and that the Almighty was guiding him. Maybe that was the reason he had come to Turkey. Maybe it was what all of his troubles in Chicago were about. He was supposed to become a conduit for the word of the Lord.

Meanwhile, his troubles in Chicago were still multiplying. When he'd picked up Indy's cable, he'd also found one waiting for him. It was from his mother, who was happy he was alive. But the news had been bad. The Nest had been condemned by the city, and unless the owners answered the complaint in thirty days, it would be taken over by the city and sold at auction. There was no doubt in Shannon's mind that it was all a ploy and that Capone was behind it. But that wasn't his concern any longer.

His bag was almost packed when he heard a knock on the door. It was Zobolotsky, and he looked grim. "What happened?" Shannon asked.

The Russian ran a hand through his sandy hair. He was fatigued and distraught. "The police are completely baffled. I don't know what we're going to do. I should have been a better father and not brought Katrina here. It's just that I thought she was supposed to be here."

Shannon didn't ask what that last part meant. "Well, I'm going after Indy and Katrina. I'm heading south."

Zobolotsky looked surprised. "What are you keeping from me? What do you know?"

"I only know that the Lord spoke to me, and I'm supposed to leave the city. I don't know where I'm going, but He will guide me."

Zobolotsky studied him for a moment. When he spoke, his voice was resolute. "I hear the devil speaking to you, not the Lord. You are mocking me."

Shannon was startled by the Russian's harsh attack. He didn't know how to respond. "What do you mean? Why am I mocking you?"

"The Lord speaks through Katrina, not you. She has proven it over and over. What have you proven?"

"Only that I'm weak, but I believe the Lord is making me strong, and I'm going to go out there and look for Indy and your daughter whether you come with me or not."

Shannon picked up his bag and was about to leave when there was another knock on the door. "Who is it?" he snapped.

The door slowly opened and the girl from the next building stepped inside. She glanced between the two men. "Excuse me, can I speak to you?"

"Who are you?" Zobolotsky asked.

"Hello, Sekiz," Shannon said. "We're kind of busy right now, and I was just on my way out."

"But it's important. It's about your friend and the pretty woman."

"You know what happened to Katrina?" Zobolotsky asked.

"I have heard things on the street. They say

that they were taken far away, but that they are still alive."

"What else do you know?" Shannon asked.

She shook her head. "That's all I know. Except . . ."

"Except what?" Shannon asked.

"There is a blind man I know. He is very old and has been blind all of his life. But he can see in strange ways. I think he might be able to see where they were taken."

"More heathen devil talk," Zobolotsky scoffed, and dismissed her with a wave of his hand.

Shannon turned to him and their eyes met. "You think so, Dr. Z? Are you so damn sure that you're going to ignore the chance that she may be right and the old man might just know where Katrina and Indy are?"

Zobolotsky looked away. When he spoke, it was in a voice that was hardly louder than a whisper. "All right. Let's go see him. I'll do anything to get Katrina back. Lord forgive me."

14

CAPPADOCIA

Indy's thoughts were taking on a life of their own. All that really existed was thought. Everything was impressions, feelings, pain and pleasure. Indy himself was a thought, and that was all he needed to know.

He could see nothing in the darkness, not even his hand. Yet he could see the inside of his mind quite clearly. Old friends paraded across the invisible screen in front of him, and each one generated a flood of emotion from compassion to wrath, anger to joy. He saw Dorian Belecamus, his archaeology professor and lover, who wanted to swallow him. His old history professor said he was remarkable, but not profound. Madelaine from his past called his name and laughed hauntingly, and a girl named Marion said she was going to punch him in the mouth one of these days. Now Deirdre appeared, and with one look she wrung his heart, drenched it in sorrow and regret, then she looked to one side and was gone.

Indy turned to see what she had looked at and there was Colonel Fawcett. He was telling him something. His lips weren't moving, but Indy could hear his booming voice. "You haven't lost any memories. They are all there—veiled."

With that single word Indy recalled his experiences with Deirdre and Fawcett in the Lost City, the city called D. The people could veil themselves and the city. There was something about dreaming, too. They ruled themselves through their dreams, and he'd had a hard time telling when he was dreaming and when he was awake. But now he knew that Fawcett had died along with Deirdre in the plane crash. Though Indy had survived, his memories had been veiled. But no more.

The thoughts and images flowed together, washing over him. He had little sense of his surroundings or the passage of time. It was dark and cool, and he wasn't in the wagon anymore. He didn't know how he'd gotten here, where he was, or how long he'd been here. Yet there was something that he should know about this place. Was this the harem that Hasan had spoken of?

Harem. The word resonated within him, and Indy saw himself as a kid again visiting Turkey with his father. They were in the Topkapi Saray, the great palace where the sultan ruled. The power of the sultan was quickly disintegrating and his father was hoping to find a manuscript related to his lifelong study of grail lore before the palace records were destroyed or moved. They were walking through the second court and his father was deep in conversation with one of the sultan's deputies when Indy saw the tall men with swords and funny hats cross the courtyard.

"Dad, did you see them? Who are they?"

His father shook a finger at him. But the deputy, a corpulent man with a trim beard, stopped and placed a hand on Indy's shoulders. "Those men are from the famous Janissary Corps. They are great warriors and great soup eaters, too. It's a ritual for them. They're headed to the soup kitchen right now."

The deputy turned back to Indy's father. "Now, what was I saying?"

They moved on, but Indy lagged behind. When he saw that his father wasn't paying any attention to him, he wandered off in the direction that the two Janissaries had gone. He came to the first of several kitchens. The Janissaries weren't there and neither was the soup. But there were sweets, trays and trays of them. A cook saw him staring at the array of candies and baked goods and offered him a gooey honey-and-almond concoction, which he gladly accepted.

When the cook wasn't looking, he crept into the next kitchen and found the Janissaries. There were six or seven of them and they were standing in a circle around the largest pot of soup he'd ever seen. They each held a bowl and spoon and lifted their spoons at the same time in a slow, formal manner.

When Indy returned to the second court, his father was nowhere in sight. He crossed the courtyard and opened a door near where he'd last seen his father. He peered into an empty council chamber, then closed the door and walked around the side of the building where he found another door. This one was to prove far more interesting. While he didn't find his father, Indy did discover something else.

In a courtyard at the end of a corridor, a dozen girls were seated on benches and an older woman was talking to them. This was the sultan's harem; he knew he wasn't supposed to be here.

He turned to retreat down the corridor, but now two chubby Negro eunuchs were moving toward him, carrying baskets filled with freshly laundered clothing. He knew they were eunuchs because his father had told him about the men who guarded the sultan's concubines. He'd also said it was strictly off limits, and now here he was.

He slipped back into the courtyard, ducked behind a column, and waited for the eunuchs to move past him. But as soon as they reached the courtyard they set down the baskets and one of them clapped his hands twice. Two women appeared and took away the clothing, passing within three feet of Indy, while the eunuchs lounged near the entrance to the corridor.

Now he had to find another way out. The women had left the baskets of laundry in the corner of the courtyard, which gave him an idea. He dashed into an alcove, reached out, and grabbed a billowy dress from one of the basket. Quickly, he pulled it over his head. It was too large for him, but he could hold the bottom off the floor.

He didn't look much like a girl with his short hair, so when he was sure no one was looking, he stepped out from the alcove and rummaged through one of the baskets until he found what he thought was a scarf. As he spread it out he realized it was an undergarment for a large woman. He cursed and was about to put it back when the laundry women returned. He ducked out of sight, and watched as they toted away the baskets. The underwear would have to do. He wrapped it around his head as best he could and steeled himself for his walk past the courtyard of concubines.

He didn't like the idea of dressing like a girl, but he knew his hero, the late adventurer Richard Francis Burton, would have done it, and if it was all right with Burton, it was okay with Indy. Burton was a master of disguises, a dauntless fighter, rider, and athlete who also spoke twenty-nine languages and dialects. He had roamed the frigid mountains of Afghanistan, the baked plains west of Karachi, unknown Central Africa, and the forbidden cities of Islam. He was a scientist who founded the first anthropological society in England, a translator of the *Arabian Nights*, and a student of mysticism. He was known to disguise himself in the garb of the native people, and he did so on numerous occasions to escape certain death. If there was anyone Indy wanted to be like when he grew up, it was Burton, and now he was getting a chance to prove himself.

He couldn't wait any longer. He stepped out of the alcove and crossed the courtyard to the far gate. No one said a word to him, but as he reached the gate he was disappointed to find himself peering into an even larger courtyard where more concubines languished and several Negro eunuchs watched over them. Life in the harem, Indy thought, wasn't for him, and the quicker he found a way out the better.

He walked along the side of the courtyard away from the eunuchs and kept his head down until he saw an old woman moving his way. There was a scowl on her face that suggested she was more than slightly curious about him. Trouble, he thought, and looked for a way to avoid her. He opened the first door he reached and stepped inside.

It didn't take but a glance to see that he'd found the common bath, and at least a dozen women in various stages of undress were sharing it. He started to back out, but bumped into the old woman. She laid a hand firmly on his shoulder.

"Do you want to take a bath, young lady?" she asked.

Indy's knowledge of Turkish was minimal, but it wasn't difficult to figure out what she'd said. He shook his head and tried to squeeze past her, but she grabbed his arm and pulled the underwear off his head.

"Who are you?" she demanded.

"I'm lost," Indy said in English. "I was with my father, but he was too busy to wait for me."

The old woman pulled him out of the common bath and marched him across the courtyard. She signaled one of the eunuchs, gave him an order, and he hurried away. She walked Indy over to an imposing door, opened it, and directed him into a large room.

A fountain bubbled in the center of it, and there were chairs and couches around the walls. She pointed to a chair and Indy sat down. He could see through a partially open door into another room with a canopied bed and an ornate fireplace.

"These are my son's quarters," the old woman said in perfect English. "He is the sultan, and I am known as the valide sultan."

"This is where the sultan lives, in the harem?" Indy asked in astonishment.

The valide sultan laughed. "Let me explain. In every traditional Moslem household, there are two parts: the greeting room, like this one where we are sitting, and the harem or private household quarters where the family lives. In the palace, of course, we have a very large harem because the sultan has a large household with four wives and many concubines.

Indy nodded. He had heard somewhere that some sultans also had boys as concubines, and he wanted to make sure that he didn't become one of them. "I'd better be going," he said, and pulled off the dress as he stood up. "My father will be worried."

"Sit down," the woman ordered. "Your lost father will be found. Not everyone has the opportunity to talk with the valide sultan. You should feel fortunate."

Katrina was frightened. They were in some dark, deep hole. She was tied to Indy, and for a long time he'd been so quiet that she'd feared that he was in a coma. But now he was muttering to himself and moving. "What did you say, Indy? Can you hear me?"

"I said I do feel fortunate to be here, but I think my father must be worrying about me."

"It's okay," Katrina said. "You're going to be all right." He was delirious; she hoped it wasn't a permanent condition. "Do you know where you are?"

It was a silly question; she didn't know herself. But she needed to make Indy aware of his surroundings. Right now she wasn't sure he even knew she was tied to him.

Indy was confused. He was a kid and a grown man at the same time and something was seriously wrong. The old woman was talking to him about a strange place in Turkey, and Katrina was speaking in his ear.

"Do you know where you are?" Katrina asked for a second time.

"Someday you should go there," the valide sultan said. "The odd shapes were caused by lava from ancient volcanoes and thousands of years of erosion. The people in the valleys have carved out very extraordinary houses from the stone, and instead of trees there are tall needles of rock with boulders balanced on top."

"What is the place called?"

"Cappadocia. Remember that name, young man."

"Indy, can you hear me?" Katrina asked.

He blinked his eyes and the sultan's palace was gone and he was no longer a kid. He was groggy and back in the dark place. It was earthy, damp, cool. He was sitting up, leaning against something that moved when he did. His hands were tied behind his back, and a rope was bound around his arms.

"Katrina?"

"I'm right here. Do you know where you are?" Her voice was near his ear, and he realized that they were tied back-to-back.

"Cappadocia," he said without thinking.

"What?"

He was confused, uncertain about what was real and what was hallucination. But the drugs seemed to be losing their hold on him. "I think that's where we are, and these men are from the Janissary Corps."

"That doesn't mean anything to me."

"I think it means we're in big trouble."

Sekiz's thick braid swayed from side to side, a dark pendulum as she walked through the narrow streets of Istanbul. She moved surprisingly fast, and Shannon did his best to keep track of the swinging braid in front of him and Zobolotsky behind him. Finally, they walked out onto the Galata Bridge, which spanned the Bosphorus River, and Shannon no longer had to worry about losing sight of either one of them.

When they reached the center of the bridge, Sekiz stopped and waited for them. "They say that this is where Asia ends and Europe begins," the girl said.

Shannon gazed at the network of winding streets on the hill rising from the west side of the river. "Is the blind man a European?" he asked as they continued across the bridge.

Sekiz laughed. "Don't you know, we are all Europeans now in Turkey. That is the new way. The old ways are over."

"How much further?" Zobolotsky asked.

"You see Galata tower over there? We're going very near it."

"Don't tell me there's a special street over there for blind prophets," Shannon said, recalling how the streets were organized in the covered market.

"No. This man is very special. He is not a Gypsy fortune-teller. You will see."

After reaching the far side of the bridge, they continued along the road until they arrived at a square. They crossed it, then walked down a narrow, stone-paved street marked Galip Dede Caddesi. Sekiz pointed to a door on their left. Above it was a sign in both Arabic and Latin lettering, which read: *Galata Mevlevi Tekkesi.* She opened the door and they entered a well-tended garden. Flowers bloomed in a riot of colors on either side of them as they followed a path toward a modest, wood-frame building.

"Where are we?" Shannon asked, but Sekiz put a finger to her lips. "Wait."

She knocked on the door of the building, and after a short time, an elderly woman looked out. Sekiz addressed her and the woman motioned toward the side of the house, then closed the door.

"This way," Sekiz said, and led the way along another path. They approached a shaded nook, sheltered by a high hedge and trees. A bearded man was seated on a bench. His head was bowed against his chest, and he appeared to be asleep.

"Who is there?" he asked in a low voice without raising his head.

"Grandfather, it is me, Sekiz."

The old man raised his head and smiled. A ray of sunlight illuminated his face. His eyes were white and filmy, his beard was gray, but his hair was as red as Shannon's own. "And who is with you, little one?" he asked as she sat next to him and took his hand.

"I've brought two friends who are from far away. They are in need of help."

The old man patted the bench next to him. "Sit down, please."

Sekiz pointed to the bench and translated her grandfather's words.

The old man clapped his hands three times. "We will have tea and talk. Now, what are your names and where are you from?"

Shannon had no idea if anything would come of this venture, but he remained patient and listened closely to Sekiz's translation. He and Zobolotsky sat down and introduced themselves.

"You can call me Alfin," the old man said. He reached out a hand and Shannon shook it, but the old man didn't let go of it. "Do you know we are from the same ancestor?"

"I don't think so," Shannon said. "My grandparents came to the United States from Ireland."

"Yes, and my distant ancestors traveled to the British Isles from this very land, which was then known as Anatolia. They were called Galacians, but you know them as Celts."

"I didn't know that." Shannon made a mental note that he would ask Indy if the Celts came from Turkey.

Alfin let go of Shannon's hand and reached for Zobolotsky's. The Russian hesitated, then extended his hand. "Please help me find my daughter."

"Your God and your daughter, and now your

daughter and your God," Alfin said, and Zobolotsky pulled away his hand.

The old woman who had opened the door of the wooden house appeared with a tray of tea and set it down on the bench. Sekiz passed cups to Shannon and Zobolotsky. She was about to hand another to the old man, but his head had nodded against his chest again. Shannon glanced at Zobolotsky, who was frowning and shaking his head.

"You, Dr. Zobolotsky, know nothing of who I am," Alfin said. It was a statement, not a question. "You should not judge what you do not know."

"I thought it best not to say too much about you," Sekiz said.

Alfin patted the air as he raised his head again. "I am from a long tradition, which our new government is trying to abolish, but they will fail. The house in front of you is a *tekke*, where we hold our ceremonies. We are known as the Mevlevi, one of the Sufi brotherhoods. We seek mystical communion with God through *sema*—chants, prayers, music, and the whirling dance."

"But the government doesn't allow them to dance here anymore," Sekiz added after she translated her grandfather's words.

"Whirling dervishes," Shannon said, sipping his tea. "I've heard about them. When I lived in Paris, a girlfriend of mine played me a recording of lute music that she said was played by dervishes."

"Did you like it?" Sekiz asked as she passed a cup of tea to Alfin.

"It was hard to listen to, and I've listened to a lot of music."

Sekiz smiled. "Maybe you have to be a dervish to appreciate it. You would like our folk music better."

"Listen," Zobolotsky interrupted. "My daughter is missing, and I will not sit here and drink tea. I must find her. Can he help us or not?"

Alfin didn't wait for a translation. "Sit still, doctor. Stay calm. I will tell you what you want to know. You came to the right person even though you do not believe it."

After a few moments of silence, Alfin set down his cup of tea. He nodded his head low on his chest until Shannon thought he was going to tip over. Then he rocked back and forth and spun his head in circles. Shannon was dizzy from just watching.

When he stopped, he spoke in a voice that was even deeper than normal. "The ones who kidnapped your daughter are known as Janissaries."

"Who are they?" Shannon asked.

"Soldiers, evil soldiers," Zobolotsky answered, "the most terrible of all."

"When the Ottoman Empire was strong, the Janissaries were the best soldiers in the world," Alfin said. "They were excellent swordsmen and could cleave a head with a single blow."

"That's impressive," Shannon said, and touched his neck.

"But they became very powerful and manipulative. They could remove a sultan from power. They are Sufis, but of another sect known as the Bektasis. They are the reason that the new government outlawed all the Sufis in 1925."

"But why would they want to kidnap my friend and this man's daughter?" Shannon asked.

Alfin was silent a moment. "Why are you here in Turkey? The question is your answer."

"I don't understand," Zobolotsky said. "We're here to climb Mount Ararat to search for Noah's Ark."

"Then that is the reason," Sekiz said without hesitation.

"But why wouldn't they want us to look for the Ark?" Shannon asked.

"The teachings of Islam say the Ark will only be revealed by God on the Day of Judgment," Alfin explained. "The Janissaries believe it is their mission to protect the Ark from those who would reveal it before God's chosen time."

"The Bible says nothing of this," Zobolotsky said. "God wants us to find the Ark to reaffirm our faith," he insisted.

Alfin said nothing.

When Zobolotsky spoke again, it was in a meeker tone. "Can you tell us where my daughter is?"

"Cappadocia is the land of the Bektasis," Alfin said. "That is where they will be found."

"Is it a city?" Shannon asked.

"No, it's a part of Turkey that was once a kingdom," Sekiz said.

"Where will we find them in Cappadocia?" Zobolotsky asked.

"In an underground city," Alfin said. "There are many of them in Cappadocia, but the Janissaries live in only one of them."

"How do we find it?" Shannon asked.

Alfin rocked back and forth, his blind eyes staring straight ahead. "You will find a house with three *peribacas*. There you will meet a man who knows where your companions are and how to find them."

"What's a *per-i-baca*?" Shannon asked.

Sekiz asked her grandfather to explain. "He says that you will know when you see them."

Alfin turned his head and seemed to stare at Shannon with white eyes. "There will be one among you who lies and cannot be trusted. This one will cause sorrow before the journey is over."

"What's he look like?" Shannon asked.

Alfin raised a hand, cutting off the discussion. "You will see for yourself."

They thanked Alfin for his time and walked with Sekiz to the gate. "I am going to stay a while longer with my grandfather." She wished them well on their journey.

"Thanks for taking us to him," Shannon said. "I think he sees better than I do." They started to leave, but Shannon stopped. "By the way, which direction is Cappadocia?"

"To the south," Sekiz said. "South of Ankara."

"South," he said, and smiled at Zobolotsky. The Russian, it seemed, was a bit more humble now than when they'd arrived.

Boris waited until Shannon and Zobolotsky were out of sight before he spoke. "It doesn't do us any good to just follow these idiots around. We've got to find out what's going on."

The brothers had arrived several days earlier, worried that they would be too late. But they'd soon learned from their contact in Istanbul that the Zobolotskys were attending a secret conference in Athens and would be delayed. So they'd waited.

Their plan had been to kill Zobolotsky in Istanbul and get it over with. When he was dead, the others would give up. But no sooner had the expedition arrived than Jones and the girl disappeared, and that changed everything. Boris knew that Zobolotsky was not to be trusted and he suspected that the sudden disappearance of two party members might be some sort of scheme to mislead anyone who wanted to follow them.

So now they'd probably have to follow them to Ararat and ambush them on the mountain. Killing them there would be the easy part. No one would be too surprised that the expedition had disappeared. Kurdish warriors were a known hazard in the region, and the mountain itself presented a variety of dangers: wild dog packs, wolves, snakes, and bears; avalanches, rock falls, sudden fissures in the ice, and frequent earthquakes, to name a few. But first they needed to know exactly what was going on.

"What are we going to do?" Alexander asked as Boris led the way to the gate.

"Our duty, brother."

"I want to get one thing straightened out between us," Zobolotsky said as they entered the hotel. "We're going to get to know each other a lot better in the coming days, so I want you to call me Vladimir from now on."

Obviously, he had a new status now in Dr. Z's eyes, Shannon thought.

"Dr. Zobolotsky," the desk clerk called out. "A message for you, sir."

Shannon watched as Zobolotsky opened the note. "It's from the kidnappers." He read it and passed it to Shannon.

> You must leave the country immediately or your daughter and your friend will die. Be on the boat to Athens tomorrow morning. The hostages will be released there. Then go home. If you return to Turkey you will die. Your last warning.

Shannon looked up. "What do you think?"

"We've got to follow their orders. We can't take any chances with my daughter's life."

Shannon thought a moment about the guidance he'd received from the Bible and about what Alfin had said. Just a minute ago, he'd been certain that they were supposed to go to Cappadocia. Now he didn't know. Then it occurred to him that Athens was also located to the south of Istanbul. "You're right, Vladimir. We've got to follow their instructions."

Now that things were looking up and it appeared that Indy and Katrina were going to be released, Shannon wished he had been the one who was swept away with Katrina. Suddenly he envied Indy's situation. He just hoped that Katrina wasn't falling for him.

An hour later, Boris and Alexander left through the gate of Galata Mevlevi Tekkesi. The old man had been very helpful. He'd been more than willing to answer their questions after Boris had threatened to kill his granddaughter.

But when they knew everything, Boris decided it was best not to take any chances. He didn't want the girl rushing to Zobolotsky and warning him. So now there were three dead bodies in the garden. The old man and the old woman had died quickly from bullets in the back of their heads. But the young girl had run screaming for the gate, and it had taken three shots to kill her.

A shame, Boris thought. *So young and pretty.* But their mission was to protect the revolution, and that was more important than any individual's life, be it a child or an old woman or an old man. And now he knew exactly what to do. The old man had told him about the meek scholars who lived in underground tunnels. They were knowledgeable about the Ark and were going to guide the expedition to the mountain. Jones and the girl had gone ahead to make arrangements while the other two had stayed behind to complete the paperwork.

He and Alexander would leave for Cappadocia this evening and complete their assignment. He didn't know anything about the Janissaries other than what the old man had told him. But it was enough to know they were just a bunch of crazy Moslem hermits. He laughed at the image of the two of them rampaging through their sacred refuge. The Janissaries would probably bury their heads in their books, just like they'd buried their lives in the ground, and clean up the mess when it was over.

15

The Janissaries

It sounded like breathing and it was coming from somewhere nearby. "Do you hear it?" Indy asked. He could see a wall a few feet in front of him and the outline of a doorway, but not much else.

Katrina shifted positions, and Indy's whip, which was bound around them, tightened. "What is it?"

"I'm not sure."

He peered across the room in the direction from which he'd heard the noise. Gradually, as the hallucinations subsided and the drug wore off, his vision was coming back to him. He could make out a shape: a figure with his back against the wall slumped in the corner. A rifle lay across his lap. His head was nodding forward and he was starting to snore.

"Company," he hissed. "A guard, and he's sound asleep."

"He must have been here all along. I didn't even know it. I can't see over there."

"Let's see what we can do to get loose." Indy drew his feet beneath him and pushed off the floor as he pressed against Katrina's back. Neither spoke as they squirmed up and down and sideways. The whip cut into his chest and arms and seemed to be tightening.

"Ouch!" he said in a raspy whisper. "What are you doing?"

"Trying . . . to . . . to turn . . . around," she answered. "Pull in your stomach."

"I don't think it goes in any further." He twisted toward her until their hips were attached like Siamese twins, then Katrina was facing his back, her chin touching his shoulder. But the ropes weren't any looser.

"I think I can do that, too." Indy wiggled his arms and twisted around. But he stuck fast halfway around.

"What are you doing?" Katrina hissed. "I'm stuck now. I can't move."

"Not so loud."

Indy glanced over his shoulder; the guard was still asleep. He tightened his buttocks, then deftly rotated his hips, and suddenly he and Katrina were face-to-face, their chests and hips pressed against one another. It was an entirely different sensation from being tied back-to-back and not exactly an unpleasant one.

"I don't think this is working," Katrina said as she adjusted her shoulders.

"It's a tough situation," Indy agreed as he wiggled his hands and rolled his hips as he tried to get hold of the whip, "but it's got certain compensations."

"What are you doing down there?"

"Down where?" They were nose to nose now.

"You know."

He moved his hips again.

"There!"

"I'm trying to reach for the whip."

"But do you need to do that?"

"What?"

His thumb touched the lower strand of the whip, but he couldn't quite hook it. He thrust his hips forward and arched his back as he reached again.

"Ah . . . You're doing it again."

"I almost . . . " He took a step forward and tripped over Katrina's foot. They tottered a moment, then toppled into the straw bedding. "You okay?"

Katrina's breath came fast, a whisper of air against his ear. "You're lying on top of me, you know."

"Yeah. Just wait. I think I can get it." As his thumbs flicked at the whip he couldn't help nuzzling Katrina's neck. Her closeness was overpowering; it aroused him. Their lips met and his thumbs stopped working. The softness of her body snuggled against him and he was pressed so firmly against her that the whip slackened and slid on its own over his thumb.

"Katrina, I . . . "

"You don't have to tell me. But I want to tell you something."

Katrina's words surrounded him in the darkness like a thick, comforting blanket. He could listen to her talk like that forever. He was still moving his hips against her, slower now, as he worked the whip over hips and thighs. He looked into her eyes. "Tell me."

"Do you know that piece of wood from the ark?" she breathed.

He stopped moving. It was the last thing he'd expected to hear from her. She was probably going to tell him it was a fake.

"What about it?"

"When I hold it, strange things sometimes happen to me. I mean, I see things happening that haven't happened yet. I knew you would come here to Turkey with us, that you were the right archaeologist."

"That's nice. I think."

"That's not all, though."

The guard suddenly seemed to gasp for breath; then he coughed. He shifted positions and Indy saw that he was a sow of a man, well over three hundred pounds. Indy waited to see if he would wake up. When he heard the guard return to the slow, measured breathing of sleep, he whispered in Katrina's ear.

"Don't tell me you saw us getting kidnapped and put in some hole or wherever we are."

"Not exactly. But I saw us like this. You know, together."

"Tied up?"

"No. Just together. But . . . oh, never mind. Maybe it was just my imagination. Besides, it wasn't you. It was Jack."

"What? You said it was me."

"Well, it was . . . later."

"Later? Maybe we should continue this conversation later." The whip was loose now and they pulled it over their legs as best they could.

"What are we going to do about our hands?" Katrina asked.

"I'm working on that." Indy used his right foot to slip off his left boot. He turned around and took the heel in his hand, twisted it, and caught the blade as it popped out. He shifted positions until he was back-to-back with Katrina again and sliced at the cloth binding.

"Careful," she whispered. "That's my wrist."

He slowed his slicing motions, but finally the cloth fell apart. Katrina took the blade from his hands and quickly cut him free.

Indy immediately crept over to the guard and patted his cheeks. "Hey, you're not supposed to sleep on the job." The guard came awake with a start, and Indy slammed his head into the wall. The man slumped to the floor, and Indy snatched his rifle. "If you're a Janissary warrior, I can see why the empire collapsed."

"Indy, there's no door. It just leads out into a stairway, and light is coming down from above."

"Let's see if we can find our way out."

Just as Indy took a step toward the door the guard grabbed his ankle and jerked him to the floor. Indy was caught by surprise and dropped the rifle. He reached for it, but the guard pulled him away like a spider overcoming its trapped prey. Indy kicked at him, but the guard quickly pinned his legs beneath him. The guy might be a slob, but he was strong.

Indy pulled back his arm and slammed his fist into the man's jaw. He connected solidly, but his hand just bounced harmlessly away.

He punched him again with the same lack of effect.

The guard grinned, spread his fingers, and lunged for his captive's throat. Indy butted his forehead into the man's nose. It stunned him, but for only an instant. The guard's forearm landed under his jaw, and Indy gagged as the man's hands tightened around his throat, his thumbs pressing hard against his Adam's apple. His face turned red, then blue, and he was on the verge of passing out when the guard's grip suddenly relaxed and he flopped over like a beached whale. Indy gasped for breath and squinted up at Katrina, who stood over the guard holding the rifle by the barrel.

"I think I might have killed him," she said.

Indy rolled over and struggled to his feet. Blood poured from a deep gash in the guard's temple. "We all gotta go sometime." Indy rubbed his raw, bruised throat. "And he left just in time as far as I'm concerned."

They moved out of the room and down a corridor. "Indy, wait."

"What is it?"

"I can't leave without the Ark wood."

"Sure you can."

"But it's an incredibly important relic. Papa is going to be really mad if I've lost it. It's priceless. It's more than that. It's—"

"Yeah, I'm sure it is. But our lives are even more valuable, and I'm sure your father would agree." When he saw the look of disappointment on her face, he added: "But let's play it by ear."

* * *

The quickest way to get to Athens was by train, so early the next morning Shannon and Zobolotsky left the hotel and took a taxi to the station. But as they neared their destination the road clogged with cars, horses and wagons, and pedestrians.

"What is going on?" Zobolotsky asked. "Our train leaves in twenty minutes."

"We'd better walk from here," Shannon said. Then he noticed a swarm of police blocking the entrance to the station. They were stopping everyone who approached. "Why don't you wait. I'll go see what's going on."

As he neared the crowd Shannon saw a British-looking man in a bowler. The man walked over to a well-dressed woman surrounded by luggage and porters. Shannon moved closer to hear what he had to say.

"What is it, dear?" the woman asked.

"It seems they're looking for two murderers. Foreigners, they say from America."

"You don't say."

"They killed a little girl, and an old blind man and his nurse, if you can believe that."

"How dreadful. But how long are we going to wait? Our train leaves on the hour."

"Oh, no," Shannon said as he backed away.

He hurried down the street to the taxi. Not only was he a suspect in a triple murder, but he was carrying a gun under his arm. "I think we better take the boat to Athens. The police are looking for a murderer."

"Who got killed?" Zobolotsky asked.

Shannon repeated what he'd heard, but kept the explanation brief and impersonal when he saw that the driver, who spoke some English, seemed to be listening intently.

Zobolotsky glanced at the driver, then back to Shannon. "That's horrible. I think you're right. The boat might be a better way to travel today."

As the taxi crawled through the traffic amid honking and shouting Shannon and Zobolotsky quietly discussed the situation. "I can't believe this," Zobolotsky said. "Who would do such a terrible thing?"

"I don't know, but that poor innocent girl. I'm ready to get out of this country. It's as bad as Chicago."

"I don't understand," Zobolotsky said.

"Maybe the Janissaries followed us from the hotel," Shannon suggested.

"Why would they do it? We were leaving the country just like they wanted."

"The note might have been there when we left the hotel," the rangy musician said. "We didn't stop at the desk. So maybe they followed us to the dervish house, thinking we already had the note. They probably know all about the old Sufi and thought he was crossing their plans."

"Could be," Zobolotsky said. "But what does that mean for us and for my daughter?"

"Nothing too good."

"Look. More police," the driver said as they reached the docks. A crowd was gathered near the gangway of a ship, and police were holding them back, checking every passenger.

Shannon suddenly realized the implications of what Zobolotsky had said. "If they would kill that easily, then we can't trust them to release Indy and Katrina, even if we do go to Athens."

"But we must do what they say," Zobolotsky insisted.

Neither had paid any attention to the driver, who now turned to them as he pulled to the curb. He was a wiry man with salt-and-pepper hair. "You know, I lived for ten years in the United States, but I came back when the last sultan was finally finished. I will tell you something about these Janissaries you are talking about. Their time is over, but some of them do not know that yet."

Shannon was surprised at the taxi driver's interest and awareness of what was going on. He must have heard and understood everything they'd said. "What else do you know about them?"

"They are still warriors, but now they are known for their gaming."

"I don't understand," Shannon said.

"I am telling you this: if the Janissaries killed those three, then they probably did it so the police would put you in jail. That is how their gaming works. They play one group off of another."

"It would have been easier for them just to kill us," Shannon said.

"These Janissaries must be smart," Zobolotsky said. "They must know that if the entire expedition was killed, it would be an international incident and the United States government would send its army to look for us and the Ark."

He's dreaming, Shannon thought, but didn't argue. Instead he pointed to the police, who were now scouring the crowd on the dock, no doubt looking for two men fitting their descriptions.

"So what do you think we should do? They're getting closer."

Zobolotsky thought a moment. "As the leader of this expedition, I have decided we should go to Ankara, and from there to Cappadocia to look for the missing members of our team."

"I will take you as far as Ankara," the driver volunteered. "I have a cousin there, and I have not seen him for many years."

"How much?" Shannon asked.

The driver waved his hand. "Don't worry; I am honest and will give you a fair price, or my name is not Ahmet."

"Done," Zobolotsky said.

So they were finally heading south, Shannon thought, and couldn't help feeling a bit smug.

Hasan sat cross-legged on the cushion in the corner of his room and turned over the piece of wood, examining it closely. He knew what it was from the moment he'd found it among Katrina's belongings. One of his brothers in America had sent him a copy of a newspaper article about Zobolotsky and his plans to search for the Ark. The article had alerted him to the expedition, and it had also mentioned the piece of wood that the explorer claimed he'd taken from the Ark.

Lute music filtered into his room from Spring House. The ceremony was about to begin. He would take the wood with him and whirl with it until he learned its secrets.

Indy's hope that the stairway from the cell would lead directly to a way out of their underground prison was quickly dashed. The light filtered from a torch at the top of a stairway; beyond the stairs was another room carved from porous rock.

Katrina moved into the room and out a door on the other side. "Look, now the stairs go down."

"Somehow I'm not surprised."

There was no choice but to keep going and see where they ended up. For all Indy knew, they could be on their way to the center of the earth. Finally, they descended to a hallway illuminated by torches, with several doorways and windows on either side. They peered into one after another and finally walked into a room with other two doorways that each led to different corridors.

"You take that one; I'll try the other. Maybe one of us will find a stairway going up," Indy said. "Let's meet back here in five minutes."

Indy had no sooner gone a dozen yards than he was confronted with more choices. A short hallway to his left led past a couple of rooms, then divided into two branches. To his right, the passageway led directly to another doorway.

"Now what?" he muttered.

He moved down the corridor to his right, but the room was a dead end. He backtracked and tried one of the branches leading from the opposite corridor. At first, it looked hopeful. There were no stairs, but the hallway rose at a forty-five-degree angle, turned, then turned again. The walls were open from above his waist, and in the faint light he could see rooms and other hallways. The place was part medieval prison and part funhouse. It was a beehive of madness.

He took a couple more turns and, when he saw

the hallway was continuing upward, decided to backtrack and find Katrina. He counted the turns as he walked, but when he thought he should be near the dead-end room, he found himself in one with three doorways. He backed out the door, tried another room, and saw that the doorway on the opposite side led to more hallways stairs.

He looked around, confused and lost. He pounded a fist against a stone wall. The funhouse was turning into a nightmare. "Swell. Now what?"

Then he heard footsteps. Katrina was probably lost in this same network of madness. But he couldn't tell where the steps were coming from or which way they were moving. He wanted to call out her name, but suppose it wasn't Katrina? For all he knew, the Janissaries were already combing these corridors for them.

He crept quietly down the hallway and peered into the darkness. Now he couldn't hear anything. Either the person had moved out of hearing range or had stopped. Suddenly he heard the footfalls again. They sounded close. Right by his head. He spun around and there were the feet moving along another hallway at his eye level.

He had to make up his mind fast. He swung the butt of the rifle around, then he saw the boots. He grabbed Katrina by the foot, and she let out a scream.

"Shh! It's me."

"Indy?" She was on her hands and knees, looking around, then she saw him. "Oh, God. You scared me. I didn't know what happened to you. This place is crazy."

"I know. Are you all right?"

"I think so. Help me down." She swung her legs over the side and slid down into his arms.

"I missed you," she whispered.

He touched her cheek, and for a moment he imagined he was with Deirdre again. Then it occurred to him that he was falling for the woman that his best friend adored. He stepped back from her. "We've got to keep moving. I thought I found a ramp that was heading up, but I'm not sure which one it was now."

"There are too many choices. It's so confusing."

"C'mon. Let's stick together."

"Don't leave me again," she said.

She didn't really mean it the way it sounded, he told himself as he picked a corridor and headed down it. They'd barely gone ten yards when the hallway opened into a chamber with a high ceiling. He stopped and gazed at the wall on his right, which was illuminated by a torch. On it was painted a fresco of a man with a cross in one hand and a sword in the other, which he pointed defiantly at a winged beast.

"It's Saint George with his dragon," the young archaeologist said. The sight of the Christian icon triggered something in his memory. "For whatever good it does, I think I know where we are."

"You do?"

"When I was a kid, I came to Istanbul with my father and accidentally met the sultan's mother. She told me that back in medieval times, thousands of Christians lived in underground cities in a remote part of Turkey. She thought I should visit the cities while I was in Turkey."

"And you think that's where we are?"

Indy shrugged. "It's a good guess."

"Why did they dig all these passages?" she asked.

"They didn't. They were already here, built by some ancient people."

"Did your father take you to see them?"

"No, he doesn't like going into confined places. He gets claustrophobic." Indy spotted a couple more inscriptions a few feet away. "Hey, take a look here."

"Oh, my God. Is it what I think?"

It was a rough sketch of a fish and next to it was an ark. "The fish and the Ark were used as Christian symbols before the cross. The fish represented the Son of God, and the Ark stood for the judgment of God and the hope of salvation."

"So you're a Christian, too. Just like Jack."

Indy cleared his throat. "No, not just like Jack. To tell you the truth, my interest is more in the history and artifacts of the times."

"But aren't you a believer in the word of—"

"Listen!" Indy said. "Do you hear it?"

"It sounds like music."

They crossed the cavern and followed a hallway leading from the far side. The sound grew louder. But then the corridor came to an abrupt end. Indy passed through a doorway on his left. A faint light filtered through a narrow window, and the sound of the lute music filled the room.

"Take a look at this!" he whispered as he peered through the window. Below them was a huge cavern many times larger than the one they'd just left. Dozens of torches burned on the walls, and a placid pool in the center of the cavern reflected the flames. But the water wasn't what grabbed Indy's attention. On the far side of the pool a dozen men were spinning in circles with their arms straight out from their bodies. They were dressed like the ones who had captured them, complete with the high hats, and now he knew who they were.

"Dervishes!" Indy said in astonishment. "The Janissaries must be a Sufi brotherhood."

"I don't understand. What are they doing?"

"They're called whirling dervishes."

"Why do they whirl?"

"To imitate the movement of the cosmos. It's their way of gaining communion with God."

"Indy, look at the one in the center," she said excitedly. "Do you see it? He's got the Ark wood."

Indy had noticed that the man held something in one hand and now he realized Katrina was right. The man was whirling faster and faster, but Indy recognized the mustache. "It's Hasan."

"The words were barely out of his mouth when the muzzle of a gun jammed up against his neck. "What a coincidence. Two more lost souls. Drop the rifle."

Indy did as he was told and slowly turned his head. He could hardly believe what he saw. It was the twin Russians from Chicago. "Don't tell me you're still mad about the trench coats."

"Get ready to die, Jones."

"How did you find us here?"

"We broke a few heads, and one of the peasants talked. They know all about these dancing bookworms."

Indy wasn't sure what he meant, but it was no time for idle chatter. He needed to act and fast. He pulled Katrina in front him and loosened his whip. "You're not going to hurt an innocent woman, are you?" he asked.

One of the twins laughed. "What kind of man are you using a woman to shield you?"

"You're right. That's not nice."

He pushed Katrina aside and snapped his wrist, unleashing his whip. The Russians were standing close enough together to allow him to lash the whip around both of their necks. A rifle fired and the bullet hit the wall next to Indy's head. Indy jerked hard and the twins toppled over. He took Katrina's hand and they rushed down the hallway.

But they didn't get more than a few yards before a Janissary, his sword at the ready, blocked their way. Behind him was another one with his sword raised over his head, and several more Janissaries had arrived to back them up. The Russians, free of the whip, bolted out of the room and into the same trap.

"I wouldn't exactly call these guys bookworms," Indy said.

16

UNDERGROUND CITIES

By the time Shannon and Zobolotsky had arrived in Ankara, Ahmet had joined the expedition. He would not only take them to Cappadocia, but would serve as their translator in their search for Indy and Katrina. That was fine with Shannon. Ahmet, it turned out, was a lute player, and while Zobolotsky slept across the backseat Shannon learned to play the string instrument with the driver's help.

They ate, then slept a few hours in Ankara, staying at the home of the driver's cousin. Then they were on the road again, heading south. "There is no place in the world like Cappadocia. You will see things there that you will not believe."

"Have you been there?" Shannon asked.

"Of course. I have another cousin there. We will find him and see how he can help. Everyone in my family helps each other."

"I have heard this name, Cappadocia, but I don't remember where," Zobolotsky said.

It was late afternoon when they entered a valley near the city of Goreme and came upon a landscape like no other that Shannon had seen. As far as he could see, there were mounds of smooth, white rock in every shape imaginable and nearly every one of them was pocked with windows.

"These are the troglodyte houses made of tufa, the rock from the volcanoes," Ahmet said. "They say that if you lived on the moon, you would be at home in Cappadocia."

"I believe it," Shannon said.

"The tufa is soft and very easy to cut. It makes a good house, and when you want to add a room for a new baby, you just carve it out."

"The people must live like animals," Zobolotsky said.

"No, like Christians," Ahmet answered. "Many Christian monks lived in Cappadocia in monasteries hollowed from the rocks."

Zobolotsky was quiet a moment. "Now I know why the name was familiar to me. Cappadocia is mentioned in the Bible."

"Don't think I've read that far yet," Shannon said.

Ahmet's cousin, Omar, didn't live in a troglodyte house, but in a rectangular stucco one, a shape that Shannon found to be a relief after looking at houses with ballooning walls, conical tops, or completely nondescript shapes. But outside Omar's house were three narrow columns of tufa that formed a triangle, and resting atop two of them were boulders.

"Those are fairy chimneys, carved by the wind," Ahmet said when he saw the two men staring up at them as they stepped out of the taxi.

"Ferry chimneys?" Shannon asked.

"Yes, *peribacas*."

Shannon exchanged a glance with Zobolotsky as they followed Ahmet into the house. He was even more amazed by the blind man's foresight. Oddly enough, it seemed they were right where they were supposed to be. Shannon didn't know how Alfin could have known about this house, but he was even more confident now that the Lord was guiding them.

Omar looked like a younger version of the wiry Ahmet, with a mustache and thick, curly black hair, and greeted them as if they were all family members. When they explained their situation, Omar nodded and gazed thoughtfully out the window.

"I know about these outlaw Janissaries. They believe as strongly in the Moslem teachings as you do in the Christian traditions. They would kill for their beliefs."

"Then they are not truly religious people."

"Maybe not," Omar said. "But they are like the Christian crusaders who killed thousands of Moslems in the name of religion."

Zobolotsky was about to say something in response, but Shannon laid a hand on his arm. The Russian turned away in disgust.

"Can you help us, Omar?" Shannon asked.

The Cappadocian stepped away from the window. "I'm not sure what you want."

"Do you know where the Janissaries are hiding? That's what we need to know."

"They are not hiding. Many of us here know where they are. But few would dare to enter their city."

"A city?" Shannon asked.

"Yes. An underground city. A very old one. It is near Derinkuyu."

"Can you lead us there, cousin?" Ahmet asked.

"Just show us where it is," Zobolotsky said. "You must understand that my daughter's life is at stake."

Omar considered what he'd heard. "For me, the family is most important. You are friends of my cousin, and if he trusts you, then so do I. I will take you there."

"Great," Shannon said.

"I not only know the location of their city, but I know a way of entering it from another underground city."

"You mean there is more than one of these cities?" Zobolotsky asked.

"There are many. Maybe six or seven, and they are all connected. When I was a boy, I spent a summer with a cousin who lived near one of the cities and we explored them. I can show you the way."

They were in luck, Shannon thought. But in the back of his mind he still remembered that Alfin had said someone would be lying to them.

Whenever the Janissaries were in the underground city, they dressed in their tunics and pantaloons, as Hasan was now. Because they had been banished and outlawed by the new government, they did not dare to don their traditional garb when they were in Istanbul. But Hasan had made an exception when they'd captured the archaeologist and the Zobolotsky girl in the old church. He'd wanted to startle them, and although Jones had nearly escaped, it had worked.

But now they'd captured two other men, and this time Hasan had been the surprised one. He had no idea who these bald-headed twins were or what they were doing here, but he was determined to find out. The shirts had been stripped off the burly pair and they were dangling on ropes from the ceiling of the chamber, their toes barely touching the floor.

"Why did you come here?" Hasan asked for the fifth or sixth time, and once again neither man answered.

He nodded toward his lieutenants. The one who had taken Jones's whip cracked it across the back of the man in front of him, then struck him again. The other Janissary twirled a barbed rope, which was attached to a short stick, and snapped it again and again, slashing shoulders and neck. The results looked about the same. The backs, necks, and shoulders of the twins were crisscrossed with cuts and welts. Rivulets of blood and sweat ran down their backs.

Hasan waved a hand and the men stopped the beating. "Now answer me."

Neither said a word.

"Salt the wounds," Hasan commanded.

The two Janissaries flung open bags of salt over the men's wounds. Both cried out in pain.

"Talk," Hasan demanded. The Russians' heads hung and their faces were contorted in pain, but neither spoke. "So that's the way you want to be."

The Janissary chieftain pulled a sword from its sheath and moved it slowly in front of the men's faces. Its blade was curved and artfully inscribed with an intricate design. "This, my twin friends, is a blade made of Damascus steel. It is sharp and strong. It can slice a floating feather in two, or it can lop off a head with a single blow." He touched the tip of the blade to one of the Russians' throat. "And that is what I am about to do."

"What do you want from us?" one of them said.

"Alexander . . . *nyet*," the other warned.

"So, you are Russians." Hasan was more perplexed than ever. He moved closer to the first man. "Alexander, I only want to find out why you are here."

"We were following the other two, the man and woman."

"Why?"

"Don't say anything more," the other one warned.

"I'll say what I want, Boris."

"Okay. Let me do the talking," Boris said, and raised his head toward Hasan. "It was a personal matter. Our business."

"A personal matter. Tell me, where did you start following them?"

"Chicago. That's where we live. Not Russia."

"So you have come halfway around the world for a personal matter. Very interesting. Now tell me the truth. What did you want with them?"

"None of your business." Boris spat the words.

Hasan tightened his grip on the sword and raised it over his shoulder. He'd get rid of this one and then the brother would tell him everything.

"We were going to kill them before they got to

Mount Ararat," Alexander said, and spared his brother's life.

Hasan lowered his sword and considered what Alexander had said. "Why?"

"We want to keep them away from the Ark. We don't want them to find it."

"I see, you want to find it yourselves. Now I understand."

"That's a lie. We don't want anyone to find it," Boris said.

Hasan looked suspiciously at the men. It wasn't the answer he'd expected. "Why not?"

"Because," Boris said, "the bishops will try to win back the people's hearts in our homeland."

Finally, Hasan understood. They were Bolshevik spies.

"Hasan," a man called from the doorway. "We have news from Istanbul."

He stared at the twins a moment longer, then walked over to the door. "What is it?"

"Zobolotsky and the other one didn't leave for Athens by train or boat," the man said in a low voice. "The police are after them and they've disappeared."

"Why do the police want them?" Hasan asked angrily as he saw his plans falling apart.

"They say they killed an old Mevlevi dervish, and a girl and an old woman."

Hasan didn't know what to believe. But he knew now that Jones and the woman would have to die, and so would the Russians. It was a perfect time for the ultimate game. He smiled, excited about the prospects. He hoped Jones and the woman would make the contest interesting.

He turned to the men who were guarding the twins. "Cut them down. There's a game to be played."

Scaling rocks wasn't Shannon's idea of fun. He and the three others—Zobolotsky, Ahmet, and Omar—were climbing along the base of a cliff, searching for an entrance to a cave—a cave that would lead into an underground city. Shannon had stumbled twice, scraping a forearm the first time and bashing a knee the second. He was limping slightly and felt a trickle of blood on his shin.

"It must be here. I remember this place very well," Omar said.

Shannon looked around, wondering how these particular rocks and shrubs were any different from the ones they'd been climbing over during the past hour. Maybe Omar was lying when he said he knew about the Janissaries' underground city. For all Shannon knew, there were no underground cities, and everything Omar said about them was a lie.

Omar let out a whoop. "Here it is. I knew we were close to it." He was kneeling in thick underbrush and Shannon couldn't see a thing. He worked his way over to Omar and glimpsed a dark hole behind the branches of a bush the Turk was holding back. "We're going down there? Into that snake hole? You've got to be kidding."

"We have lanterns," Ahmet said. "It won't be so bad."

Shannon gave Zobolotsky a sour look.

"Think of Katrina," Zobolotsky said.

If Zobolotsky knew just how much he thought about her, he wouldn't say that. Katrina was a soft, persistent ache in chest, and yes, of course, he was committed to Indy. But he was hesitant to follow them to a similar fate. Maybe there was another way. But if Indy and Katrina were underground, how was he going to help them up here? He knew that Indy would help him if their positions were switched, and what good was it to love Katrina if he never saw her again? It was all about loyalty and friendship, love . . . and faith. That was it. He had to remember that he was guided, and there was no reason for fear.

They lit their lanterns and crawled into the hole. Omar took the lead, followed by Shannon, Zobolotsky, and Ahmet. Shannon held his lantern in one hand and felt his way with the other. The ceiling was low, and he was already claustrophic. He'd barely gone five feet when he felt animal droppings on his hand. He wiped his palm on his pant leg, then duck-walked several more feet until he could stand in a crouch. The floor of the cave descended gradually, and soon the walls were wide enough to stretch out both hands and the ceiling rose to nearly seven feet.

"How far do we go, Omar?" Shannon asked.

"One city is right below us now. The one where we are going is maybe two miles."

"Two miles? Are you sure you remember the way?"

"It's very easy. Take a look. You see, the cave branches here. To the left, it goes down to the city, and to the right is our underground road to the other city."

"I'll take your word for it," Shannon said as they moved on.

A couple of minutes later, they came to a stairway. "Do you remember these steps?" Zobolotsky asked as they started the descent.

"Yes, I think so. They must have been here." Omar sounded uncertain.

"When were you last here, Omar?" Shannon asked.

"When I was ten or eleven."

"That's a long time ago."

"I'm only twenty-seven."

"So am I, but I can't remember much of what I did when I was ten," Shannon said.

"If you would've explored these cities, you probably would remember very well," Ahmet said.

Shannon squinted through the dusky air. "I hope so."

A short distance after they reached the bottom of the steps, the passageway split again. This time Omar stopped. "I don't remember any other forks, but I think we should stick to the right."

Great. Just great. At this rate not only would he never see Indy again, he'd never see the sun or breathe fresh air. "I'm placing my life in your hands, Lord," he muttered, but the words came out louder than he expected.

"God is good," Ahmet said.

A doorway appeared on their left, and when they held up their lanterns, they saw another passageway that appeared to run parallel to them. Omar shook his head and they continued walking. No one said a word, but they were all thinking the same thing. Something was wrong.

Just ahead of them another stairway descended sharply and curved left and out of sight.

"No, this can't be right," Omar said. "Let's take a look at that other corridor we just saw and find out where it goes."

Shannon was feeling more uneasy than ever, but he didn't say anything. They'd barely gone ten yards on the adjacent corridor when they reached a series of interconnected rooms. Some of the rooms had windows looking into adjacent rooms or passageways, and there were holes in the wall revealing stairways leading to other levels or other parallel paths.

"This is madness," Zobolotsky said as he held his lantern up and the beam illuminated a ceiling that looked like an upside-down staircase. "I think we should go back to the first junction and take the other path."

"I agree," Omar said. "We must be in the wrong city now. Let's go back."

They retraced their steps out of the rooms, but now they were confronted with a corridor that split into three arms. "I think we were in this one," Zobolotsky said.

"No," Shannon said. "I'm sure it was the center one."

Shannon dropped down on one knee and tried to find their footprints, but the stone floor revealed nothing. "I had the feeling this might happen."

"Have faith," Zobolotsky said. "The weak of heart always perish first."

Shannon had faith, all right, but it wasn't in Zobolotsky's sense of direction.

"I didn't see all these different routes when

we came by here," Ahmet said, shaking his head.

"These cities are deceptive," Omar said. "I think you are both turned around. "Jack's way is right, but the direction is wrong."

"Good God," Shannon moaned.

"God is good," Ahmet replied.

"Maybe it was a mistake to try to escape." Katrina was huddled next to Indy in their cell; two guards stood at the door. "Hasan said he was going to let us go if Papa left the country."

"He'll probably still do it." Indy sounded more optimistic than he felt.

"But I killed that guard."

Indy heard footsteps in the corridor. "I think we're going to find out really soon."

Hasan appeared in the doorway and said something to the guards, who grabbed them by their arms and yanked them out of the cell. Indy's right foot was tied to Katrina's left one and he stumbled as they were dragged into the corridor.

"Where are you taking us?" Indy demanded.

"To larger quarters," Hasan replied. "Much larger quarters." Without any further explanation, he accompanied them along the passageway and down a set of stairs. They hobbled through a series of corridors and rooms, down another set of stairs, and then they were in the expansive cavern with a pool in the center.

Katrina paled. "Indy, I can't swim. Don't let them throw us in there. I'll drown."

Hasan snapped another order; the guards pulled out knives, and the blades flashed in the torch light. Indy and Katrina backed away, but the guards grabbed them, spun them around, and cut the bonds on their hands and ankles.

Hasan gestured impatiently. “Okay, go on. You’re free to find your way out.”

Indy looked warily around. “What’s going on?”

“There are at least six doors leading from this room and you can take any of them. You may find a way out; you may not. There are many hidden passageways, some that we’ve never explored. Who knows where they go?”

“Why are you doing this, Hasan?” Katrina asked.

“To give you a fair chance. It’s a game we play with our children. Only the smartest ones can find their way out of the labyrinth.”

“Oh, hey, it’s just a game.” Indy laughed nervously. “Maybe we don’t want to play.”

“You have no choice. Our game is a deadly one, as you’ll see.”

The pair didn’t wait any longer. They hurried along the shore of the lake, away from where Hasan and guards stood.

“What do you think’s going on?” Indy asked.

“I was going to ask you the same thing.”

Then Indy saw the answer to his question standing twenty yards away under the light of a torch. “Look over there.”

The hulking Russians watched them like hawks ready to dive for their quarry.

“This is the right passageway; I’m sure of it,” Omar said triumphantly.

Shannon just nodded; neither Zobolotsky nor

Ahmet said a word, either. They'd tried several routes and now Shannon felt thoroughly lost. He no longer had any sense of where they were or which way they had come from. They could spend days wandering around here and never get out, much less to another underground city. But as they continued along the corridor and didn't reach any forks or stairs or rooms, Shannon's hopes rose.

Then Omar stopped and looked up at something.

"What is it?" Zobolotsky asked wearily.

"Yes, I am certain. This is the way." Omar pointed to the wall. "You see those three connected circles. They represent the Trinity of God. I remember this very clearly."

"It's hard to believe that Christians lived in the ground like this," Zobolotsky said.

"They were safe here and free to tend to God's work without interruption from the everyday world," Omar said.

"Like a monastery," Shannon said.

"Exactly," Omar answered.

"My cousin, you have found the way, but we must hurry now," Ahmet said.

They moved quickly along the narrow path, covering a mile in fifteen minutes. After another ten minutes of steady walking they stopped to rest. "This place makes me claustrophobic. I can barely stand up," Shannon said. "There must have been one helluva threat above the ground if they took this route rather than walking in the sunshine and fresh air."

"Maybe it was only used in emergencies," Ahmet suggested.

"Like now," Shannon said. "We better get going."

"Wait a minute." Zobolotsky held up his hand. "Omar, what's going to happen when we get to the other city? Do you know where the Janissaries are?"

"I think I can remember how to find the lake. They're probably close by."

"The underground city has a lake?" Ahmet asked in amazement.

"It's a spring, their water source."

"Then let's go," Shannon said.

The Russians were not attractive men, and now, with blood covering their upper torsos, they looked monstrous. But ironically, all Indy could think of as he stared at them was that the pair would never make it through the door of the Blackstone Hotel in Chicago.

"Why don't we talk about this?" Indy said as he and Katrina backed away. His eyes darted around for the nearest door. "We all want to get out of here. If we work together, we can do it."

Hasan suddenly stepped out of a dark doorway that Indy had just spotted. "That wouldn't be fair, Jones. Not fair at all, and we would have to end the game very quickly."

"What do you want from us?" Katrina's voice quavered.

"I'm glad you asked. You can answer a question for me." Hasan stepped out into full view and held up the Ark wood.

"That belongs to my father."

"Yes, he says it's from the Ark."

"It *is* from the Ark."

"Then here is my question. Why does no one believe that he found the Ark?"

"Some people believe him. But many people want more evidence. That's why we came to Turkey."

Hasan held up the Ark wood. "I know the Ark is on Mount Ararat, but this piece of wood is not from the Ark. I whirled with it and saw that it was ordinary."

"Fine. Just give it to us and show us the way out of here," Katrina said.

Hasan laughed. "I'm afraid, Miss Zobolotsky, that will not be possible. Judgment Day is not upon us yet, and God's command to me is to protect the Ark from being revealed before that day."

"The Ark is about life, and a new beginning, not the end of everything. Finding it won't bring on the Judgment Day," Katrina said.

"Then you do not know the word of God." Hasan took a few steps toward them. "You will not climb the mountain, and you will not ever look at this piece of wood, either." He hurled the Ark wood into the lake.

"No!" Katrina raced toward the dark waters and dived toward the spot where the piece of wood had splashed.

"Hey, you can't swim," Indy said as Katrina disappeared beneath the water.

When she surfaced, she gasped for air and slapped the water.

"You weren't kidding, either." Indy dived after her, and the shock of the cold water nearly drove the air from his lungs. He surfaced next to her and crooked his arm around her neck. He was already shivering, but he only had a few strokes to reach the shore.

Katrina struggled frantically against him. "The wood," she gasped. "I've got to get it."

"Don't worry about it." Indy struggled to shore with her. They were both on their hands and knees in the shallows of the pond when Indy looked up and saw the twins standing in front of them. They grabbed his arms and jerked him to his feet.

Before he'd even caught his breath, both men pulled back their arms and simultaneously slammed their fists into either side of his face. The concussion of the double blow snapped his head back, and he fell to the ground, out cold. The Russians took him by the arms and legs and heaved him into the lake. He sank into the icy spring waters, a string of bubbles drifting from his mouth toward the surface.

Then the bubbles burst, and ceased.

17

Death Game

The first thing Shannon saw when they reached the cavern was the last thing he expected to see. The two Russians from Chicago were pulling someone from the lake. At first, he couldn't see who it was, then it became all too clear.

"It's Katrina," Zobolotsky said. "Stop them."

Shannon pulled his revolver from his shoulder holster and fired three rounds above their heads. He wasn't the greatest shot, and he didn't want to hit Katrina. The Russians looked up, then hurried away from the lake with Katrina. "You missed," Zobolotsky yelled. "Shoot them."

Shannon took aim, but the Russians were holding Katrina up so that her body blocked his shot. Then they ducked through a doorway and were gone.

"You let them go," Zobolotsky snapped.

"I could've hit Katrina."

"After them," Zobolotsky barked, and the four men raced across the chamber.

She's still alive, Shannon told himself. She's got to be. But he couldn't help thinking that the Russians might've been shielding themselves with a corpse.

High above the floor of the Spring House, Hasan watched as the intruders disappeared from sight in pursuit of the Russians. He stared a moment at the pool to make sure Jones hadn't surfaced, then moved away from the window.

"God is helping us carry out His will," he said to his two lieutenants. "The rest of the expedition has arrived. We couldn't have asked for anything better. All the players in the game are with us."

"What about the other one?" one of the men asked.

"Who, Jones?" Hasan walked out the doorway and down the passageway. "You can fish his body out later. Let's see about the living ones right now."

The instant Indy had struck the icy water, he regained consciousness, but his arms and legs wouldn't work. It was as if the connection between his mind and his muscles was out of order. He could move his feet, but his legs wouldn't kick. He held what air was left in his lungs and drifted with the spring's current.

To his surprise, he started picking up speed. But he was moving sideways, instead of upward. Then he felt a rocky surface below him. His shoulders bumped against walls and his head struck a ceiling. He was being hurtled through a water-filled cave, and his lungs were bursting. He couldn't last much longer.

The pounding on his body awakened something in him, and for all the good it did him, he'd regained control of his limbs. But he was out of air and desperate. He clawed at the ceiling. Drifted, drifted. It was almost over. Then his arm shot through a hole and his elbow hooked on a ledge.

With his remaining strength, he pulled his head up through the hole, but he was still underwater. His hand poked through the surface and touched something soft and spongy.

Above Indy, the cook for the Janissaries, an overweight man in his early sixties, leaped off the wooden toilet. He was so startled by the hand that had grabbed him that he ran into the wall in his rush to flee. He tottered, fell back, and struck his head on the edge of the toilet.

Indy burst through the surface of the water. He gasped for air, coughing and gagging. He was still in the water, but he was breathing. He would make it. His head was inside a wooden box with an oval hole. He kicked his legs and pulled himself up. He blinked against the assault of light, then saw that he was in a small room and a man was lying next to him with his pants down. A dead man. It dawned on him that he'd surfaced through a toilet and that the spongy object he'd felt had been flesh. He pushed the box off his shoulders, tossed it aside, and climbed out the hole.

"I'm glad you don't bolt your toilets to the floor," he said to the dead man as he stepped over him. He walked into the next room and found himself in a huge kitchen. In the center of it was a gigantic black iron caldron. He walked over to it and smelled soup. "These guys really do like soup," he muttered.

He heard someone coming, ducked behind the caldron, and peered around the side. A Janissary with his sword drawn was skulking through the kitchen.

"Mustafa," the man called out. "Mustafa."

Indy crept around the pot on his hands and knees and saw the man as he lifted a ladle from the pot and tasted the soup. He grabbed the Janissary around the knees and lifted him into the air. The Turk's yell was cut short as Indy dumped him headfirst into the iron pot.

"I hope the soup's good."

He retrieved the Janissary's sword and darted out of the kitchen and down the corridor. He had no idea where he was, but he had to find Katrina. He heard footfalls ahead of him and slipped into the nearest room. On a table in the corner of the room was his whip. He scooped it up and hooked it on his belt.

The sounds of footsteps grew louder. He heard voices speaking Turkish. There were at least two in the party, probably more, he thought as he pressed up against the wall. When they passed by without pausing, Indy crept to the door. He was about to step into the passageway when he heard footsteps and breathing. One of the Janissaries was probably trying to catch up with the others who'd just gone by. This was his chance. He'd force the man to show him where Katrina was being held. He waited just inside the doorway until the man was within a few feet, then reached out, grabbed him by the throat, and shoved him against the wall. He raised the sword to within a hair's breadth of the man's nose.

Then he saw who it was. "Christ, Jack. What the hell are you doing here?"

"Having a heart attack."

"I could have killed you."

"Likewise." Shannon held up his revolver. "Another half second and I'd have blown your guts out."

Boris and Alexander pulled Katrina's limp body into a room. They'd been ready to toss her into the lake after Jones when they'd heard the shots. Boris instinctively lifted the body to shield himself, then they rushed toward the nearest door. Only after they were safe did he see who was following them. No wonder the girl hadn't been struck by a bullet.

She wasn't dead yet, but she wasn't his concern right now. They had to deal with Zobolotsky and his party, and they weren't the only problem he and his brother faced. The old blind bastard had lied about the Janissaries. It was obvious they were warriors, not scholars, and there were too many of them. They were probably hiding out in this maze because they were outlaws.

But first they'd deal with the Zobolotsky bunch. They laid Katrina in the corner of the room, crouched on either side of the doorway, and waited. Their disadvantage, Boris knew, was that they weren't armed. That wouldn't have been any problem if they'd just faced Jones and the woman. But now they had to rely on surprise, because the others were armed.

"I'll grab the one with the gun first, and you get Zobolotsky. Then we'll take care of the other two."

"I hear them," Alexander said.

The sound of footfalls in the passageway grew louder. They were less than a hundred feet away, but Boris didn't dare peek around the corner. He tensed, readied himself to pounce as soon as the men came into view.

"Father, watch out," Katrina shouted.

Boris cursed in Russian as he turned to see Katrina sitting up. Then Alexander stepped into the hallway. The fool, he thought. Boris grabbed his arm, pulled him back into the room. "This way."

There was a window on the opposite wall that led out into another passageway. Boris dived through it, rolled over. "Hurry," he snarled.

"What about her?"

"Leave her."

Alexander flopped through the window and Boris roughly pulled him through.

"Ah, my back!" Alexander said.

"Forget about your back. Think about your life."

Now they would have to find another way to catch them.

"Jack, we've got to find Katrina," Indy said.

"What do you think we're doing? Where've you been, anyhow?"

"In the toilet."

"What?"

"Where's Zobolotsky?"

"Didn't you see him go by here? He was just ahead of me."

"I just heard someone speaking Turkish."

"That was Ahmet and his cousin. They're with us," Shannon explained.

"Tell me about it later. Let's go."

With Indy in the lead, they raced down the corridor. But they hadn't gone far before they heard voices coming from one of the rooms. They stopped, pressed up against the wall, melted into the shadows.

"Oh, Papa, you're here. You're here."

"It's Katrina," Shannon said, and bounded toward the room.

Zobolotsky was hugging her, and when she saw Indy and Shannon, she looked as if she were going to fall over. "Indy, I can't believe it. You're alive." She ran to him and wrapped her arms around him.

"I'm like a cat. I've got a few extra lives."

"Yeah and you may need another one in a minute," Shannon grumbled.

"Jack. You're here, too," Katrina said, and embraced him. "I'm so glad to see you."

"You are? I mean . . ."

"It's no time to stand around," Zobolotsky barked. "We've got to get out of here."

"Papa, they took the Ark wood and threw it in the lake."

"No, they didn't," Zobolotsky said. "I've still got it. I fixed a fake one for you to carry just in case something like this happened."

Katrina looked startled. "That's wonderful, Father."

"Yeah, she almost killed herself going after

the other one," Indy said. He headed to the door, but stopped and turned to Shannon. "Do you know the way out of here?"

"I don't know. We came from another underground city," Shannon explained. "Omar, you can take us back the same way, can't you?"

The Turk nodded. "Yes. But only if we can find our way to the lake. Right now I'm lost, too."

"The problem with going back to the lake is that's where the Janissaries are," Indy said.

"Don't forget about our Russian friends," Shannon added. "They're around here, too."

"So you've seen them, too," Indy said.

Zobolotsky moved into the corridor. "We've got to make up our minds."

"Indy's got a good sense of direction," Shannon said. "I say we follow him back to the lake."

"My good sense of direction says we go up to get the hell out of here. If we find the lake and your route to the other city on the way, then we'll take it."

Zobolotsky took his daughter by the hand. "Let's go."

Hasan knew the maze as well as anyone, and it didn't take him long to figure out how Zobolotsky had entered. He told one of his men to make sure that the path to the adjoining underground city was guarded. None of them was going to escape.

The maze was a network of pathways, most of which went nowhere. When the brotherhood had first descended into the city two years ago, Hasan had been angered and annoyed by the lack of order. But as he gradually learned his way around, he realized that the maze had been built that way intentionally, to foil any intruders who managed to enter the city. Knowing one's way around was a powerful advantage, which the members of the Zobolotsky expedition and the two Bolsheviks would soon realize, if they didn't already.

Hasan stepped into a narrow room with a long, rectangular window at head level. There were at least a dozen rooms in different parts of the city that were identical to this one, and months had passed before he'd realized their purpose. They were specially built for observation, and through this particular window he could see five or six levels above him and at least a dozen paths.

He scanned the area and after a few seconds spotted the Zobolotsky party. They were carrying torches now, which made it a simple matter to find them. But when he raised a pair of binoculars to his eyes and studied them, he counted two extra members. The Zobolotsky girl was with them and, to his surprise, so was Jones. Somehow, the archaeologist had survived and escaped undetected, and the girl must have been rescued from the Russian twins.

He was disappointed in the Russians, but mildly amused by the others. They were nothing compared to the challenge presented by the government, which was intent on abolishing the Sufi brotherhoods, especially the ones linked to the Bektasis order and the Janissary Corps. This game was going to be enjoyable, even though it would be one-sided.

He could see the group was attempting to

climb the maze to the surface, but they'd embarked on a dead-end path. When they backtracked, as they would be forced to do, they would try again and then again, and each time they would find themselves either facing a blank wall or circling back on paths they'd already trod.

He scanned the rest of the maze that was visible, searching for the Russians. It took a while longer to locate them. They weren't carrying torches, which was smart of them, but it also made the going more difficult, since many of the passages weren't lit by wall torches. He spotted the pair moving along the same passageway as the expedition. They were several levels higher and near the end of the route. They weren't looking for Zobolotsky and the others. They were searching for a way out.

But they'd soon turn back, and in a matter of minutes the two parties would encounter one another, and that was another count against the expedition. Their chances of surviving to see another day were virtually nil; their chance of making it to Ararat nonexistent.

They were coming down a flight of steps after striking a dead end when the two Russians were caught by surprise. A double surprise, it turned out. "I hear them coming," Boris hissed. "Get over here fast."

They crouched in the darkened alcove next to the stairway as the expedition marched their way. They weren't ready to attack; they could only defend themselves if they were discovered. They'd both agreed that finding a way out was their top priority, and if they came upon Zobolotsky and the others, so be it. They'd take care of them as best they could, then continue their search for an exit.

Coming here had been so easy. The peasant had been more than willing to help them after he'd understood that his life was in danger. He'd led them into the city, and when they'd reached the first burning torches on the wall, Alexander had crushed his skull against the rock wall. That had angered Boris, not for any moral reason, but because the body could attract attention. Now that didn't matter; finding the original path did, though.

The expedition moved into view and with it another surprise. Leading the way was Jones. The bastard was still alive, and somehow he even had his whip again. That damned whip. He'd like to strangle Jones with it, and maybe he would.

The archaeologist was followed by the gangly redhead with the gun, Zobolotsky and Katrina, who both carried torches, and two others who looked like Turks. Each one's attention was on the steps and none saw them crouched just a few feet away.

"Six now, Boris. We were only supposed to get two of them. We should've never come here."

Boris didn't know whether he meant the underground city or Turkey itself. But knowing Alexander, he probably meant both. "Listen, we're not the only ones who are surprised. The Turks weren't expecting these other guys, either."

"So what's that mean to us?"

"It means we kill them all, and hope the Turks let us out of here for doing their dirty work." Boris noticed a hole in the wall above their heads. "Boost me up so I can see what's up in that hole."

Alexander bent over. "But they'll be coming back as soon as they see it doesn't go anywhere."

"That's what I'm counting on." Boris stepped on his brother's shoulders and Alexander stood up. It was too dark to tell whether it was a room or another corridor, but it didn't matter. He had another idea. "Okay, you get back by the steps, and when they come down, I'm going to jump on the one with the gun. You take Jones. The others will be easy, and we'll have the gun. Just don't let any of them get past you."

Indy ran his hands over the wall, searching for a lever or at least a crease in the wall to indicate that it was a door. But the longer he searched, the more he became convinced that the wall was just that—a wall that was not going to magically open and lead to the great outdoors.

"No, the damn thing just ends," he said. "We've got to go back."

"Oh, no," Katrina moaned. "How far back down do we have to go?"

"Five levels if we want to stay on the main route," Omar said. "But there are other paths we could try, too."

"Maybe we should break up into groups of two and look for a way out," Ahmet suggested.

Indy shook his head. "That'll make it too easy for the Russians. They'll pick us off one at a time. But I don't think the Russians are stupid enough to attack this many of us."

"I bet ole Hasan is just sitting back waiting for us to give up," Shannon said as he gazed wistfully at Katrina, who stood next to him.

"The Janissaries are just playing with us," she said. "It's like a game for them. They're waiting to see what the twins do."

"I have an idea," Zobolotsky said. "Katrina, I'm going to take out the Ark wood. I want you to ask the Lord for guidance."

"Amen," Shannon said. "We need guidance, but what's that got to do with the piece of wood?"

"You'll see," Zobolotsky said.

Anything was worth a try, Indy thought, remembering what Katrina had told him about the Ark wood and its effect on her.

She sat on the floor and carefully unwrapped the cloth from around the piece of wood. Shannon was looking around uneasily. "We're cornered here if anyone comes after us."

"Have faith," Zobolotsky said. "I can see that you have not been a Christian for long."

Shannon scowled and looked like he was about to start an argument when Indy drew him back from the others and asked in a quiet voice what had happened to them in Istanbul. Shannon told him about the murders and their escape. "Now I realize that it must have been the Russians who killed them, not the Janissaries."

"That poor girl," Indy said.

"Shh!" Zobolotsky raised a hand. "Please."

Katrina's eyes were closed, and she held the Ark wood to her chest.

The image Katrina saw was that of a woman surrounded by light. At first, she couldn't make out the woman's features, but even before they became clear, she knew it was her mother. At the moment of her realization, the light seemed to brighten. Her mother smiled at her, then the light descended until it surrounded Katrina. She thought it would blind her, but she was overwhelmed by a feeling of peace and tranquillity.

She saw herself rising on the light beam, moving straight up through a tunnel until the night sky was above her. She was standing on ground in the white valley with the strange houses, but now she knew where it was. It was no longer an imaginary landscape, but a real one that existed above the underground city. She also knew why it was dark and light at the same time. The sun was down, but a bright moonlight flooded the valley.

Then the valley was gone. She still saw the light, and in it, blocking her way, stood the silhouette of one of the Russians. The light faded and she was aware of herself again sitting on the floor of the passageway. She looked up and saw the others staring down at her.

"Did you see a way out?" her father asked. When she didn't answer immediately, he spoke again. "Did the Lord show you the way?"

She didn't want to tell him that she had seen her mother. That would cause only confusion and denials. "I saw a way, I think, but I'm not sure where it is."

"We'd better get moving," Indy said.

He sounded impatient; he wanted more. She rolled up the Ark wood, feeling angry and foolish at the same time. "Actually, I do know where the way out is."

They waited for her to continue, and she drew out the moment. Maybe she'd seen her own death. Maybe that was the only way out. But there had been something else.

"Well?" her father asked.

"We'll find it when we find the twins."

18

THE SHAFT

"Do you know it's almost two in the morning?" Shannon asked as they walked along the corridor. "No wonder I'm exhausted."

As far as Indy was concerned, there was no time down here. No day; no night. Only the dim, smoky light of the torches and the flickering shadows. "Yeah, I could use a cup of coffee, but I don't think we'll find a coffee shop on this route."

"How can you make jokes?" Zobolotsky said as they descended a stairway.

Indy stopped at the base of the step. He was fed up with Zobolotsky and his stern demeanor and was about to tell him what he thought when Shannon pulled his gun.

"What was that?"

"Where?" Indy whirled around.

"Over there, in the corner. I heard something."

"Don't shoot," someone said from the darkness. Indy had no sooner heard the plea than a massive figure dropped from above and knocked Shannon off his feet. The gun flew from Shannon's hand and vanished in the shadows.

Indy raised the sword he'd been carrying, but the man in the corner sprang at him like an animal, grabbed him by the neck, and tossed him against the wall. He snagged Indy's arm, twisted it, and the sword clattered to the floor. Shouts and screams and moans reverberated around him; arms flayed. One of the men picked up Omar and Ahmet by their throats and was strangling them. Indy glimpsed a bald head as he kicked out both legs and knocked over the attacker. The other Russian was applying a bear hug to both Shannon and Zobolotsky, who punched wildly at him.

Indy fumbled with his whip, but the twin he'd knocked down rolled over on top of him. He pulled the whip from his grasp and wrapped it around Indy's throat. He jerked it so tight that Indy knew his neck could snap at any moment. He was to about pass out when Katrina jammed a torch in the Russian's face. The whip slackened as the twin staggered around bellowing like a wounded bull.

Indy rolled over just in time to see Katrina jam the torch down the back of the other twin's pants. He let go of Shannon and Zobolotsky and roared in pain as he tried to pull out the torch.

By the time Indy got to his feet, the twins had hobbled off into the darkness, and the torch that had saved them was smoldering on the floor. Indy was wobbly, but managed to help the two Turks to their feet. Zobolotsky was crawling on the floor, muttering about the Ark wood, and Shannon was hugging Katrina.

"Hug her for me, too," Indy said. "Hug her for all of us. That torch trick saved us."

Indy spotted the Ark wood on the floor, illuminated by a faint, silvery light that had suddenly appeared. "There it is, Vladimir. Over here." As Zobolotsky snatched it Indy turned his head to see the source of the light. It was filtering through a hole high in the wall.

"The light. That's moonlight," Katrina said excitedly. "That's where one of the Russians was, blocking the light. That must be it, our way out."

Shannon boosted Indy, who crawled through the hole. He found himself inside a closet-sized room. A few feet in front of him was another wall with a similar round hole. But above him was what looked like a narrow elevator shaft that went up and up, and far above him a full moon spilled light down the shaft.

"It's an air shaft," Indy told the others. "It goes up at least a hundred feet."

"Maybe we can climb out," Katrina said.

Indy ran his hands over the smooth wall. No handholds. Nothing to grab onto. He ducked back down and saw that Shannon and Katrina had joined him in the tight quarters.

Shannon had picked up the sword from below and now he poked it at the wall. "I wonder how long it took to cut that shaft."

That gave Indy an idea. "You have a knife, Jack?"

"Yeah, but I didn't have any time to get it out. The Russians were all over us."

Indy sat down and twisted the heel of his boot, which was still soaked from the lake and his travels through the sewer system. He pulled out his blade. "You can use it now. We've got work to do."

Hasan had watched the Bolsheviks limp down a passage and head up another dead-end trail. He knew that there'd been a confrontation, and the Russians looked hurt. Twenty minutes had passed and the others still hadn't reappeared. What could they be doing up there? It was just another dead end. Maybe the Russians had finished them off.

"Do you think they're dead?"

Hasan looked over at his lieutenant with disdain. "How should I know?"

"Do you want me to go see?"

Hasan took in a deep breath and exhaled. He'd hoped that this game would last longer, that he would follow them through the maze and watch their battle. But now it seemed it might already be over. A disappointment.

He spotted the Bolsheviks again. They were moving closer to the Green Road, a passageway that would lead them to the top.

"Go see what happened to them, and let me know. Then head off the Bolsheviks before they get onto the Green Road. Nobody escapes."

The inside of the shaft was made of the same solidified volcanic ash that covered the entire valley, and it was an easy task to carve handholds and footholds. They were making progress, scooping out holes every couple of feet, with each one taking no more than thirty seconds to carve.

But Indy didn't know how much time they had left before Hasan would investigate. He was almost certain that the Janissary chieftain knew where they were, if not what they were doing, and before too long his warriors would show up.

Indy had wrapped the hilt of his blade with a piece of cloth and had worked his way more than fifty feet up the wall, taking turns with Shannon, while Omar and Ahmet were working on the other side of the shaft, using their own knives.

"Indy, I'm going up," Ahmet called out. "I'll get the taxi."

He turned to see Ahmet climbing hand over hand, stabbing two knives in the friable tufa. He was surprised, but he knew Ahmet was doing the right thing. They would need to get away as soon as they were all out. He watched Ahmet's progress. The first few overhead pulls had been quick and smooth, but he was slowly losing strength and each stab was becoming an effort. Then, with only a few more feet to go, he stopped to rest.

Indy knew it was a mistake. The only way Ahmet could make it was to continue climbing. The knife wouldn't hold his weight for more than a few seconds. He saw the knife slowly pulling out and Ahmet slipping. That was it; he was about to fall. He'd knock Indy off the wall; they'd both die. But at the last moment Ahmet slammed the other blade into the tufa, catching himself in time. His narrow escape seemed to give him renewed vigor and strength, and he quickly scaled the remaining stretch. He flopped over the top and his legs disappeared from sight.

"Here comes the knives," Ahmet yelled.

Swell, Indy thought. Just swell.

He saw a silvery glint of steel in the moonlight as the blades dropped along the opposite wall. One fell straight down, but the other struck a prominence and veered off course, heading directly for Indy. He turned his head and ducked. The hilt of the knife struck his fingertips, missing his head by inches. His fingers throbbed with pain, but he refused to let go.

"Okay down here, Indy," Shannon yelled. "You ready for me?"

"Yeah, I'm coming down." He passed Omar ascending the opposite wall and wished him well. When he reached the bottom, he gave Shannon a pat on the back. Then he saw that Zobolotsky and Katrina hadn't been idle. Since he was last down here, they'd been taking the fallen pieces of tufa and enclosing the hole.

"Good idea. Let me help."

"It's better than standing here waiting for the next piece to fall on our heads," Katrina said.

"Sorry." He brushed his hand over her hair.

"It's nothing," she said.

Zobolotsky scowled when he saw Indy touching Katrina. "How did you allow these brutes to capture Katrina in the middle of a city in broad daylight?"

"Papa, he couldn't help it."

"It's no time to argue," Indy said just as a chunk of tufa struck him on the neck. He rubbed his neck, then picked up the piece and added it to the wall. The hole was not much more than a wide slit now. That was when he heard the Janissaries.

"They're coming," he whispered.

There was no time to do anything but hold their breath and hope the Janissaries didn't see what remained of the hole. The sound of voices grew louder; Indy knew there were at least a half dozen of them, maybe more. Then the Janissaries were right outside the wall.

Clots of tufa rained down on them. Indy squeezed his eyes shut, expecting swords to plunge through their false wall at any moment. But the Janissaries kept moving, and climbed the steps toward the dead end. As the sound of their steps receded, Indy and Katrina and her father dropped to the ground and grabbed the tufa.

"Thank the Lord," Zobolotsky breathed.

"We're not out of this yet," Indy warned. The Lord might have double duty to perform before this night was over, he thought as they finished the wall.

It wasn't a beautiful-looking wall, and it definitely wasn't a sturdy one. But the Janissaries might miss it altogether and assume they'd gotten to another passageway. Indy squinted as he gazed up the shaft. Shannon was within twenty feet of the top and Omar was even closer.

"Go ahead," Indy said. "By the time you two get up there, they should almost be done."

"What about you?" Katrina asked.

"I'm going to wait until I hear the Janissaries leave, then I'll be right behind you."

As they started to climb, Zobolotsky followed his daughter on the same route. "Don't do that," Indy said. "If she falls, she'll knock you down. Take the other one."

Zobolotsky turned and glared at Indy. "Stop trying to run this expedition, Jones. If Katrina starts to fall, I might just be able to save her. And if she falls, I might as well go with her."

Something about Zobolotsky bothered him. It was more than his moodiness and arrogance. But there was no time to think about it. The Janissaries were returning down the steps, and this time he heard them talking right below the false wall.

Get going, keep moving, Indy ordered in his mind.

"Hey, what are doing?" Shannon yelled down. "I'm not done yet."

"Jack, shut up," Indy whispered through his clenched teeth.

The Janissaries were quiet a moment, then they were jabbering excitedly. Indy cursed under his breath and backed away from the hole just as a sword pierced the false wall and a hand and arm followed it.

"Oh shit." He snatched his whip off his belt. The quarters were tight, but there was space above him, and he came down with an overhand release that caught the intruder's sword and snapped it out of his hand. Indy pulled it over to him and picked it up just as the entire false wall caved in. The Janissary, who'd lost his sword, looked up warily.

"Looking for this?" Indy held the sword like a spear and jabbed it toward him. The Janissary threw himself over backward onto his companions below, and Indy still clutched the sword. "Just kidding."

He looked up to see the progress above him.

Omar had reached the top, but Shannon was still a few feet away and Zobolotsky and Katrina were right below him. He considered darting up Omar's side, but thought better of it. He had to hold the Janissaries off as long as he could.

Another one had mounted the hole. Indy could see his head and shoulders, but no sword. Then his right hand appeared and in it was a gun. Fortunately for Indy, the man didn't see him right away. By the time he did, the sword had slashed down and severed the man's hand. Indy looked at the curved blade. "Like cutting butter. And that was left-handed."

The Janissary disappeared from sight, but another warrior quickly replaced him. He swung the sword, but the Janissary blocked it with his own blade, then thrust the sword with lightning speed at Indy. For an instant, Indy thought he must be dead, but then he saw that the sword had plunged under his armpit and was buried at least a foot in the tufa.

"Indy, hurry!"

He looked up to see the others peering down at him from the top and didn't hesitate another second. He draped his whip over his shoulder, gripped the sword with his teeth, and climbed as fast as he could. He'd barely taken a dozen steps when he glanced over his shoulder and saw several Janissaries already mounting the carved steps.

"Swell. Lots of company."

He could make it to the top ahead of them, but he wasn't sure how long he could hold them off once he'd climbed out of the shaft. Suddenly, he realized he wasn't scaling the shaft nearly as quickly as he'd hoped. He'd made the mistake of climbing the steps that Omar and Ahmet had carved. They'd made longer and shallower steps and that was why Omar had finished ahead of Shannon. But now Indy climbed with an uncertainty that slowed his progress.

He was nearly halfway up when his right foot slipped, then his other one slid out of its hole. He dangled, kicking his feet, and then he saw one of the Janissaries reaching for his ankle. Indy found one of the footholds, and the Janissary found the other one as he missed Indy's foot.

"That's mine," Indy snarled, and jammed his boot hard against the man's hand and wrist. The Janissary grunted, pulled his hand away, and swayed out from the wall. That was all Indy needed. He kicked out his leg, catching him across the chest, and the man toppled off his perch. He struck the man below him, knocking him off, and then two more Janissaries. They plunged like screaming dominoes to the bottom of the shaft.

"That wasn't so hard," he said, congratulating himself.

A sword suddenly slashed the wall, nicking his forehead. Blood streamed down his cheek as he turned and saw the opposite wall covered with a string of sword-bearing Janissaries. "Oh, shit."

He scrambled up the wall as fast as he could, not worrying about the depth of the footholds or their spacing. Now the longer steps worked to his advantage. As he neared the top he saw Shannon and Omar silhouetted in the moonlight as they reached down to him. They grabbed his wrists and jerked him out of the shaft.

He rolled over, pulled the sword from his mouth, and stabbed it at the first Janissary coming up the wall. But the man had stopped short, and he was waiting with a revolver aimed at the top. Indy was already jabbing at him when he saw the gun, and before he had a chance to react, the gun fired. The bullet careened off the sword's blade just above the hilt, and he felt the pressure between his eyes.

"C'mon," Shannon barked.

Indy flung the sword down the shaft, and retreated. Maybe he'd knocked the gun away or even knocked the man off the wall, but he wasn't sticking his head over the side to find out.

"Indy, hurry!" Katrina yelled.

He turned to see the others already fifty yards away, dashing toward a pair of headlights. He raced after them as the taxi made a U-turn, and they scrambled inside. The car was already moving and Shannon was holding the backdoor open as Indy leaped onto the running board. He looked back and saw half a dozen Janissaries with raised swords closing the gap.

"No more room, guys." Indy slipped inside and slammed the door shut.

"Step on it, Ahmet," Shannon shouted, and they pulled away.

"This is much more fun than driving in Istanbul," Ahmet said. "Where are we going next?"

"Mount Ararat, of course," Zobolotsky said. "That's why we're here."

"Then I'll take you."

"You'll need help driving these roads," Omar said. "I'm going along, too."

"The expedition is ready to find the Ark," Zobolotsky said in a commanding voice.

Indy looked over at Shannon. "Now for the real excitement."

"You don't exactly look like you're ready to climb a mountain," Shannon replied.

Indy's shirt was nearly in shreds. His face was streaked with dried blood and bits of tufa. "I could be worse off. I've still got my whip."

"And your jacket and fedora are in the trunk," Shannon said.

"When I was coming to pick you up," Ahmet said, "I saw two men in my headlights. It was only for a very short time, but I'm sure they were those Russian twins."

"Guess they found their way out, too," Katrina said.

"And I bet they find their way to Ararat," Indy said.

19

On the Mountain

The midafternoon sun was brilliant on Mount Ararat, the sky a deep blue, and the day had been a pleasant one. They'd left their encampment before dawn and had been climbing for more than eight hours. The six of them were strung out in three pairs. Indy and Shannon were in front of Ahmet and Omar by a couple of hundred yards, and Zobolotsky and Katrina brought up the rear.

Indy filled his lungs with mountain air. After all they'd gone through, they were finally here and scaling the famed peak. Even after a full day, his enthusiasm hadn't waned. The openness and brightness were a stark contrast to the dim, hazy world of the underground city they'd fled nearly a week ago.

After their escape, they arrived at the Cappadocian city of Kayseri by dawn and rested for a few hours. But they feared the Janissaries would hunt for them, so they left by midafternoon. For the next several days, they traveled from village to village across eastern Anatolia, the ancient name still used in this part of Turkey. Indy had jotted down the names of the villages and cities along the route, thinking that someday he'd write about this sojourn.

They drove through Sivas, Malatya, Adiyaman, and Kahta, where they stayed at a temple on a mountain called Nemrut Dagi. Before they left the next morning, Indy had inspected a collection of statues left behind by some pre-Roman king and his relatives. Each day he was more and more impressed by the antiquities he saw in the villages and countryside, and he wondered about the ones that still remained hidden.

They'd moved on to Sanliurfa, Mardin, and Diyarbakir, where Indy briefly examined ancient walls and the exteriors of mosques built more than a thousand years ago. The following morning, they'd headed east through Bitlis, then along the southern shore of Lake Van and to the city of Van, where they spent another night. Then it was on to Agri and east to Dogubeyazit, where they'd bought supplies for the climb. Yesterday afternoon, they'd arrived at a hamlet called Eli, the last outpost before the ascent. It was located at 6,400 feet on Agri Dagi, the Turkish name for Mount Ararat.

The escape from the underground city had gone as smoothly as Indy could have hoped, considering that they faced opposition on two fronts. There'd been no sign of either Janissaries or the Russian twins, but Indy hadn't let his guard down. The chances were good that they were being followed. The worst part of the journey had been listening to Zobolotsky's pompous espousal of how they were being guided by the Lord and how he would spread word of the Ark across the globe after they returned to civilization. It was almost as if Zobolotsky thought he was the resurrected Christ, and Katrina some sort of virgin mother of prophecy.

Although Zobolotsky probably suspected that something had happened between Indy and Katrina during their forced stay together, he said nothing to Indy about it. Instead, he'd kept Katrina close to him and appeared by her side every time Indy was alone with her for more than a minute or two. Shannon, on the other hand, had repeatedly prodded Indy for details and it was clear that he was jealous.

Indy didn't know what was going to happen between himself and Katrina, if anything. He was attracted to her as much as ever, but so was Shannon. It hardly mattered, though, because neither had any time alone with her. And she prudently kept whatever her thoughts were on the matter to herself.

Indy turned his thoughts from the tangle of relationships and gazed up at the mountain's two peaks, still visible in spite of the clouds that were settling on them. The one on the left was Buyuk Agri or Great Ararat, the other was Kucuk Agri or Little Ararat. The Ark was supposedly located in a saddle between the peaks at about fourteen thousand feet.

He tried to imagine a flood that would place a boat at such an altitude. It would take one helluva storm to generate that much water, a deluge beyond imagining. There were a thousand arguments against the existence of the Ark. Yet, if Zobolotsky had actually seen it, Indy was hard pressed to dispute it, unless Zobolotsky was lying.

"Hey, hold on," Shannon called from a few yards behind him. He was gasping for air as he caught up to him.

"What's wrong? We're almost there."

"I know, but don't you think it would be a good idea to let Vladimir lead the way from here?"

Indy dropped his pack and leaned against a block of stone. "I suppose you're right. We don't want the good doctor worrying that he's got a mutiny on his hands."

When they'd stopped for lunch, Zobolotsky had pointed out a sheltered area high above them, and they'd agreed that it would be the best spot to make camp. It was just below where the snow began and would protect them from the wind. Now they were less than five hundred feet from the spot.

"I think he's worried that you're going to steal his thunder," Shannon said. "And I'm worried you're going to steal his daughter."

"C'mon, Jack, will you cut it out about Katrina and me? Your imagination's getting the better of you."

"Sorry, it's just that she seems to be brooding about something all the time, and I wonder if it's you. She won't even look at me."

"It's probably not about either of us." Indy gazed out over the range of mountains and valleys below them. He could see several lakes that looked like pale blue ponds. The roofs of the houses in the village where they'd camped were mere specks. "I was hoping we'd go a little farther. I'd really like to get to that saddle by early tomorrow afternoon."

Shannon had set down his pack next to Indy and was rummaging through it. "It looks like we're almost there to me. I bet we could be asleep inside the Ark tonight if we really pushed it. At least, if everyone went at your pace."

"I doubt that. It's not going to be so easy tomorrow. You can count on lots of snow and wind and freezing temperatures up there. To say nothing of hidden fissures."

Shannon took out his Bible. "We're in God's country, Indy. I hope you don't mind if I read a few lines aloud before the others get here."

Indy shrugged. "I'm all ears." Thankfully, Shannon had kept his pontificating to a minimum during the last few days. Indy didn't know if he could have put up with two Bible thumpers in the crowded taxi.

Shannon opened the Bible and an envelope fell out. "Oh God, here's that cable of yours I picked up in Istanbul. I forgot all about it."

Indy glanced at the envelope; it was from Marcus Brody. "That's quite a while for you not to crack open the Good Book, Jack," he said as he opened the envelope. "You're not losing your commitment, are you?"

"Not at all. But being around Vladimir so much has made me see that you can get sort of carried away."

"Amen." Indy unfolded the sheet of paper and read the cable:

INDY: HE'S A FRAUD. NO ONE NAMED ZOBOLOTSKY IN 19th PETROPOVLOVSKY REGIMENT. PROBABLY NEVER CLIMBED ARARAT. MARCUS

"Oh, no."

"What is it?" Shannon asked.

"Take a look." He passed Shannon the sheet of paper.

"What's it mean?"

"It means we've been taken."

"Now that I think about it, he doesn't seem like he knows any more about Turkey than I do," Shannon said.

"And he's only made a couple of general comments about his last trip," Indy added.

"So what're we going to do?" Shannon asked

Indy shook his head in disgust. "He's got some explaining to do before I take another step up this mountain with him."

Katrina was glad to see that Indy and Jack had finally reached the campsite. She was exhausted from the day's trek and she wasn't even carrying any of the supplies.

"Do you remember it being so tiring, Papa?" she asked.

"I've tried to forget about that part," he answered. "I'm only thinking about the Ark, and that we will soon see it."

She could hardly believe it herself that they would actually reach the Ark tomorrow. She was anxious not only to see it, but to photograph it. She'd been so relieved to find out that the police had recovered her cameras from Aya Sophia.

But she felt guilty that Omar and Ahmet were carrying her equipment as well as the other supplies.

She would've liked walking with Indy or Jack, at least part of the day. But she knew Papa wanted her to stay by his side. Ever since their escape from the underground city, he wanted her to have as little as possible to do with either of the men. He'd made Indy his scapegoat for all their troubles, and she felt sorry for him.

In spite of the intimacies she had shared with Indy, it was Jack who preoccupied her. She thought about him so much, she couldn't even look at him anymore for fear he would see it in her eyes. He wasn't as handsome as Indy, or as self-assured. But he was struggling to find himself and she could understand that. She knew all about it. And he was a jazz musician; that fact alone fascinated her. She had never heard jazz before she migrated to the United States, and even though her father was against it, whenever she heard the music it triggered something deep inside her.

She knew it was no use telling Papa how she felt, not about jazz or Jack. It would only make things worse. At least for now. Besides, there was really nothing to say. Jack hadn't really told her how he felt about her. He seemed to watch her a lot, but he'd hardly spoken to her. She remembered, though, how he'd hugged her in the underground city after she'd driven away the Russian twins with the torch. It had been an emotional moment, when, for a few seconds, the barriers had broken.

The two Turks had caught up with Indy and

Jack, and she and her father were only a few yards away when she heard the sound of barking. Several huge dogs—or maybe wolves—raced across the sparse landscape toward them. "Look, Papa!"

"Dikkat! Dikkat!" Omar yelled. "Hurry, danger."

"Up here!" Indy shouted from the top the rock he'd been resting against.

"Papa, run!" she screamed.

As they raced toward the rock the barks grew louder and were mixed with howls. Indy pulled Jack up, then both men helped Omar and Ahmet. They were just steps away when her father slipped. She stopped to help him and saw the charging dogs, their teeth bared leaping at them. She froze; it was too late. She covered her head with her arms and squeezed her eyes shut.

But the animals stopped short. She heard their snarls, felt their hot breath on the back of her neck. Slowly, she raised her head.

"Don't move!" Indy said in a low voice from the rock.

The dogs growled and pawed the ground. There were five or six of them. They looked like wolves, but they wore spiked collars around their necks. Then, beyond the dogs, she saw several men standing on the prominence staring down at them.

"Are they Janissaries?" Jack asked.

"No," Omar responded. "They're Kurds."

Slowly, the men picked their way through the rocks. They wore long beards, turbans, and simple outfits woven from raw wool. As they neared, Ahmet called out to them.

"Merhaba! Hello!"

The men didn't reply.

"Lutten kopegi tutun. Hold your dogs."

One of the men said something and the dogs whined and backed away, wagging their tails and holding their heads low. The men stepped forward, and examined the expedition's gear, and spoke among themselves.

"What do they want?" Zobolotsky asked.

This time Omar spoke to the men, and they answered him. "They want to know what we're doing here."

"Tell them," Katrina said.

Omar gave what seemed like a long, rambling speech. Katrina understood none of it. The one who seemed to be in charge, the oldest of the band, responded with a few terse words.

"He wants to know if you are Russians," Ahmet said. "They don't like Russians on their land."

Katrina knew that they were near the Russian border, and she'd heard Omar say there were hostilities between the Russians and the Kurdish tribesmen.

"Tell him we're Americans," Zobolotsky said.

"I already did," Omar said.

"Then ask him if he knows about the Ark," Indy suggested.

The old Kurd listened to the question, then waved his hand toward the mountaintop as he answered.

"He says that it's impossible to climb higher on the mountain. It's a holy place and is protected," Omar said. "The Ark is up there, of course, but they never would try to look for it.

He says if we try to find the Ark, we will only meet our deaths."

"Optimistic fellow," Jack remarked.

At that moment, the old Kurd pulled a long knife from his belt and hurled it at Katrina. It landed next to her foot, where it had pierced the head of a snake.

The Kurd picked up his knife and tossed the snake. He directed a few words at Katrina, then said something else to Omar. He motioned to his band, and they moved away without another word.

"What did he say?" Katrina asked.

"He said the snake was poisonous and was about to strike you," Omar replied. "Then he told me that we better not kill any of their sheep or they will kill us."

Indy jumped down from the rock. "That sounds like a fair deal."

Katrina looked down at the ground where the snake had been and rubbed her hands over her arms. When she raised her head, Jack was staring at her. She could tell he wanted to say something. She smiled shyly at him and looked away.

"Let's move on to the shelter and get the camp set up," Zobolotsky said.

Indy spoke up. "Not quite yet. I've got a problem. I don't think you've ever been here before, Vladimir. I think you're lying about seeing the Ark."

"What are you talking about? You saw the Ark wood yourself, and you know that it is holy."

"All I know is that you were never in the Nineteenth Petropovlovsky Regiment."

"Why do you say that now that we are almost to the top of the mountain?"

"Because it only recently came to my attention. Okay?"

"You're crazy, Jones. Let's go, Katrina. We'll carry our own luggage. We don't need these madmen."

Katrina was startled and surprised by what Indy had said. But now something that had happened a few years ago suddenly made sense. Everything fell together and she knew that her father had been lying to her for years.

"He's telling the truth, isn't he, Papa?"

"What, are you against me now, too?"

"Don't you remember, Papa? I told you about the man who came to our house and was so glad that you were alive. He said he was in the army with you, but that you had disappeared during a battle with the Germans in 1917. When I told you about it, you said it must be another Vladimir Zobolotsky. But it was you, wasn't it? You were never in Turkey, were you?"

Zobolotsky looked away.

"Mother and I didn't hear from you for a long time, then you came home with this story about Turkey. Why, Papa, why?"

"Stop it." His face was lined with anguish. In a softer voice, he said, "All right. It's true."

"But, Papa, what about the Ark wood? Is it just another lie?"

"No, it *is* from the Ark."

"But you just said—"

"I know what I said." He ran a hand over his face, gathering his thoughts.

Katrina could tell he was going to give a lecture, but she sensed this one was going to be like no other she had heard from him.

"I was a young doctor and I was sick of death," he began. "We were being sent to the front lines and I knew most of the men would die. Millions were dying. The villages were stacked with bodies. I was overwhelmed by blood and death. It was horrible. So I fled back to Russia, but I could not go home because I would be arrested for deserting. Instead, I joined the Bolsheviks."

Katrina could hardly believe what she was hearing. It was as if her father had been transformed into another man. She didn't know him anymore.

"What's this got to do with the Ark?" Indy asked.

"I'm getting to that. I didn't tell the Bolsheviks I was a doctor, because I would have been too valuable. At that time I was very naive, and wasn't sure of where I stood about these political matters. They made me a courier, and that was when I found out about the Ark."

He explained how he and another man had captured a White Russian courier en route to the czar. They found that he was carrying photos and descriptions of the Ark and explanations of how it was found, and deep inside the man's satchel, Zobolotsky had found the Ark wood.

"You see, I was a religious man, and when I found this, I knew it was a message from God. I could not be a part of the godless Bolsheviks. I wanted to take the satchel myself, but the other Bolshevik courier wouldn't allow it. I know now that I should have killed him and sent the White Russian on his way to the czar, but everything happened so fast. All I managed to get was the Ark wood."

"What happened to the rest of it?" Indy asked.

"The courier delivered it to the command post. I suppose it fell into Trotsky's hands. As for myself, I fled home, and in the confusion of the revolution I escaped with Katrina to America. I never forgot what I saw in the courier's satchel, and of course I took the Ark wood with me. I knew that one day I would come here."

"Why didn't you just tell the truth?" Katrina implored.

"At first, I was afraid to admit that I had associated with Bolsheviks. I was worried that I wouldn't have been allowed to enter the United States. Then once I had told my story and people listened, I couldn't change it. No one would believe anything I said about the Ark if they found out I had lied about climbing the mountain."

"You're damned right there." Indy pulled the cable out of his pocket. "I wouldn't be here now if I'd picked up this cable while we were in Istanbul."

Katrina took it from him and read it, then handed it to her father without saying a word. In spite of Papa's explanation, she didn't understand how he could be such a religious man and at the same time live so long with a lie.

Her father crumpled the cable and tossed it down. "The important point, Jones, is that the soldiers of the White Russian Army did climb the mountain and find the Ark, and so will we."

"Unless the whole thing was a fraud," Indy said. "Maybe none of it was real. Maybe it was just a ploy by the czar to keep the Russian people on his side and against the revolution."

"I don't believe that," Katrina said. But now she was wondering about the Ark wood. Had she taken the real Ark wood or the false one from the safe that night in Chicago? Did it matter? Maybe it was all just her belief and had nothing to do with the wood.

"We'll find out soon enough."

"Now, can we move on to the shelter?" Zobolotsky asked.

The words were no sooner out of his mouth than the crack of a firing rifle cut through the cool mountain air. There was a moment of stunned silence, then Katrina screamed as her father collapsed. She dropped beside him. "No! No!"

Indy and Omar and Ahmet were yelling in Turkish and Jack and Indy in English. Two of them grabbed her father under the shoulders and another carried him by his feet. This couldn't be happening. She couldn't believe it.

A bullet ricocheted off a rock near Katrina's head. Jack pulled out a gun, dropped to one knee, and fired wildly. Then he wrapped an arm around her shoulder and they rushed toward the shelter.

In her mind she saw Papa a few hours earlier, pointing to this place where they would camp.

And where he would die.

Indy had no idea where the rifle had been fired from or who had fired it. What he knew was that Zobologsky was dead.

Shannon and Katrina were huddled together under the shelter of rocks as long shadows fell across the mountain. Her head rested against Shannon's chest and his arm was draped around her shoulder. Zobolotsky's body was covered with a tarp just a few feet away. Two hours had passed since the first volley had been fired, and they'd heard only one other shot, distant and muffled, fired about half an hour ago.

Indy stood on guard, his rifle pointed out toward the fading light. Omar and Ahmet had left to investigate after the last shot was fired, and they hadn't returned. He ducked back down under the shelter. "I'm going to start the kerosene stove and heat up the soup."

"Good idea," Shannon said. "Give me the rifle."

Indy tilted his head toward Katrina. "She going to be all right?"

Katrina looked up and nodded. "I'm okay," she said in a barely audible voice.

Just then several more shots were fired. Indy spun around, but it took him only a moment to realize that the shots had been fired from well out of their range.

"What the hell's going on out there?" Shannon asked.

"Don't know, but I'll find out." Indy crawled out of the shelter. "Be back in a little while."

"Indy, it's going to be dark in a few minutes."

"Good. They won't see me."

He moved off in the direction from which he'd heard the gunfire. He was worried that by now Ahmet and Omar were beyond help. But he couldn't just leave them out here.

He hadn't gone far before he saw a long shadow moving over the rocks, then another. Monstrous shadows. They were coming his way and he could see rifle shadows, too. He ducked behind a rock and took aim.

The one in the lead was in his site when he disappeared behind a rock. When he came into view again, one of the last rays of sunlight fell across him and Indy recognized Ahmet. Omar was behind him; they were alive.

"Hey, over here," Indy said in a hushed voice when Ahmet was with ten yards.

Both men ducked behind rocks, then Omar called out, "Indy, is that you?"

Indy stood up and ran over to them. "What was the shooting about?"

Both men started talking at once in a mix of Turkish and English. Indy couldn't make any sense of what they said. Finally, he took Ahmet by the arm. "Try again. Slowly this time."

"Okay. We walked in the direction of the shot we heard, and when we got close, the Kurds jumped out and captured us. We thought they were going to kill us, too."

"But it was the sheep, you see," Omar said.

"No, I don't see. What sheep?"

"The two Russians, the twins. They are the ones who shot Dr. Zobolotsky," Ahmet said. "Then they must have decided to celebrate their victory. So they shot a sheep for their dinner, but the Kurds saw them."

"And they killed them?"

He shook his head. "No, they only shot them in the legs so they die slowly. The Kurds showed us what they did, then they let us go. They only wanted us to see what they did to those who killed their sheep."

Indy looked up in the direction the Turks had come from. He knew that a wounded man could be as dangerous as a cornered animal. He didn't put it past the Russians to come after them, even with wounded legs.

"Let's go take a look," he said.

"This way," Omar said. They climbed over rocks for several minutes. The light had faded almost completely when they reached the base of a rise.

Ahmet pointed to the top of it. "We can see from up there."

They'd taken just a couple of steps when they froze at the sound of a ferocious growl that made the snarling dogs sound like puppies. "What the hell was that?" Indy asked.

Boris wasn't as badly wounded as Alexander, who was bleeding heavily from the bullet in his thigh. They had to get the bullets out, and Boris was ready to operate on his brother. After that, he'd tackle his own wound. He didn't trust Alexander to do the job, especially after he was done with him.

"What are we going to do? We can't climb down the mountain," Alexander complained. "We're going to die here."

"Shut up and pull the tourniquet tighter." Boris poured vodka over the wound. "Drink this. It'll help." He passed him the bottle; Alexander took several gulps.

"Okay, get ready."

Boris dug his knife into the wound, and Alexander screamed. But the scream was lost amid a bone-chilling growl from right behind them. Boris's knife slashed out of control down his brother's leg. He turned his head and saw two huge bears hovering over them. They must have stood ten feet tall with arms thicker than his own thighs. One of them bared three-inch incisors and growled again.

Boris raised an arm, and the bear swatted his massive paw at him, shredding his forearm.

"No! No!" Boris scooted on his back as fast as he could.

"Boris, help me," Alexander screamed.

The other massive beast picked up Alexander, wrapped his arms around him, and squeezed. Then he shook him as if he weighed nothing. The bear growled at Alexander, shook him again, then ripped out his throat.

But Boris didn't see it. He only saw the razor-sharp claws slashing at his head, then felt his face being torn from his skull.

From the top of the rise, Indy peered down and saw the Russians receiving the same savagely brutal treatment they had so readily dished out. They were sprawled on the ground, and a pair of gigantic brown bears were viciously tearing them apart. A few yards away, as yet untouched, was the carcass of the sheep, which the Russians would never eat.

Too bad, guys. Too bad.

20

THE FINAL ASCENT

A day later.

The snowfield seemed endless to Katrina, a continent of white that stretched farther than she could see. They were all tied together and carried sticks and prodded the snow as they walked. If Indy tumbled into a fissure, they could surely pull him out. The same might be true if Jack were pulled in after Indy. But if Katrina followed them into a chasm, she figured the two Turks would quickly join them. It would be a sudden end to the expedition, which had already lost its leader.

If Jack hadn't stayed at her side, comforting her through the hours after her father's death, Katrina didn't know if she would have had the courage to continue the ascent. Although she appreciated Jack's support, her feelings were as frozen as the ice and snow that surrounded them. The emotional numbness was self-imposed, a requirement for her very survival.

She couldn't break down or the expedition would collapse and her father's dream would never be realized. So she pressed on, scaling the mountain with a determination that she had hardly known she possessed.

The clouds were only a few hundred feet above them, and still descending. Katrina fought off a sense of hopelessness. The Ark could be buried beneath the snow and ice of any of the valleys and canyons they'd already climbed through. But if the Russian army report, which Papa had intercepted ten years ago, was correct, the Ark was visible during the summer months.

She tried not to think about how she had turned against her father in his last few minutes of life. She didn't want those feelings roaming free. He'd been a good man. That was what she thought, and she was going to fulfill his last wish. Just before he'd died, he'd whispered in her ear. "There. The Ark. See it?"

Nature wasn't their only adversary. Shannon hadn't forgotten about the Janissaries. Every time they'd had a good view of the landscape above and below them, he had stopped the procession and taken out Zobolotsky's binoculars which Katrina had given him. First, he would peer up the mountain, searching for a sign of the Ark, then he would turn his gaze to the snowfields below them. Each time, without a word, he put away the glasses and they continued climbing, a sojourn they'd all agreed to complete.

After Indy had told him and Katrina about the

fate of the Russians, he asked who wanted to go back down the mountain in the morning. Although Shannon was curious about what was ahead, he was ready to call it quits, if that was what the others wanted. To his surprise, Katrina had spoken adamantly against turning back. This was her father's expedition and he would not only want to be buried on the mountain, he would also want them to complete his quest, she'd said.

After her speech, no one dissented. Jack was proud of Katrina and more infatuated than ever with her. Although she had yet to open up to him, she accepted his comfort and support. He even felt she needed it, and this gave him hope; perhaps they would have a future together beyond their time in Turkey.

In the morning they'd buried Zobolotsky's body in the shelter where they'd slept. Katrina had kissed her father, then laid the Ark wood on his chest and crossed his hands over it.

"You sure you want to do that?" Indy had asked.

"The Ark wood belongs with him."

Shannon knew exactly what Indy was thinking. If it was wood from the Ark, it was a treasure that belonged to humanity, and besides, Zobolotsky had stolen it. But Indy did the right thing and kept quiet. He and Jack draped the body with a tarp, and then with the help of Omar and Ahmet, they'd covered it with a mound of rocks.

Katrina asked him to read something from the Bible before they left. He agreed, of course, and she requested Luke 17, verses 22 to 26, which was what her father had been reading over and over during the past few days.

Shannon had looked it up, read it three times to himself, and then as the others waited he'd read it aloud.

> "Then he said to the disciples, 'The time will come when you will wish you could see one of the days of the Son of Man, but you will not see it. There will be those who will say to you, "Look, over there!" or, "Look, over here!" But don't go out looking for it. As the lightning flashes across the sky and lights it up from one side to the other, so will the Son of Man be in his day. But first he must suffer much and be rejected by the people of this day. As it was in the time of Noah, so shall it be in the days of the Son of Man."

Shannon thought he knew why Zobolotsky had read the verses over and over. They could be interpreted to mean that the discovery of the Ark would herald the return of the Son of Man. Zobolotsky must have seen himself as a Christ-like figure, who'd suffered and been rejected. His quest had been the butt of jokes among Indy's peers and the press. His chief allies had been people who were more concerned with the political implications than the spiritual ones. But Zobolotsky also lied and deceived. He was a man, not a God.

Shannon could also see how the Janissaries could interpret the words to mean that the discovery of the Ark would bring on Judgment Day. Maybe they were right. Maybe this was a mistake. Maybe it wasn't time for the Ark to be found. Who was he to be responsible for what could be the virtual end of the world?

He stopped. "Wait a minute."

Indy turned and frowned. "Now what?"

Katrina looked concerned. "Are you okay?"

Shannon bent down, picked up a handful of snow, and smeared his face with it.

"What are you doing?" Indy asked.

"I just want to clear my head. I think the altitude is getting to me."

Katrina bent down next to him. "Can you make it?"

"Sure. But do we want to make it?"

Katrina gave him a puzzled look as they both stood up. "What do you mean?"

"I was starting to think that this might be a mistake, that maybe we shouldn't be here."

"Do you want to go back?" Indy asked.

"Do you?"

Indy gazed up toward the peak of Big Ararat, which rose above them. A thick layer of clouds had nearly engulfed the mountaintop. "You know, if the Janissaries hadn't threatened us and tried to kill us, I'd say forget it. Let it rest. But I think we should complete this. If nothing else, it's a matter of principle."

"But what if the Janissaries are right?" Shannon asked.

No one said anything for a moment. Then Omar kicked at the crusty snow. "If we were not supposed to be here, then we wouldn't be. Simple as that, I say."

Shannon wasn't so sure about that. Their leader had already died, and maybe it was a warning for the others. He felt like he was carrying the weight of the world's future on his back instead of a knapsack. But who were the Janissaries to determine when Judgment Day would come, and why should they be able to kill to enforce their beliefs?

"Let's go see what's waiting for us."

"Jack, don't take it so seriously, okay?" Indy said as they prepared to move on. "Chances are we won't find anything."

Shannon wasn't sure what Indy meant. "Are you telling me that you came all this way and you don't believe in the Ark?"

"Look, for me, it's not a matter of belief. Maybe there was an ark; maybe there were lots of arks that set out during some great flood in ancient times. Maybe there is one of them on this mountain. But *the Ark* was just a legend."

As they plodded on, Shannon puzzled over what Indy had said. As far as he knew, the Bible didn't say anything about a bunch of arks. Indy always put a twist on things that made them difficult to understand. Indy was smart, but he didn't study the Bible. Jack wasn't even sure what Indy believed. Except he knew he didn't believe the earth was created a few thousand years ago. He'd told him that. The more he thought about it, the more bewildered he became. If Indy was right, then was the Bible wrong? But how could that be?

Things were much simpler when he was onstage and playing his music. There were no such questions to ponder. That was when he was struck by an odd thought, a strange connection that he might not have glimpsed on another day or at a lower altitude. The truth about the Ark might be like the beauty of a jazz riff. There were different ways of playing it, and you played what you felt. But your interpretation wasn't necessarily the only right way to play it.

"Maybe that's it," he muttered to himself. "Maybe it was something like that."

In the dream, they had found the Ark and were about to enter a gaping black hole that was a doorway to the interior. He heard noises coming from inside. Animal sounds. Maybe animals lived inside the Ark. But what animals would live at this altitude?

Indy took a step inside and the shriek of animals was deafening. He was knocked to the ground, overrun by a flood of animals. They stampeded over him and the others, crushing them and burying them.

It was a silly dream, not even worth repeating to any of the others. Yet it bothered him, and he couldn't get it out of his mind as they trudged across a snowfield hours later. The sound and the rush of animals had been ferocious, and he'd woken from it sweating and out of breath.

Indy's thoughts were interrupted as his stick plunged straight down through the snow. Shannon didn't notice he'd stopped and walked into him. Indy tottered on the brink of the hole, then Shannon yanked on the rope and he was pulled away.

Indy turned and grinned, but his face was as white as the snow. "That was close." He pointed his stick toward a ledge above them. "Let's try to work our way up there since we can't go any farther in this direction."

No one argued with him, especially since the craggy landscape along the route he had suggested was relatively free of snow. They backed away from the hidden crevice, then turned upward. Now the angle of the climb was much steeper and the going slowed. At this altitude, it didn't take much to tire them, and every few minutes they stopped for a short rest.

Finally, Indy reached the rocky slope leading to the ledge.

"Can you see anything?" Shannon asked.

Indy gazed into another canyon, and at first he didn't see anything different from the other canyons they'd crossed today. But then he saw it. "Pass me those binoculars." Indy lifted the lenses to his eyes and focused as the others joined him. "Very interesting."

"Jack, do you see it?" Katrina whispered as the others joined Indy on the ridge.

"I sure do."

Omar and Ahmet dropped to their knees.

Three hundred yards away, a massive black rectangular-shaped object rested on the floor of the hollow. If what they were looking at was Noah's Ark, it resembled a ship about as much as the strange tufa structures in Cappadocia looked like log cabins, Indy thought as he gazed through the lenses.

"I only wish my father was here with us now," Katrina said.

"Maybe he is," Shannon said.

"What do you see, Indy?" Katrina asked.

He lowered the binoculars. "Let's go down and take a closer look."

Shannon held out his hand. "Let me see."

Something was definitely wrong. Shannon was sure of it, and as they crossed the hollow he became more and more suspicious about the Ark. It seemed to fit the description of the Ark of Genesis, which depicted a vessel that was more barge than boat. But magnified through the lenses, the contour had changed. Now, as they neared it, he realized that what they'd seen was an optical illusion created by shadows and reflections.

He could see that great chunks had been scooped out of the front and side. It narrowed in the center and was shaped more like a letter *K* than a rectangular block. It didn't look like it was made of wood, either.

Indy was the first to touch it. "It's a rock."

Shannon searched for an explanation. "Maybe it's petrified wood."

"I don't think so, Jack. There's no wood grain of fiber. It's igneous rock."

At that moment, the sun broke through the clouds and they turned their eyes skyward. At first, the sun blinded Indy. He blinked, shaded his eyes, and then he saw it. No more than two hundred feet above them, a massive black box, shaped like a coffin and virtually the size of an ocean liner, protruded from a glacier. The sight was overwhelming, nearly beyond Indy's comprehension, and totally unexpected.

In spite of all the time he'd had to think about

it, he was unprepared for what he saw. There was no doubt in his mind that he was gazing up at the Ark. His knees wobbled; his heart fluttered. He turned his head away.

"My God!" Shannon whispered. He dropped to one knee and bowed his head.

Katrina's hands were folded in prayer, and tears rolled down her cheeks. The two Turks had dropped to the ground and bowed their heads in the snow.

Indy forced himself to look again. He saw it was really there. "The Ark," he said under his breath. "At least, an ark . . . " Whatever, it was going to change everything. It would prove that the Genesis deluge was more than legend, that the earth really had undergone massive changes. It was the discovery of all time.

21

HARK!

Even though it seemed they could nearly touch the immense vessel, it took nearly an hour for them to scale the last barrier separating the expedition from the Ark. The break in the clouds had been temporary, and the dense shroud of fog, combined with blowing snow, made the going particularly treacherous. Indy could barely see his feet and repeatedly stabbed his stick at the hard-packed snow in front of him as he edged forward.

"It's taking forever," Shannon said. "I hope we didn't walk right past it."

"It would be hard to miss, Jack, even in this soup." And then he saw it fifteen feet away, a vast black wall in the haze. "Take a look!"

Although Indy was anxious to reach it, he took his time, feeling every step before he committed himself to it. The wind gusted along the wall of the Ark; every stride was an effort. The rope connecting them was icy and felt like an iron rod protruding from his back.

Finally, the Ark was within his reach. He rubbed the snow away and scraped at the ice on the wall. He pulled off his glove and touched the Ark. He leaned close as the others gathered around. It wasn't stone or wood. The surface looked like a hard black resin similar to the layer of pitch he'd seen on the Ark wood.

"We've found it, haven't we?" Katrina shouted above the whining wind. "We've really found it."

"I don't think it's a rock."

"Of course, it's not," Shannon said. "It's the Ark."

They were all touching it now. "This is the holiest of holy places," Katrina said. "We are blessed to be here."

Indy took a couple of steps back and craned his neck. From below he'd estimated that the Ark rose at least forty feet from the snow, but now it was impossible to tell. He tried to gauge its length, its width, but the structure vanished after a few feet in the clouds and blowing snow.

"What's wrong, Indy?" Shannon shouted.

"We'd better start back. We can't stay up here tonight, and it's going to be dark in a couple of hours."

Katrina shook her head. "I want to stay up here. In the morning when it's clear, I can take my pictures."

"Let's look for a door," Shannon said. "We can stay inside."

A door, he thought. Sure. And a welcome mat decorated with a pair of giraffes.

Usually he was the one willing to take chances. But not in the damn cold. He hated every minute he spent in the snow and ice and blowing wind. Give him a desert or tropical jungle any day over these conditions. And the longer they stayed up here, the less time they'd have to find a suitable shelter in the canyon.

But he didn't argue. He turned and edged along the Ark toward the end that they hadn't been able to see. Except for the top few inches, the snow was packed hard and formed an incline. The vessel was probably resting on a glacier, and someday, with the right conditions, it might slide down into the valley. It could take years, centuries even. Or it could slip this summer. Or tonight, maybe.

The end of the vessel was buried in snow, and the incline allowed them to reach the top. Indy stepped out onto the flat, snow-covered surface and was nearly blown off the mountain. The wind howled; sixty miles an hour, at least, he thought.

He dropped to his hands and knees and was about to back down, but the others were already following him. Swell. Just swell. He crawled ahead until he reached the other side. The wind seemed lighter here, and there was less snow in the air. But there was no incline. If they dropped to the snow fifteen feet below, they probably wouldn't be able to climb up again, and he wasn't in favor of finding a new route down. Not at this hour.

"Look! There. Do you see it?" Shannon was hanging over the edge, pointing.

Indy leaned forward and peered through the haze. The wall was covered with snow and ice, but Shannon was pointing at a black hole.

"It's a way inside," he yelled. "C'mon."

Indy wasn't so sure it was an opening. He remembered the illusion the fake ark had created. "Jack, wait!"

But Shannon had already slipped out of the loop of rope tying them together, shed his knapsack, and dropped over to the side. He sank to his thighs in the snow and waved for them to join him.

Then everyone was wiggling out of the rope. Ahmet and Omar took Katrina's hands and lowered her over the side. She dropped next to Shannon, who gave her a hug and pointed.

Maybe something was there. At least a shelter for the night. The two Turks quickly rigged the knapsacks to the rope and lowered them over the side.

"Say, aren't you guys worried about what might happen when the world knows about the Ark?" Indy asked. Even though they were Moslems, they'd had no reservations about the climb.

"If it is time for Judgment Day, then we are ready," Ahmet said. He leaped down, and Omar followed him.

"I don't know if I'm ready," Indy said to himself, then plunged after them. He hit a soft spot and fell forward and was buried to his neck in snow. He rose up and gazed toward the wall.

Wisps of fog hung in the air, and the wind had died to a whisper. In front of him, a gaping hole opened in the side of the vessel, and all Indy could think of was his dream of the Ark's doorway and roaring animals charging and burying them.

Shannon and Katrina stepped toward the black hole and were about to enter the vessel when they stopped. They didn't move, and Indy wondered what was keeping them from entering the Ark. Then Hasan emerged from the darkness, aiming a rifle at Shannon's chest. Behind him were two other Janissaries.

"So glad the expedition finally made it," he said and smiled. "It was faster going up the other side."

Indy knew they were trapped, but he didn't think that Hasan had seen him. He quickly burrowed down into the snow, covering his head, disappearing from sight.

"Where are the other two—Zobolotsky and Jones?" Hasan demanded as soon as Shannon and Katrina and the two Turks were ushered inside.

"They didn't make it," Shannon said. He thought he'd seen Indy drop from the roof, but now he wasn't sure. "We had some trouble with those bald twins."

Hasan motioned the two men with him to look around. "Where are the Russians?"

"The Kurds and a couple of bears took care of them."

"Too bad. Well, take a look around. I hope you find this place interesting, because you're going to stay here a long time."

"This is the Ark," Katrina said. "You can't deny that it exists."

He smiled at the young woman. "I never denied the existence of the Ark. It's the revelation of it that concerns me."

"Why didn't you just stay in your hole?" Shannon said.

Hasan's thick mustache curled up into an ear-to-ear smile. "You are the ones who will stay in the dark until Judgment Day when your bones will be crushed by the hordes praising the return of the Son."

"And you will be judged as a murderer," Shannon snapped.

Hasan's jaw tensed. "The Janissaries are servants and warriors of God. We are one with His wishes."

"Then why did He let us find the Ark?" Shannon asked.

"Jack, don't push him," Katrina said.

"You are fools, but you are no longer a danger. God has tested us, and we have shown Him that we are ready to defend the Ark from all infidels who would expose it to the world."

"What makes you think you know when Judgment Day is coming?" Shannon persisted.

"Only God knows that. He will reveal—"

The sharp crack of a gunshot cut the exchange short. "On your faces, and don't move."

Indy knew every minute now was precious. Hasan was going to kill his friends, and he wasn't about to let it happen without a fight. Slowly, he lifted his head until he could see the wall and the black hole. One of the Janissaries prodded the snow with the barrel of his rifle near the spot where Shannon had landed. He moved closer to another landing spot and stabbed at the snow.

Then he moved nearer and jabbed the snow

near Indy's feet, missing his boots by inches.

C'mon, Indy thought. Closer. A little closer.

Indy couldn't spring from the snow with any effectiveness; it was too deep. Finally, the man moved along toward Indy's head and thrust the rifle into the snow. Instantly, Indy snatched the barrel; the man struggled and tumbled on top of him. They rolled over and over, fighting for the weapon.

Then a shot was fired, but the rifle didn't kick. The Janissary's grip relaxed, and Indy realized the man had been hit. He shoved him up, out of the snow, and the air cracked with the report of another shot. Indy burst through the snow into a sitting position, simultaneously raising the rifle. He spotted another Janissary, fired.

The man crumpled to the ground; Hasan darted from the hole. Indy rolled over, burying himself in the snow again. Hasan fired wildly, and the sound of the shots echoed from the top of the mountain and down through the valleys below.

Indy rose up to return the fire just as a low rumbling erupted. He took aim at Hasan, but he couldn't hold the rifle steady any longer. The ground shuddered; the rumbling grew louder. It was as if the mountain were talking back, and indeed it was. Talking and moving! The sound grew to a roar; the mountain rocked. Avalanche!

The gunfire. Of course.

Indy crawled toward the hole and collided with Hasan. The Janissary raised his rifle, swung it at him, but missed. Indy jabbed the butt of his rifle into Hasan's gut and dived for the hole.

He took one look back as he rolled over and saw a tidal wave of snow fifty feet high roaring down the mountain; the sound was deafening. "Oh, Jesus."

He rolled again and disappeared into the hole just as the maw of the avalanche swallowed the Ark. Snow exploded over and around him. The vessel shuddered and he was tossed onto his back.

They were moving! The Ark slid forward, over the edge of the canyon, a giant toboggan sweeping into the valley over the snow and ice.

Indy tumbled and careened about like a circus performer somersaulting from a trapeze. But there was no partner to catch him, no net to save him. He didn't know up from down; all he knew was that his body was being pummeled. Then, with a tremendous jolt, the Ark came to a rest and he was catapulted through the air, a human cannonball, and his head cracked against something hard.

"Hark!"

Indy blinked his eyes at the sound of the voice. At first, he saw nothing but the darkness. Gradually, his eyes adjusted and he saw the old man. "Who are you?"

"You know."

Indy tried to make out his features. He had a bushy beard and white hair falling over his shoulders. "Merlin?"

The old man laughed. "Think about where you are."

Indy looked around, trying to get his bearings. He saw the ruins of cages. "Noah . . . don't tell me you're Noah."

"Then I won't."

"What do you want?" Indy asked.

"You're in my Ark. You're my guest. What would you like?"

"To get out of here alive."

"Is that all?"

"Is this really happening?"

"What do you think?"

"I don't know. Where are the others? I don't want to lose them. I want to see them. I want all of us out alive."

"So be it."

"Indy! I think he's coming to his senses. Indy, are you all right?"

Noah's voice still echoed in his mind as he heard Katrina. He blinked his eyes. His head pounded. Katrina, Shannon, Ahmet, and Omar were crouched around him.

"It's a miracle," Shannon said. "We thought you were outside buried in the avalanche all this time."

Indy saw faint light in the distance as he rose up on his elbows. He was near a wall and a pile of snow. "What happened?"

"The Ark slid down into the valley," Shannon said. "But that was yesterday. We've been tunneling through the snow all morning, and we broke through."

"I was piling snow here from the tunnel when I saw you," Katrina said.

Indy sat up and rubbed his face. He was cold and sore and numb.

"Indy, listen," Shannon said. "Do you think you can walk? We've got to get out of here before the tunnel collapses. There's a lot of snow on the Ark."

They helped him to his feet. He felt dizzy for a moment. "I think I'm okay."

As they moved toward the tunnel his vision of Noah came to mind. "Hark?"

"What was that?" Shannon asked.

"Never mind. I'll tell you later. Let's go home."

Epilogue

A month later
New York

"So at that point, we were ready to make our descent," Indy said as he relaxed in an overstuffed chair in Marcus Brody's office.

"You must have been exhausted." Brody rested his chin on his hands as he listened in fascination.

"We all were. It was a tough day, but we made it to a shepherd's hut, and the same Kurds who had shot the Russians gave us our first meal in two days."

Indy brushed a mote of dust off of his tie, which he wore with a brown tweed suit, as he waited for Brody's response.

"Indy, I haven't heard such an intriguing tale since . . . I guess since you told me what happened to you in the Amazon." He stood up and moved around his desk, working his way through a maze of pottery, statues, and stelae. "I hate to say this to you, but I think it's in your best interest if you keep this episode to yourself when you go to the interview. Especially the part about your talk with Noah."

Indy laughed. "Don't worry about that, Marcus. But I wasn't the only one who saw the Ark. We were all inside it."

"Yes. You and a jazz musician who found God, an Istanbuli taxi driver, a Turkish peasant, and a young lady whose father was obsessed with the Ark. They won't be taken seriously and neither will you."

Indy adjusted his black, wire-rim glasses. "Well, it's up there."

Brody raised a hand. "Don't get me wrong, Indy. I believe you, but I'm just trying to be practical. Think about it; even if you did convince a team of scientists to accompany you and you raised the necessary funds, what are the chances that you would find it?"

He probably could find the valley again, but the Ark was buried under tons of snow. "I see what you mean."

"Maybe it's best that way."

Indy smiled and leaned forward in his chair. "Don't tell me that you believe this stuff about Judgment Day."

Brody walked over to a window and stared out. "Not so long ago, you would've laughed at the suggestion that there was an ark, any ark on Mount Ararat."

"That's true." Indy stood up and shook Brody's hand. "I've got to go, Marcus. I'm late already."

"I hope it goes well at your interview. I think you'll make a great addition to the archaeology staff.

"Thanks. I'll let you know what happens as soon as I find out."

Indy left the office and descended the steps of the museum. He caught a taxi to Grand Central Station and hurried inside.

"There you are," Shannon said. "I thought you weren't going to make it. We're all ready to board."

"I know."

Katrina stepped forward and hugged Indy. "I wish you were going to California with us."

"I'll be out to see you. Best of luck."

She kissed him on the cheek. "Thanks. I've got something for you." She reached into her purse and pulled out a long, slender object wrapped in cloth.

"What is it?"

"The Ark wood."

"What? You left it with your father."

"No. That was just cloth wound tightly together. It was a gesture. I didn't see any reason to leave the real one, but I didn't want to say anything right then."

Indy held it up. "I know just the museum director who will find a place for it."

Indy turned to Shannon. "The jazz scene in San Francisco will never be the same after you arrive, Jack."

Shannon grinned and took Katrina by the hand. "We'll see, Indy. We'll see."

"You're a lucky guy, Jack. One helluva lucky guy."

"I know."

"Well, I've got my own train to catch."

Indy started to leave, but stopped and turned to Katrina. "By the way, did you hold the Ark wood one last time?"

She smiled, and exchanged a glance with Shannon. "As a matter of fact, I did."

"And?"

"I saw a little boy. He had sort of a funny name. Noah Indiana Shannon."

ABOUT THE AUTHOR

ROB MACGREGOR is an Edgar-winning author who has been on the *New York Times* bestseller list. He is the author of seventeen novels, ten nonfiction books, and numerous magazine and newspaper articles. In addition to writing his own novels, he has teamed with George Lucas, Peter Benchley, and Billy Dee Williams.

Here is a preview of the
Indiana Jones adventure
Indiana Jones and the Unicorn's Legacy
by Rob MacGregor

PROLOGUE

1786
Yorkshire, England

Jonathan Ainsworth hardly recognized his father, who sat hunched over on a wooden bench. After five months in this damp, shadowy cell, he was a changed man. He'd lost twenty-five pounds, his hair was gray and motley. His shoulders were slumped.

"Father?"

Michael Ainsworth slowly raised his head as the jailer unlocked the cell. For a moment, Jonathan feared his father wouldn't know him, that he'd lost his mind. He hadn't seen him since the day the trial ended. Then he saw a faint smile and a glimmer of light in his father's bloodshot eyes, and he knew that, despite the conditions, he still maintained his sanity.

The cell door slammed shut. The noise echoed eerily along the hallway. The smile on his father's face changed to a look of concern. "Jon, you shouldn't have come here. It's not a place for a boy."

"It's okay, don't worry about me." His father still thought of him as a child, but he was twenty-one, full grown, and the head of the house. "I wanted to visit sooner, but . . ."

"How are the young ones taking it?"

He sat down on the bench next to him. "Mary had a hard time. She still cries for you. I think Charles has accepted it. Of course, he's a little older."

"And your mother?"

"She's doing her best." He wanted to say that there was a particular reason why he had come today and not his mother, but he couldn't do it, not yet.

Michael Ainsworth coughed, a deep, wracking cough that took possession of his body and throttled it. "Is there trouble?"

"They can't do anything more to us than they've already done, Father."

Ainsworth grasped his son's wrist with surprising strength. His eyes flared. "What have they done? Tell me everything."

"We're losing the house. We can't make the payments any longer. We can't get credit. People don't trust us." It was worse than that. They were openly hostile. But he didn't want to burden his father. He only wanted him to understand that they had to move to London, where no one would know them, and that Mother wouldn't be able to visit him as often.

"Talk to Mathers. He said he was so concerned about you children. Maybe he'll help you find a job."

Frederick Mathers was a barrister like his father. They'd been partners until a couple of years before Ainsworth's arrest. In the trial, Mathers had testified to his father's good character, but it had been a weak plea for leniency and the judge might as well have been stone deaf. "He's helped as much as he can. He can't do anything more. We have to leave, Father. It's no good for us here."

The elder Ainsworth nodded. "You're right. Now listen closely to me."

Jon leaned toward his father, whose raspy voice was barely audible. He hoped this wasn't going to be a confession. Ainsworth had maintained his innocence throughout the trial. Although Jon knew that his father was guilty as accused, he didn't want to hear him admit it.

"What is it, Father?"

"My trunk in the closet."

"The authorities went all through it, Father. They went through everything we own."

Ainsworth shook his head. "It has a false bottom. Tear it out. You'll find some money. Not much. But it will help you."

"Why didn't you tell me this before? We could have used it for your defense."

Ainsworth shook his head. "It wouldn't have done any good. With the money, you'll find what looks like a staff made of twisted ivory and gilded silver. It's beautiful, but you must destroy it. The staff is what's caused all of my problems. All of them. And yours as well. Do you hear me?"

"How could a staff do that?"

"You'll find a letter I wrote that explains it all. Read it, then break the staff into as many pieces as you can and scatter them. That will break the spell."

"Yes, Father. I'll do as you say."

Ainsworth held up a finger. It shook as he spoke. "I knew this probably sounds like nonsense to you. But please believe me. The staff is evil. Its powers are unfathomable."

"I'll do what you say, Father."

Jonathan Ainsworth left the cell with one thought in mind. His father was mad, raving mad. It was horrible to see him this way. But the money would help, and maybe he could sell the staff. The family needed every cent they could get.

1

DIVING INTO THE ICE AGE

1924
Montignac, France

Indy stepped into the frigid water that flowed into the dark cavern and mentally prepared himself for what was ahead. He glanced along the riverbank to make sure no one was around, then waded into the cavern.

The water slowly swallowed his legs. He winced as the icy fingers lapped at his groin. "Are you sure about this, Jones?" he asked himself in a whisper. "It's worth a shot," he answered. "Worth a shot." He grimaced as his bare foot stepped on a sharp stone. "I think."

He'd waded about a hundred feet when the roof of the cavern sloped downward and met the river. There were easier caves to explore in the foothills of the Pyrenees. At least a dozen had been found that contained evidence of Paleolithic inhabitants, who had painted the walls with surprisingly detailed drawings of animals. In fact, they'd already visited a couple of them near *Le Tuc d'Audoubert.* However, the nine graduate students and their instructor had hoped to stumble on a new cave during their ten-day excursion. Today, their final day of prowling the hills near the Trois Frères region, was the last chance before they headed back to Paris.

Indy figured it was this cavern or nothing. Even though it was less than a mile from camp, no one had bothered with it after they'd seen how the cave ceiling dipped into the water. Yet, the more he'd thought about it, the more he'd become convinced that there were caverns inside. The late Ice Age, after all, had been cold and dry so that the water level must have been lower. That meant there was a good chance the cave had been inhabited like others here in southwestern France.

He sucked in his breath, filling his lungs, then ducked under the surface. The water was so cold that he shot to the surface and sputtered.

Damn it, Jones. Either you do it or get out of the water.

He took another deep breath and dove. When he was a kid, he could easily hold his breath for three minutes. If anything, his lung capacity was larger now. So was his body, of course. But he had a plan to avoid trouble. He'd swim for a minute and surface. If the ceiling was still underwater, he'd turn back. He had two minutes to make it. He could do it.

He took leisurely strokes, letting the current do most of the work. Thirty seconds...forty. The current was stronger than he'd suspected. He wondered how difficult swimming against it would be. Maybe he'd better surface. He swam up and almost instantly struck his head against a wall. He ran his hand over the smooth surface and noticed how quickly he was drifting downstream. Suddenly and unexpectedly, a streak of panic raced through him. He was losing ground and running out of air. He wanted air. Now.

No. You can make it back. He turned upstream, losing another few yards in the process. Then he kicked hard against the current, and one foot shot through the surface and splashed. Indy's mind was as numb as his body, and it took a second for the significance to register: a splash required air. He arched his back, twisted, and shot through the surface. He drew in a deep, reviving breath.

He treaded water and continued drifting in an envelope of darkness. He reached for the ceiling, but couldn't touch it. He could be inside an immense cavern, and he wouldn't know it. He worked his way across the current until he touched a wall. It was worn smooth.

"Hello," he shouted. His voice sounded flat. Then his head struck the ceiling. "Ouch!"

The roof was coming down again, and he didn't know how much longer the pocket of air would last. No reason to go any further. He swam against the current, his heart pounding in his chest. He was gasping for breath, and his head was above the surface. He'd never last three minutes underwater. He reached out, touched the wall, and found a handhold.

He rested and regained his wit. He was doing fine, he told himself. He slowly worked his way upstream along the wall until the ceiling touched the water again. Nothing to worry about. He'd make it out easily, he repeated to himself. No problem at all, and he'd come back with candles and matches in a waterproof container, and find out what was here.

It was time. He took a deep breath, dived, and swam furiously. The deeper he swam the less the current seemed to pull on him. But he knew he couldn't stop or even slow his pace. A minute passed. Then another. He kept swimming. His lungs were ready to burst. This was harder than he thought. Then his stomach scraped on the bottom. He pushed off and his head punched through the surface and into the light. He was back.

"Jones, what are you doing?"

Indy slogged out of the cavern and squinted against the bright sunshine. Roland Walcott, the lab instructor who was officially in charge of the fieldwork, was standing on the riverbank, his hands on his hips.

"I think I found a cavern."

"You think you did, or you did?"

"I've got to go back with candles. I couldn't see. You've got to swim underwater a ways before you can surface."

Walcott gave him an odd look. "I heard you were a bit daft. Now I believe it." He shook his head and turned away, neither giving support nor disapproval for Indy's plan to venture back into the cavern.

"Friendly guy," Indy muttered and walked back to the camp alone. Walcott was nearly thirty years old and was a perpetual student, who couldn't seem to finish his Ph.D. He'd heard that the burly Englishman spent most of his time drinking in the *boîtes* and lacked ambition. At the same time, Walcott was nosy and competitive. He appeared to thrive on one-upmanship, taking advantage of his experience. On this trip, Walcott seemed intent to do as little as possible, which was fine with Indy. It was better than dealing with someone who set all kinds of limitations on what he could do.

"Indy, you're all wet. Where've you been?"

He looked over at Mara Rogers, another American attending graduate school at the Sorbonne, and the only student among them who was not working toward a Ph.D. in archaeology or anthropology. She was an art history student who was Walcott's special guest, so to speak. She was a rangy, good-looking woman with clear blue eyes, high cheekbones, and full lips. Her mane of blonde hair was tied in a ponytail.

"I was swimming in the river, where it goes into the hills," he said.

"You mean you followed it underground?"

"Yeah."

She considered what he said a moment, then motioned toward the table. "C'mon, sit down and tell me about it. I saved some lunch for you."

When he finished describing his feat, he was surprised that she didn't seem to consider it particularly unusual.

"Are you going to go back?" she asked.

"Sure, and this time I'm going to be better prepared."

"Does Roland know what you're doing?"

He'd better watch what he says now, he thought. He didn't know exactly how close she was to the lab instructor. "Yeah, I saw him down by the river. He knows."

"May I come with you?" she asked. "I'd like to see the cave."

"Oh, I don't know. It's sort of dangerous. You'd have to have to be a pretty strong swimmer."

"They used to call me the long-legged fish when I was a kid. We had a public swimming pool just a block from our house in Albuquerque. I'd swim every day for an hour or two."

Indy liked Mara just fine, but she was here with Walcott and he didn't want his plans messed up. "What about Roland? He might not like it."

"I don't need his approval for anything. If I want to go for a swim, I'll go."

But if Walcott saw them together, he might get angry and order Indy not to go into the cavern. He was trying to think of a way of discouraging Mara from joining him when four of the other students approached.

"Hey, you two seen Roland?" one of the men asked.

"He's off somewhere by himself," Mara answered.

Indy expected Mara to tell the others about his venture in the river, and he saw his discreet plans vanishing. Everyone would want to join him, and Walcott would nix the whole thing. But Mara didn't say a word about it.

"Well, if you see him, tell him we're going to follow the gully for a few miles and see what we find."

Indy and Mara wished them luck, and watched them walk off. "Thanks for not making a big deal about the cavern."

"No reason to. We don't know if anything's even there yet."

Indy had hoped that Walcott would show up and occupy Mara, but when the lab instructor hadn't returned by the time he'd finished eating, he'd reluctantly agreed to take her along. He figured she'd probably change her mind anyhow once she stepped into the icy water, and if Walcott crossed their path, he'd just keep going and let them work out the details.

"Why didn't you go with Roland when he left camp?" he asked as they headed toward the river.

"I didn't feel like it. He's not my boyfriend, you know."

"Oh, I wasn't sure. You two have been together all the time."

"That's just it. I'm tired of tagging along with him everywhere, and that's what I told him before he left. I'm sorry if I hurt his feelings, but that's how I feel."

"I was sort of wondering what you saw in him."

"We've been friendly for a while, but to tell you the truth, the only reason I came along was because I'm fascinated by these cave paintings."

When he'd heard that Walcott was bringing along a woman from the art history department, he'd thought the worst. He figured she'd make a fuss about sleeping in a tent with other people and being required to help with the cooking and other chores. But Mara was nothing like his image of an art historian. She was willing to do whatever was required and she hadn't complained once, not even when she'd found a field mouse in her sleeping bag the first night.

"So do you really think we've got a chance of discovering a new cave?" she asked as they hiked along the riverbank.

"I know we'll find a cave. It's just a question of whether anyone lived there ten thousand years ago and left a calling card."

"It would be great if we did find a completely unknown cave. I'm so glad you let me come along."

Indy smiled, but didn't respond.

"You didn't have any trouble getting away?" she asked.

"I made room for it. I wasn't going to miss it."

"No, I mean, that is . . . I was wondering if you had to leave a girlfriend back in Paris."

Indy laughed. "Not really."

"What's that mean?"

"Well, there's no one who I had to tell I was leaving." The truth was he hadn't given anyone a chance to get too close, not since he'd become involved with his first archaeology professor, who'd taken him to Greece. But that was nearly two years ago now, and he was starting to look at women in a new light again.

When they reached the base of a hill where the river disappeared into the narrow cavern, Indy sat down on the bank and took off his boots. He glanced at Mara, wondering if she was going to change her mind now that she was here.

"Don't look," she said and carried her pack behind a clump of juniper.

Indy opened his pack and made sure the watertight container with the candles and matches was still secure. The only other thing in the pack was his whip. He didn't like carrying the extra weight, but he hadn't been able to find any rope, and besides the whip was a good-luck piece.

He heard Mara singing softly to herself and glanced quickly over his shoulder just as she tossed her blouse on the top of the bush. He saw arms and legs through the thicket, and then her slacks landed next to her blouse. He smiled to himself as he turned away.

"You're not looking, are you?"

"Of course not."

"I'm glad I brought my swimming suit along," she called to him. "I thought it was silly at first. But I guess I knew I was going to get a chance to wear it."

"You could've gotten along without it."

"What do you mean by that?"

Indy laughed. "You could've worn your clothes on this swim. The water's cold."

"For a moment I thought . . . oh, never mind."

He liked Mara more all the time. He was already thinking ahead to when they were back in Paris. He could see them together sitting by the fountain at the Place Saint-Michel, walking through Luxembourg Gardens, or losing themselves in the Louvre.

"Is this going to be like the sewers?"

"What?"

"You know, *les égouts*, the Paris sewers. You have been down there, haven't you?"

He admitted it was a part of Paris he hadn't visited.

"Oh, you've got to go. It's like an underground city."

"I'd probably need a guide," he said. "Maybe you can show it to me when we get back."

"Indy!" she shrieked. "My God . . ."

He leaped to his feet and dashed over to where Mara was pressed against the juniper, her bare limbs rigid, her arms crossed over her chest. "Look!"

He followed her gaze to where a black shiny snake

was curled near her feet. Its body was as thick as his wrist and its tongue was flicking in and out. He slowly bent down, reached for a rock. The snake turned its head, watching him. He froze; he couldn't pick up the rock. It was as if the snake had hypnotized him. The creature abruptly slithered toward him, over his bare foot, and away.

As Indy straightened up, Mara embraced him. "Oh, my God. You weren't even afraid of it."

His eyes were wide with terror. His heart was pounding. He watched the snake disappear between two rocks. "Not at all. It was just a snake."

"I was scared to death."

Suddenly, Indy was aware of Mara's closeness, of the feel of her body against him, of her face against his neck. She stepped back, self-consciously pulled up the strap of her swimming suit that had slipped off her shoulder.

"Well, shouldn't we go for our swim?" she said.

She looked great, he thought. "Are you still up for it?"

"You don't think there are any . . ."

". . . snakes in the water? Naw, water's too cold. Snakes are cold-blooded. They get sluggish in the cold."

"Oh, good."

They walked down to the water hand-in-hand, and Indy was surprised by how easily they seemed to get along, how effortlessly they'd come together. It was as if they'd known each other for years. He felt comfortable around her, and it amazed him.

Then Walcott crossed his mind again. This was where he'd last seen him. Indy looked up, scanned the hills, searching for the Englishman. He imagined him somewhere up there staring at them, growing angry, and charging down to ruin Indy's plans.

"What are you looking at?" Mara asked.

"Oh, nothing."

She stuck her foot in the water. "Oh, it *is* cold. But I guess that means I have the advantage now."

"Why's that?"

"Didn't you know women have an extra layer of protective fat?"

Indy stepped into the stream. He thought of a response about how she could warm him up, but kept it to himself. "Lucky you." He reached into his pack and took out his whip. "Let's not lose each other."

He tied the end of it around her slender waist. "Good idea," she said. "Won't it get all stiff from the water?"

"The whip? I'll oil it after it dries. It'll be as good as new." He jammed the other end under his belt. There was about ten feet of whip between them, enough so they could swim without kicking each other. His only concern was that Mara might panic and fight him. In that case, they could both drown. "You sure you can hold your breath for a couple of minutes?"

"I've got excellent lung capacity." She drew in a deep beath and her full breasts rose.

"Yeah, I see." They waded into the opening, the stream pulling them forward as the light dimmed. "You think you can swim against this current?"

"Stay there," she said and without another word moved downstream to the end of the rope. She ducked down and disappeared beneath the surface. A moment later, he glimpsed her as she wriggled past, then he felt the tug of the rope and she rose like a mermaid.

"Not bad."

She rubbed her arms. "Then let's get on with it."

They moved down to where the ceiling met the water. Indy glanced back at her. "Ready?"

They plunged into the dark waters, and this time it seemed to take only seconds before he felt air above him and popped to the surface. The first time he'd gone further downstream than necessary, but it was also the knowledge that he'd done it once that made the underwater journey go so swiftly.

Mara bumped into him, then surfaced. "That wasn't hard at all. But where are we? I can't see a thing."

"Right now we're just drifting downstream. Here's the wall. Hey, there's a ledge here."

"Where?"

He took her arm. "Here."

"Got it."

Indy braced himself on the ledge, then reached into the pack and found the soap dish-sized aluminum container with the candle and matches. There was no water inside, a good sign. The match roared in his ear as he struck it, and a pellucid light filled the cavern. He lit a candle, passed it to Mara, and lit another one.

"Look, Indy!"

"What is it?"

The ledge was narrow and the ceiling was only a couple of feet over their heads, but that wasn't what had attracted Mara's attention. Just a few yards away, the stream split into two branches. The one veering to the left opened into an immense cavern whose ceiling was at least twenty feet above their heads.

"What a difference a little light can make." Indy let go of the ledge and side-stoked into the channel, holding the candle over his head.

He squinted up at the wall, looking for a sign of a cavity. Their only hope was that there were caverns untouched by the water and undiscovered by man since the Ice Age.

"Look up there," Mara said. Indy followed her gaze toward the ceiling. High on the wall was a gap couple of yards across and half that high.

As Indy moved toward the wall, his feet touched a

narrow underwater shelf, and he stood up. He pulled Mara up with him. "You cold?"

She rubbed her arms. "A little. How about you?"

"I don't feel a thing. I guess I'm numb."

She touched a finger to his mouth. "Your lips are blue." She leaned forward and kissed him gently.

"I think they're warming already."

He handed Mara his candle and reached around her waist. "I'll take the whip and if it looks promising, I'll help you up."

"It's so steep. You think you can make it up there without falling?"

He coiled the whip and hooked it on his belt. "It'll be a snap. If I fall I'll land in the water." He reached up, found a handhold, then a foothold, and he pulled himself up.

Slowly, he worked his way up the wall and finally when he was within a few feet of the hole, he realized that he could see into the cavern without a candle. The light was faint, but it meant there was a hole to the outside. He pulled himself over the lip of the gap and crawled inside.

"Oh, my God, Mara," he said.

"What is it?"

"You've got to see this."